BANE OF THE DEAD

Book 1 of the Seraphim Revival

JACOB HOLO

Jacob Holo

Cover Art by Adam Burn
Internal Art by Phouthong Phimmarath
Cover Design and Internal Layout by H. P. Holo

ISBN-10: 1514236958
ISBN-13: 978-1514236956

The Seraphim Revival

Bane of the Dead
Throne of the Dead
Disciple of the Dead

Also by Jacob Holo

The Dragons of Jupiter

Time Reavers

Dedication

To Ben. For encouraging this story.

BANE OF THE DEAD

Book 1 of the Seraphim Revival

JACOB HOLO

In the far future, the people of Earth have reached the stars and found they are far from alone, but not in the way they expected.

The galaxy teems with countless human civilizations, and the two greatest are the Aktenai and the Grendeni.

Called the Forsaken and the Fallen in their shared tongues, these two empires are eternally at war.

Chapter 1
Truth and Lies

The voices in his head were right.

It may have taken fifteen years to find, but here on the far edge of the galaxy was the terrible truth he sought.

Only one obstacle remained.

"We're alone out here," Jack said, slipping into his uniform jacket. "No hope of support. No chance of rescue. You with me, buddy?"

The seraph said nothing.

"That's the spirit. Let's do this!"

Jack clasped his storm-gray uniform jacket at the neck. White six-winged hawks adorned the cuffs and the sides of the collar, marking him as a seraph pilot of Aktenzek. His bright blue armband bore the Earth Nation seal: the moon and Earth within a halo of sixteen stars, a testament to his origins.

Jack rubbed the itchy stubble on his chin. He ran his fingers through an unruly mop of brown hair and jogged towards the *Scion of Aktenzek*'s seraph hangar.

The pressure door slid open, and he watched it part from both sides. With each step, his connection to the seraph strengthened. He entered the hangar and looked up.

The bay was just large enough to contain the mighty girth of the seraph. Soft white lights illuminated its form. Spindly mechanical arms moved above and around the seraph, transporting its armaments down out of the ceiling and affixing them via conformal pods. When finished, the arms retracted upward.

The seraph was truly gargantuan. It stood in the manner of a man, towering high above Jack, who wasn't as tall as its smallest finger.

Jack slowed to a walk. This part of the hangar came level with the seraph's chest. A slender gangplank extended from the ledge to the cockpit. The seraph's head swiveled down and watched him approach. Six blade-like wings extended from its back, retracted into tight clusters of three. The armor was a seamless, immaculate white. Designers had given this seraph a smooth set of muscular curves.

Strings of black runic characters adorned the forearms, legs, and wings. They spelled out the Litany of the Mission, a simple ten-verse invocation held sacred by the Aktenai:

Who are we?

We are those forsaken by our kind.

What is our purpose?

To repent for our greatest sin.

What was our sin?

The creation of the Bane.

How must we repent our sin?

We must kill the Bane.

Who will judge our worthiness?

The Keepers of the Gate.

Jack knew it by heart. The words filled him with dread.

"Well, this might be it," he said. "We could turn back, you know."

The seraph did not speak.

"Yeah, I thought you'd say that."

Jack hurried across the gangplank and entered the spherical cockpit in the chest. He turned and slid into the man-shaped alcove. The seraph's skin sealed him inside, leaving no evidence of an opening. The walls closed in, contracting around his body, entombing him in darkness.

Jack shut his eyes and took a deep breath. The mundane senses of his body faded. The multi-spectral "eyes" and "ears" of the seraph filled his mind. He clenched the giant hands of the seraph and shuffled from one foot to the other, restricted by the cramped confines of the hangar.

Jack didn't pilot the seraph. He *was* the seraph.

He let a trickle of power flow out from his frail, almost forgotten, human body. Raw, chaotic fury surged through his arterial network, energizing his limbs and wings. The black script of the Litany ignited with blinding blue light. His internal systems came online one after another, sipping at an endless reservoir of extra-dimensional energy.

Beneath his feet, the first of three doors flinched open. Clamps descended on rails and affixed to his shoulders and wings. With a surge of motion, the launch catapult thrust him down. He passed through doors that snapped open and shut in the span of an eye blink.

The catapult flung Jack into the dark of space. He floated free of the *Scion of Aktenzek*: a white, armored figure falling from the vast cylindrical vessel. He spread his wings and redirected power to them. Edges along each blade-wing flared with light.

Jack flew ahead of the carrier.

"Well, don't keep me waiting," he said. "You know where I am and where I'm going. Time to finish this."

He didn't wait long.

The first Disciple frigate folded space several hundred kilometers away. The sleek, silver-skinned enemy craft materialized within an expanding ring of distorted light, then turned its nose to face the *Scion*. Once aligned, it fired the centerline fusion cannon that took up the bulk of its interior.

A beam of white light smashed into the *Scion*, carving a ragged blister across its hull. Almost immediately, mnemonic armor flowed over the glowing wound, remembering and restoring its original shape. The fully automated carrier had impressive self-repair capabilities, but it was also his only way home. If it fell, so did he.

"Here we go, buddy!" Jack shouted.

He rocketed towards the enemy craft. The frigate fired again, but this time Jack swung into the beam's path.

Focused atomic energy met his chaos barrier in a brilliant flash of competing forces. White ribbons splashed off him like water, leaving his armor untouched.

Jack aimed the fusion cannon housed in a conformal pod along his left arm. The weapon drank in a portion of his barrier, energized the barrel, and focused the nuclear charge into a tight plasma lance.

The beam hit with all the force of a capital ship's main gun, emitted from a weapon one-fiftieth the size. Plasma cleaved the Disciple vessel in half. Secondary explosions snapped across its length and obliterated the rest.

Two more Disciple frigates folded space, both larger than the first and positioned further out. They fired their main guns and unleashed a steady stream of fusion torpedoes from twin launchers.

Jack turned and sped towards them. He shot the lead ship. His beam hit from the side and punched clean through, blowing the nose off the craft. His second shot stabbed through the center. Two ruined halves tumbled away, shedding life pods like a rain of silver droplets.

Three more frigates entered the system even further away and commenced their attack runs.

The *Scion* took hit after hit. Beams seared its armor, and torpedoes exploded against its hull. Damage indicators opened in Jack's mind. A nuclear inferno breached the outer hull, and radiation flooded two of the aft compartments.

"Good thing that's not where I sleep."

Jack closed the alert and fired again. He raked the beam across the closest ship, cleaving it at a diagonal. Explosions brewed up within the wreck, shrouding it in fire.

Fusion beams slashed across space. The *Scion* spun its hull, spreading the hits across its surface. More damage warnings flashed in his mind.

Jack twisted around and rocketed towards the new trio of frigates.

"They're trying to split me off from the *Scion*!"

The seraph did not speak.

"I can't help it! Their cannons have better range!"

Jack flew across their formation and unloaded shot after shot. Beams carved red-hot holes through the Disciple ships. Superheated alloys cracked the first frigate apart, then the second.

The last frigate unleashed a swarm of forty torpedoes from its external racks. Jack blasted the ship apart and swung past its spreading wreckage. He deployed a wave of tactical seekers from weapon pods attached to his legs.

The tiny guided projectiles ignited their overloaded drive blades and sped after the torpedoes, intercepting over half of them. The rest slammed into the *Scion* in one infernal detonation after another. The hull heated and bulked. Damage alerts opened faster than he could read them.

But when the translucent gauze of plasma dissipated, the *Scion* remained.

"Whew! That was close."

As if to prove him wrong, a Disciple dreadnought folded space almost on top of the *Scion*. Its reflective armor gleamed in the starlight. Three whole frigates could have fit within its long flattened hull.

"Where the hell did you come from?" Jack shouted.

The dreadnought oriented its three cannons on the *Scion* and fired. A trio of plasma jets scorched the carrier, opening another breach. One of two engine compartments vaporized. Radiation polluted half the interior.

Jack dumped power into his wings and raced in.

The dreadnought opened fire again. Armor scattered from the *Scion*'s hull in molten globules.

"The substructure is exposed!"

Jack aimed his arm cannon and fired. The fusion beam struck the dreadnought amidships. Fierce plasma scarred the armor with a livid orange slash, but it failed to penetrate.

"I can't punch through that hull in time!"

No one responded.

"Oh yeah? Watch this!"

Jack closed with the dreadnought, diving in perpendicular to its path. He didn't slow down. Instead, he crashed feet first into the ship, forming a crater. The impact forced the mammoth warship off course. Its shots flew wide, arcs of plasma fading into the depths of space.

Drive blades along the dreadnought's rear powered up, reorienting the bow onto its target. Fusion torpedoes deployed from six launch tubes, adding to the incoming fire.

Jack grabbed the leading edge of the ship and flipped himself inside one of its fusion cannons. The long tube ran almost the entire length of the craft, lined with gravitic focusing rings.

At the far end of the dark barrel, the next ignition spark appeared.

"Oh, this is going to hurt."

Jack raised a forearm and shielded his face.

The cannon discharged. Blinding light filled everything. Plasma sleeted over his barrier, cooking him. He grunted in pain, but his barrier did not waver.

The cannon finished firing, and Jack ran down the barrel, keeping his arm up. More damage registered on the *Scion*. Its launch catapults were gone.

A faint glow brightened ahead.

"Oh, no you don't!"

Jack sprinted in. The shunts along his left forearm glowed brighter. Blue energy extended from above his wrist, forming a blade as long as he was tall.

Jack stabbed the chaos sword into the ignition mechanism. The spark vanished. Machinery melted and floated away. He cleaved through the back of the cannon, then let the sword fade into a dusting of winking motes.

Jack jammed his hands into the breach and forced the armor apart, exposing over a dozen of the dreadnought's crewed decks stacked one on top of the other. Startled men and women in dark red pressure suits stared at him. The interior must have already been depressurized for combat.

"Surprise!" Jack swung a leg through the breach and stepped in, his shin crashing through three decks at the same time. Disciple warriors scattered out of his way as he smashed through the ship's interior, crumpling the walls and floors of a dozen decks with each stride as if they were made of paper.

When he reached the bridge, Jack clawed the reinforced exterior aside. The Disciple captain stood in the center of a circular room ringed with tactical displays. Red messages flashed urgently on most, but the captain glared defiantly at the seraph, unwilling to retreat.

Jack pointed his arm cannon at the man.

"Heh. Nothing personal."

He triggered the weapon. A fusion beam vaporized the whole bridge and everything behind it. Jack emptied his cannon with shot after shot, turning the dreadnought's interior into a white-hot inferno. He spread his wings and flew out through the giant barrel. Behind him, the dreadnought drifted away, its armor bulging out.

Jack arced towards the *Scion*. The carrier was lacerated with glowing crisscrossed patches of superheated alloy, at least where it still had armor. Several molten holes laid its copper-hued internal systems bare to the vacuum. He opened the *Scion*'s internal diagnostics and took a long, thoughtful look.

He sighed.

"Good. Half the seraph bays are intact, two fold engines are still working, and my room is in one piece."

The seraph said nothing.

"No need to be mean. It worked, didn't it?"

The *Scion* sent him a navigational request. Its fold engines were finally charged for the next jump. His internal fold engines were also ready.

"Let's see if all of this was worth it."

Jack and the *Scion of Aktenzek* vanished.

They reappeared three light-years away, materializing near a Seeding world.

After fifteen years and more than eight hundred worlds, Jack no longer doubted his mission. Already he had found more Seeding worlds than anyone had thought existed, some with thriving human civilizations older than anything in Earth's history. Humanity was everywhere in the galaxy, spread across countless planets. Many of those were primitive blasted wrecks from long forgotten wars, but even more flourished with life, art, and culture.

He had known for a while what he sought was somewhere out here amongst the uncharted Seedings. If nothing else, he owed the Disciples that small piece of gratitude. How else could they have recognized him? Why else would they have hunted him?

No, what he sought was out here, and it was close.

Jack turned to the planet.

The face of a sun scorched his vision. Hot needles of pain pushed into his eyeballs.

Jack gasped and jerked his gaze away, shielding his head with an open hand. In the cockpit, his true eyes watered.

"What the hell was that?" he muttered.

Like every other onboard system, the seraph's scanners dipped into Jack's ability to channel chaos energy. Besides a few tertiary fusion toruses, a seraph had no power generators. Instead, the pilot supplied everything the seraph's drives, barriers, and weapon systems required.

A pilot's very soul served as the connection point to a vast extra-dimensional sea of energy. The instinct to protect oneself resulted in the barrier field. The urge to move quickly drove the drive shunts. Without a compatible pilot, a seraph wouldn't budge.

The chaos scanner worked in a similar fashion, amplifying Jack's ability to detect other users of chaos energy, called chaos adepts. With a thought, he accessed the scanner and lowered the gain to one percent.

Slowly, he turned back to the planet and peeked through spread fingers.

The world was lush and beautifully Earth-like. Vast oceans separated the many and varied continents. Deserts, jungles, and mountains filled its lands. Ice barrens capped the poles. Upon seeing the planet, homesickness tugged at his heart.

But that wasn't all.

A point of light glowed near the equator, though it illuminated nothing around it. This glow represented a chaos adept of unprecedented power. After all the close battles, fruitless trails, and careful research, *here* was the very person he sought!

Jack turned the gain down even further.

His optical scanners picked out points of interest from across the surface. This world, like so many others, was embroiled in war. Vast fleets of metal ships plied the seas. Primitive propeller aircraft dueled in the skies. Legions of troops engaged in brutal trench warfare. The technology bore striking parallels to Earth's Second World War.

These massive wars were not alone noteworthy. Jack had seen more than his share of such conflicts among the Seeding worlds, even before leaving Aktenai space. But the patterns were strange because no fighting occurred near the point of light.

In a radius of over two thousand kilometers, almost as if the peoples of this world were afraid to approach too closely.

His optics enlarged the area near the light.

"Oh, how quaint."

The castle resembled something plucked from a romanticized version of Earth's age of chivalry. A tall stone wall encapsulated the cathedral-like keep and its patchwork gardens. He noted the anti-aircraft batteries along the parapets and artillery cannons behind its high walls.

Perhaps an outside force had accelerated this world's advancement. He'd seen situations like that before where more advanced Seedings had experimented on lesser cultures. Regardless of the reasons, its inhabitants would likely be armed as well.

The chaos adept he sought was indoors, so Jack could gather no further information from orbit. He linked a station keeping order to the *Scion of Aktenzek* and descended towards the planet.

Jack expanded his barrier into an aerodynamic wedge and powered through the upper atmosphere. He left a burning friction comet in his wake, broke through a layer of cottony altocumulus clouds, and slowed.

The surface beneath him was a range of rolling hills. He skimmed across them, following a winding paved road. When the castle came in sight, he dropped down and landed with feathery lightness in front of the drawbridge.

The outer wall barely came up to his knees. Rays from the morning sun shone off its smoothed walls. A checkered quilt of gardens in full bloom stretched across the interior, with a path cut through the middle. White-and-silver banners flapped in the wind along the flagstone path leading to the keep.

"Your move," Jack said. He crossed his arms.

Men in black uniforms and white berets ran to their artillery pieces. Jack laughed when they struggled to bring their weapons to bear. Weapon barrels gleamed from meticulous polishing, but their rotating axes were rusted solid. Apparently, this castle didn't see much action. Only one adventurous crew managed to turn its artillery piece around.

The shell hit with so little force his barrier didn't even become visible. It ricocheted off, landed a kilometer way, and blasted a house-sized crater in the foothills.

Jack shook his head and wagged a finger at them.

The crew hesitated before loading another shell.

"All right. So you haven't seen a seraph before. What about your guest?"

A dozen women in plain black livery rushed across the garden grounds, shouting urgently. After a stunned pause, soldiers aimed the lone artillery piece away from the seraph. They backed away from the gun and retreated indoors.

"Well, that's encouraging. I wonder …"

Jack trailed off when he saw her.

She emerged onto the balcony of the keep, wrapped in the fierce glow of chaos energy. If not for that, Jack would have guessed her age at around eighteen.

Her flawless skin resembled soft cream. Silver rings clasped her silken raven hair in three places down her back. She wore black garments similar to the servants, yet trimmed with white and silver at the collar and wrists. Her hair swayed in a gentle breeze.

The woman looked up and beheld the seraph with a knowing gaze and a slender smile. Oh, yes. She knew exactly what it was.

The woman stepped inside and reemerged on the ground floor. She strode across the gardens giving orders. Whenever she pointed or spoke, the liveried servants hustled into action. Four of them brought a table of rich dark wood and set it out within the centermost garden. Two others placed high-backed chairs on either side. A dozen more followed, setting trays of food and drink on the table until it overflowed.

With her eyes affixed on the seraph, the woman gestured across the table with an open palm.

"Why not?" Jack said. "I didn't come all this way for nothing. Right, buddy?"

The seraph was silent.

"I know, but don't worry. I'll be careful. I've got you to back me up."

Jack focused on the distinction between his true body and the seraph. The connection between man and machine lessened to the point where he no longer was the seraph. The cockpit walls spread into a spherical chamber and the outer hatch opened. Light played against his real eyelids. He took in a deep breath and opened them.

The first thing he noticed was the scent in the air. It was rich with the aroma of flowers and evoked a sense of nostalgia for Earth, even if the plants were of alien origin. Each garden patch used a different design. One had checkered patterns of blues and greens. Others spiraled outwards in swirls of crimson or traced angular shapes in purples and yellows.

Jack brought the seraph's hand towards the cockpit and stepped onto the giant armored palm. He lowered the hand to the flagstone path and walked off.

White banners crossed with silver diagonal bands flapped in the breeze. Jack kept his gaze fixed on the woman, but the seraph's scanners remained vigilant, their input flowing into a corner of his mind.

Jack stopped a few paces from her. She appraised him with strange eyes that possessed brilliantly silver irises. Despite her youthful face, her exotic eyes held no fear, only a powerful sense of confidence and comprehension. This was no ordinary human. But then again, neither was he.

He spoke in the Aktenai tongue. “Can you understand what I’m saying?”

The woman tilted her head to one side as if thinking, then nodded solemnly.

“It has been a long time since I used this language,” she said, her words thick with a peculiar accent that emphasized harsh consonants.

Jack recalled hearing that accent before. It was somewhere on Aktenzek, but where precisely or from whom escaped his memory.

“My name is Jack Donolon.”

The woman smiled and bowed her head at the neck. “You may address me as Vierj. It is what my family used to call me.”

Vierj clapped her hands. Two serving girls sprinted out from the keep and hurried to the table. In moments, his plate was served and his drink poured. The girls retreated, positively oozing fear, both of him and of Vierj.

“Please sit,” Vierj said. “Eat something. Consider yourself my honored guest.”

“Thank you.” Jack pulled out his chair.

Vierj sat down across from him and leaned forward onto her elbows.

The seraph’s scanners detected no trickery in the food. Much of the food smelled too spicy for his tastes. He selected a bowl of zesty vegetable soup, took a spoonful, and blew on it.

Vierj made no move to eat or drink, but merely observed him with a calm demeanor.

“Do you like it?” she asked.

Jack put the spoon in the bowl. “You don’t seem surprised that I’m here.”

"I knew someone else like me would eventually come searching. It was only a question of time."

Jack grimaced. "Someone like you …"

"You and I are the same," Vierj said. "I am sure that is why you have come. I can feel the change beginning in you, as it did once in me. You must have at least suspected this."

Jack nodded slowly. He sighed, leaning back in his chair.

"Yeah, I guessed it."

He had so hoped to find someone different from this woman, someone different from *himself*. But, the truth was too obvious now. All he had left was his original plan.

But how to set it in motion?

"What is the matter?" Vierj asked.

"I guess I expected someone different," Jack said, stirring his soup absently.

"This is not an uncommon response for someone educated by the Aktenai."

"Yeah, I guess so."

Perceptive woman, Jack thought. It was strange, hearing such statements from her. She looked about half his age. But however young she appeared, Vierj's words betrayed her wisdom and experience.

She leaned closer. "Tell me, what do you know of the Gate?"

So we are coming to this already. She isn't wasting time.

"Not much, I fear," Jack said. "The Aktenai say it's a way of escaping this universe to a paradise they call the Homeland. They have the Gate and very few of them know where it's hidden. I know the Grendeni also want it. The Gate is one of the reasons those two civilizations continue to wage war."

Vierj nodded. "It sounds like not much has changed. I myself tried for a very long time to locate it. The Aktenai hid it well."

"What do you want with the Gate?"

Emotions flashed in Vierj's silver eyes. Jack briefly saw something horrible and disturbing in them.

"To pass through it, of course," she said. "There are old crimes that have long gone unpunished."

"Revenge?"

"If you will." She smiled as if amused. "You are the one who sought me out. Do you not intend to aid me?"

"It doesn't matter," Jack said. "No one except the Aktenai Choir knows where it is, with the possible exception of the current sovereign. And it's not like you or I can just walk up to them and ask."

"I have waited in hiding long enough. Now that there are two of us, we need not fear the Choir's bigotry."

Jack kept his face neutral. He could see where this was leading, but he dared not appear overly eager.

"Yes, there are two of us," he said. "But the Aktenai possess vast fleets, and the Choir is sheltered within the planet's core."

"Those obstacles could not stop us."

"What about other seraph pilots?"

Vierj's glanced up at the winged giant beyond the castle walls. "Yes, I suppose you are correct. How many are there now?"

"Hard to say. Their numbers were severely depleted when I left, but another generation of pilots should have reached maturity by now. Hundreds, probably."

"I see. We should be cautious then. That is, if you are willing to aid me."

"It's not that simple. You must understand how difficult this choice is for me. We would be fighting against my friends. You are asking a lot."

"Would these friends of yours be so loyal if they knew what you are?"

Jack masked his elation carefully. Things could not have gone more perfectly if he'd tried. Indeed, he had refrained from any overt manipulation, for Vierj was clearly intelligent. However, the opportunity now presented itself. Here was what he had long sought. Now all that remained was to carry his plan through to its blood-soaked end. He *had* to seize this moment.

But he hesitated.

Jack had been honest when mentioning the difficulty of this decision. This path would lead him against his former comrades, and undoubtedly many would fall. He and Vierj would cut a bloody path into the very heart of Aktenzek. They both wanted the Gate's location, though for very different reasons.

And Jack feared two people most of all, two pilots of Aktenzek who had saved him from the depths of despair. They were his friends. More than friends, they were almost like family, the only family he had ever known. How could he face them as traitor and murderer? The separation of years and distance did nothing to dull his feelings for those two.

Jack found it difficult to return Vierj's calculating gaze. How could he falter at this critical moment? Could he face them in battle? Could he kill them to achieve his goals?

The answer had to be yes, as dark and evil as that answer was. There could be no turning back now. He had no choice but to use this dangerous woman and move his plan forward.

Finally, Jack met Vierj's stare with absolute certainty. "I'll help you."

A smile graced her face, and her eyes shone with unexpected tears. For the first time since meeting her, Jack saw her as genuinely happy. She turned away and wiped under her eyes.

"It has been so lonely," she said.

Jack reached across the table. He placed his hand on hers and clasped it tightly in his.

"Yes, but you're not alone anymore," he said.

"When shall we leave?" Vierj asked.

"Right now if you like. My ship is in orbit."

"Now, then. This barbaric planet has nothing I want."

"Your seraph?"

"Gone. Stolen from me a long time ago."

"I see. Then let's go."

Jack rose from his seat and extended his hand. Vierj took it and stood.

He knew it would take them two years to reach Aktenzek, and that their return would herald the Aktenai people's darkest hour.

But I will not turn back. Not now. Not ever.

2 Years Later

Chapter 2

Forsaken

Seth Elexen spread his six wings and ascended past the asteroidal clutter of Earth's orbiting industries. Shunts across his black angular armor burned with purple light. He cleared the converted asteroids of the Earth Defense Array and turned gently towards the twin fortress planets of Aktenzek and Zu'Rashik.

Few remained in the solar system that would not have recognized his seraph's silhouette. Purple runes burned across his armor, proclaiming the Litany of the Mission. Thin gray scars traced across old battle wounds. The edges of his six black wings blazed with fire. He shot through the congested space lanes between Earth and the twin fortress worlds.

It wasn't often that Seth got to cut loose and just fly wherever he wanted. It felt refreshing to push his seraph-body as fast as he could for the simple joy of doing it.

Aktenzek and Zu'Rashik closed quickly, enlarging from twin white pearls to worlds that filled his view ahead. Perhaps he would descend into Zu'Rashik's interior and inspect the new fortress planet's construction firsthand.

Twenty years ago, the last great battle between the near-invincible

Aktenai armada and those ragtag Earth Nation defenders had come to its startling conclusion. Only the defection of three seraph pilots, Seth included, had prevented Earth's total annihilation and had set the stage for the present day Earth-Aktenai Alliance.

For twenty years, the Earth Nation and the Aktenai had cooperated, merging Earth's plentiful pilots and Aktenzek's technological and industrial might into unstoppable legions of seraphs.

But the situation was not entirely harmonious.

"Hey, Seth? You there?" a pleasant female voice called in.

Seth grimaced. "Yeah, Quennin. Go ahead."

"You okay? You sound kind of gloomy."

"Sorry. Just dreading whatever you're calling about. What can I do for you?"

"If you want, I can handle this one," Quennin said. "I'm already heading out."

"No, that's fine," Seth said. "I'm not even halfway to Zu'Rashik yet. I can get there first."

"Okay. Well, you know that little joint-operations exercise that's being held over near the *Resolute*?"

Seth checked his schedule. "The Earth Nation 17th Annual Joint Seraph Deployment Venture?"

"That's the one."

"I'm not due over there for a few hours."

"Right, that's not the problem. The Aktenai at the event are hosting a close-combat tactics exchange."

"Why do I feel this horrible sense of foreboding all of a sudden?"

"Or were hosting it, as of a few minutes ago. I don't think you can really call it an exchange anymore. It's turned into more of a demonstration."

Seth spun around, angled his wings, and accelerated straight for Earth.

"Now, this may be me overreacting," Quennin said. "But I think one of us should get over there. Right now."

"Let me guess, we're experiencing some inter-Alliance friction."

"I suppose that's one way to put it."

"Next you're going to tell me Tevyr is involved."

"Why, yes, Tevyr is in attendance."

The edges of his wings burned hotter, and he rocketed towards Earth.

"I think there's going to be an incident," Quennin said.

"Not another one."

Seth focused his optics on a small asteroid base that served as the Joint Seraph Deployment Center.

The JSDC building had been constructed on an old mined-out asteroid in Earth orbit. Not only did the asteroid have numerous excavated caverns for confined-space combat exercises, but the surface was covered with old industrial silos, refineries, and emptied factories. All this, plus an Aktenai-provided gravity grid, allowed for highly varied combat simulations.

Above the JSDC, a flame-red Aktenai seraph dueled with five metallic gray Earth Nation seraphs. Tevyr's red seraph fought ferociously, his barrier flashing bright green every time he struck a foe. Like Seth's own armor, the runic Litany of the Mission burned brightly with Tevyr's personal chaos frequency.

One aspect of seraph operations the Earth Nation had never truly appreciated was close-quarters combat. Seraph barriers were nearly impenetrable at long range, even with intense fusion cannon bombardment. The best way to breach a seraph's barrier was to engage it with another seraph, and most pilots could tighten and sharpen a part of their barrier, forming it into a coherent dagger of energy.

Fortunately, Tevyr had not activated his chaos daggers, and Seth sighed with palpable relief at this. If the brash Aktenai pilot had been so inclined, his opponents would now be floating around in a lot of small pieces.

That isn't to say Seth found the predicament much more pleasing. Instead of using chaos daggers, Tevyr had disabled one EN seraph and now swung it as a bludgeon against the other four. Barriers or not, the EN seraphs showed heavy damage. Seth spotted the hapless bludgeon's wing clusters drifting away from the melee.

"Well, at least he's winning," Seth muttered.

Seth redoubled his efforts to reach the melee before it escalated further.

The EN seraphs spotted Seth approaching and immediately scattered. Seth closed rapidly with Tevyr and his mangled seraph-bludgeon. Tevyr tossed the abused seraph aside, as if that made him any less guilty.

Seth concentrated, right fist compressing tightly. Purple snaps of barrier energy arced out of the digits. He pulled the fist back, flew in at incredible speed, and swung.

There was a brief, blinding flash of green and purple light as his fist connected. Tevyr's barrier compressed. His shoulder imploded inward. Kinetic energy exchanged between the two seraphs, leaving Seth at a relative standstill and Tevyr speeding down into the JSDC asteroid.

Tevyr's seraph hit so hard that the asteroid's outer surface cracked open, sending him careening through the asteroid's mined-out caverns.

Seth fanned his wings out and turned slowly in space, facing the EN seraphs. With a mental command, all seraphs present entered a common channel.

"Would anyone care to explain the situation to me?" Seth asked.

The channel was silent for long seconds.

"Anyone? Anyone at all? I'm sure one of you is about to share a fascinating tale with me."

The least damaged EN seraph flew forward slightly. He grabbed the still-spinning seraph-club and steadied it. The pilot's name registered as Jared Daykin.

"Umm, we made a wager, sir." Jared glanced over the mangled remains of his team. "And we appear to have lost."

"I see. A wager, was it?"

"Yes, sir."

"And not an attack on another Alliance pilot?"

"No, sir. Nothing of the sort. Simply testing some of the tactics we learned today."

"By letting one of your own be swung around like a club?"

"Well … the tactics were a bit on the unconventional side, sir. I will grant you that. We may have gotten a little out of hand."

"A *little* out of hand, you say?" Seth asked.

"But this was purely due to our unfamiliarity with the tactics in question," Jared added quickly. "Please accept my apologies on behalf of the Earth Nation. It was entirely my fault. We should not have engaged in such, uhh, advanced tactics without additional practice beforehand."

"I see. Well, that is quite an interesting piece of fiction you just spouted."

Jared's wings twitched. "It's all true, sir."

Seth frowned. "I will take your apology under consideration. All five of you are grounded until further notice. Land immediately."

"Yes, sir." Jared slung the seraph-bludgeon under an arm and led the others to the JSDC asteroid's hangar.

Seth linked to the red seraph on a private channel. "And as for *you*!"

Tevyr finished freeing his seraph from the crater. He shook his wings out, looked up, and shrugged.

"What did I do?"

Seth let out a slow seething exhale. "Indeed. Besides using one of the Earth Nation's seraphs as a close combat weapon, indeed, what have you done?"

"It's not what you think."

"Land at the JSDC. We will discuss this further in person."

"Understood," Tevyr said glumly.

Seth pushed out of the pilot alcove and stepped onto his seraph's open cockpit hatch. The JSDC facility might have been an Earth Nation facility, but the seraph bays were of Aktenai manufacture, staffed by Aktenai technicians. Aktenzek still flatly refused to share the core seraph technologies with the Earth Nation, but this compromise had worked so far.

A gangplank extended from a ledge level with the seraph's waist, and Seth walked across it. Spindly armatures like insects legs descended from the ceiling and clawed at his seraph, removing conformal weapon pods and opening patches in the mnemonic skin for servicing.

Seth's interface-suit's textured, storm-gray skin fit tightly around his body. He took off his helmet and ran gloved fingers through a short crop of damp black hair. He glanced over his surroundings with dark eyes.

The armband on his i-suit was a vivid purple that matched his chaos frequency and bore the Aktenai seal. To his Earther allies, it resembled an inverted cursive *i* holding a white sphere. To him, it was life and purpose given form.

One of the several seraph technicians in the bay approached. He stood a head taller than Seth. More people did.

"Pilot Elexen, does your seraph require any special attention?" the technician asked.

Seth handed over his helmet. "Not at this time. The standard checks will do."

"Of course, Pilot." The technician bowed his head.

"Has Pilot S'Kev arrived yet?"

"I believe so." The technician motioned to Seth's right. "She should be in the next bay over."

"Thank you." Seth headed over to meet Quennin.

Seth passed through the open airlock separating the two seraph bays. Within the second bay, another red seraph was being raised up. But unlike Tevyr's, this one sported chaos shunts stylized as large kite-shaped crystals, one embedded in each forearm, leg, and wing. A single larger crystal pushed out from the center of the chest.

Its familiar sight brought a smile to his face.

The bay machinery finished hauling the seraph into position. A gangplank extended from the ledge, and a tall figure walked out, clad in a gray i-suit like his own.

Quennin S'Kev removed her helmet and handed it to the waiting technician. Thanks to Aktenai medical science, age had failed to blemish her beauty, and the tight i-suit complemented the fit curves of her tall, elegant body. She pulled her long red hair out of her i-suit's neck ring, allowing it to sway with each step. A silver clasp, decorated with a single emerald, gripped the hair near the nape of her neck.

Quennin stopped next to him and smiled warmly, her bright green eyes lighting up.

Seth bowed his head slight. "Beloved."

"Have you talked to Tevyr, yet?" she asked.

"No, I thought having both of us present might help."

"It didn't last time."

Seth shrugged, then motioned to the exit. "Shall we?"

"I'll follow your lead this time."

A few bays down, the flame-red seraph loomed above, its Litany shunts dark against its bright armor. Tevyr waited outside the seraph's cockpit, a nervous expression on his face. A small crowd of EN pilots had gathered in the overlooking balcony.

The teenage pilot was already taller than Seth, though quite lanky. He made Seth think of a shorter person stretched to his current height by some archaic Earth torture device. Tevyr's hair matched the fiery color scheme of his seraph. He tried to massage his right shoulder through the i-suit.

Seth glanced up at the seraph, eyes drawn to the collapsed right shoulder and limp right arm.

"I didn't hit you with a dagger, Tevyr. If there had been any real damage, your i-suit would have fixed it."

"I know, but it still stings."

"Well? Don't make me wait any longer. Explain yourself."

Tevyr stopped rubbing his shoulder, looking troubled. He turned to Quennin, only to be confronted by her crossed arms and stern gaze. Clearly, no sympathy or support was forthcoming from that direction.

Tevyr took a deep breath and inclined his neck. "I started it, Father."

"Very well. I think that's enough flying for this exercise. Your seraph is grounded until I decide otherwise. You can assign command of your squadron to Pilot Nezrii."

Tevyr Elexen did not move. He kept his head bowed, his eyes downcast.

"You can use the additional time for more studying," Seth continued. "I understand your scholastic scores are disappointing."

"My scores are above average, Father."

"And when your scores have risen *far* above mere average, I will consider them acceptable. Is that understood?"

"Yes, Father."

Good, Seth thought. *You acknowledge your failure and accept your punishment. You don't whine like some Earther child, complaining about fairness or parsing every last word.*

Seth looked up at Quennin. She nodded her agreement.

"Now go!" Seth said sharply. "You have work to do."

"Yes, Father. Mother." Tevyr bowed to each parent, then departed the seraph bay.

With Tevyr gone, the crowd of EN personnel in the balcony dispersed.

When they were alone, Quennin shook her head. "You could have been a little easier on him. I don't think any animosity was involved, just two groups of young pilots trying to show off. And those EN pilots weren't faultless either."

"Which is why I grounded them, too."

Quennin sighed. "He's had to grow up so fast."

"Do you think I was too harsh?"

"A little. He's still just a kid."

"He is also a warrior of Aktenzek. The time for such antics has passed."

"Did you see him take on all five at once? They couldn't touch him. His technique is superb."

Seth nodded. "He's a stronger pilot than I was at his age."

"You think he'll be better than you someday?" Quennin asked.

"Could be." Seth gazed up at the seraph. Tevyr had chosen the flame-red colors of his mother's seraph and the Litany shunts of his father's. "Is it a good thing or a bad thing for a father to be surpassed by his son?"

Quennin kissed him lightly on the cheek. "I think you already know the answer."

Chapter 3

The Kids

Tevyr Elexen lived in that period of life when evolution told him to leave the safety of family, seek a mate, and sire children. Society was not so keen on the idea and instructed him to dutifully repress those base urges. He was not yet an adult, not ready for the rights and responsibilities associated with the title.

Paradoxically, Tevyr was a pilot: one of the elite warrior youths of Aktenzek, one of only a handful of human beings in the entire universe who could pilot the awesome power of a seraph. He was a dangerous master of tactics and strategy, possessing lightning reflexes and brilliant cunning.

All of which made his grounding even worse. Since Tevyr couldn't prove his superiority through flying, he had been reduced to *this*.

"Are you going to move or not?" Tevyr rested his head on a fist.

"Almost got it." Jared Daykin sat opposite Tevyr in the JSDC's pilot mess hall. Most of alpha and epsilon squadrons sat, ate, and talked at the rows of rectangular tables. The Earther was trying to find a way out of the trap he'd blundered into. With hands at the sides of his face pulling the skin back, he stared intensely at the playing board. His fingers flexed, gripping his sandy-blond hair tightly.

Tevyr surveyed the game with no small degree of satisfaction. He was winning, and he enjoyed winning.

"You don't look like you're enjoying this at all," Tevyr said.

"Shush. I'm concentrating."

"You've been concentrating for ten minutes."

"I've almost got it figured out."

Tevyr took a moment to appreciate the layout of white and black game pieces. His two bishops were projecting a nasty V of potential attacks into the heart of Jared's formation. Jared could counterattack, but then he'd exchange either a queen or rook for a mere bishop.

No, the Earther's only option remained to fall back and accept additional losses.

Such a simple game, really.

Jared reached for the black queen, but hesitated.

"*Jared*?"

"I've almost got this figured out."

"Would you like to start over?"

"No, I'll get you yet." Slowly, Jared grasped the black queen and dragged it deeper into his defenses.

The moment Jared's hand left the game piece, Tevyr picked up a bishop and knocked over Jared's last knight.

"Check."

Jared's eyes narrowed. He tightened the death grip on his hair.

Tevyr draped one arm over the back of his chair and slouched. "Aren't you supposed to be a genius?"

"Just in my seraph. My brain accelerates."

"And how does that work, exactly?"

"Don't know. How can you generate two chaos daggers at once when I can't?"

Tevyr shrugged. "Don't know. Just do."

He took the moment to brush a few specks of lint off his uniform. Even though Jared served the Earth Nation's seraph squadrons, his uniform shared much with Tevyr's. Both were storm-gray ensembles with white six-winged hawks at the cuffs and collar.

The main differences were the colored armbands. Tevyr's green armband displayed the Aktenai seal: an inverted cursive *i* done in black, looped around a white sphere. Jared's bright red armband displayed the Earth Nation seal, with the Earth and Moon centered within a halo of sixteen stars.

A young woman walked over to their table carrying a tray of steaming Earther slop and one of their fizzing iced drinks. Yonu Nezrii wore her long black hair in a complex braid, twined with a translucent blue ribbon. Tevyr tried not to leer. He made a point of studying the ceiling instead of the ample breasts straining her uniform.

"I hate you," Yonu said, sitting sat down next to him.

Tevyr blew out a breath. "Nice to see you too."

"Why is it whenever you screw up it means extra work for me?"

Tevyr chuckled. "Funny how that always happens, huh?"

"Yeah. Real funny," Yonu said. "I don't even want to run your squadron. By the way, Dekin and V'Zen are at each other's throats again. I scheduled a duel to sort it out."

Tevyr rolled his eyes. "What else is new? I wish they'd start sleeping together and get it over with."

"Seriously, I don't have time to waste on their drama. Speaking of which, shouldn't you two be studying for the history exam?"

Jared shook his head. "Not until I beat him."

"Then you might as well leave your test blank," Yonu said.

"I'm not doing that bad."

"Oh, come on. Even I can see you're getting thrashed." Yonu set a d-scroll next to her tray and let it open. Historical texts and images activated on its translucent surface.

Yonu poked her fork into a repulsive slab of something called "meatloaf." She thumbed through the d-scroll's contents with her free hand.

"How can you eat that stuff?" Tevyr asked.

"It's actually quite good. You should try it." Yonu took a large bite and chewed with a cheerful grin.

"No, thank you."

In truth, the Earth food wasn't all that bad, just weird to Tevyr's taste buds. However, Yonu's other explorations into Earth trends were far stranger. She had actually had her ears pierced! Admittedly, the twin sapphire gems accentuated her beauty in an exotic way, but that sort of bodily mutilation was unheard of anywhere in Aktenzek.

"I still can't believe you let them pierce your ears," Tevyr said.

"It's a fascinating, if primitive culture," Yonu said. "It is our responsibility as members of the more advanced society to make efforts to understand them."

"You just did it to annoy your mom."

"Well. Maybe that too."

"So, you hear that, Jared?" Tevyr said. "Yonu says Earth culture is primitive."

"Whatever."

"Are you even listening to us?" Yonu said.

"Yeah. Sure."

"What have we been talking about?"

"Stuff."

Tevyr snapped his fingers in front of Jared's face.

Jared looked up from the chessboard. “Tevyr?”

“Yeah?”

“Are your parents getting divorced?”

Tevyr’s jaw flopped open.

Yonu dropped her fork.

“Jared, how can you even ask something like that?” Tevyr said.

“Don’t know. Just curious, I guess.”

Yonu leaned over and whispered, “I told you. Primitive culture.”

“What was that?” Jared asked.

“Nothing,” Yonu said.

“Okay. First, Pilot Seth *Elexen* and Pilot Quennin *S’Kev* aren’t married,” Tevyr said. “Aktenai don’t get married. They bond.”

“Oh,” Jared blinked. “Right. Forgot.” He let go of his hair and sat up. The quick removal of his fingers left his disheveled mop standing up. “What’s bonding again?”

“Oh, curse this,” Tevyr muttered.

“It’s really simple,” Yonu said. “Aktenai bond when they conceive a child. They stay bonded until that child reaches maturity. At that point, they are free to part ways if they desire or stay bonded. Typically they’ll conceive another child at this point if the bond continues.”

“My parents have that decision coming up soon,” Tevyr said.

“Mine too.” Yonu winked at Tevyr.

Aktenai pilots were almost always raised in male/female pairs. The Choir selected those pairings with care, but also expected them to bear fruit. Tevyr had already received words of encouragement from his parents.

And Yonu’s parents too, for that matter.

“So, *NO*,” Tevyr said, “my parents aren’t getting divorced.”

“I get it now.”

"Do you really?"

"Are they going to have another kid?" Jared asked.

"I don't know! Go ask them yourself!"

Yonu shook her head and took another bite. "So primitive." She thumbed down a screen of text on her d-scroll, then highlighted a line with a finger. The text updated via her neural link.

"What are you working on?" Tevyr asked.

"My speech for tomorrow."

"What's the topic?"

"Jack Donolon, the pilot massacre, and the founding of the Alliance. You?"

"Veketon and the creation of the Choir."

"Uhh," Yonu said. "That's so boring. I bet half the class is going to do something on the Original Eleven."

"Maybe, but the speech practically wrote itself. Just pick any old text and reword it a bit." Tevyr wiped his hands off. "There. Done."

"That won't save you from the questions."

"It's our venerable master Veketon. Seriously, what are they going to ask me that I don't know?"

"If you say so." Yonu selected another line and deleted it with her neural link.

"How about you, Jared?" Tevyr asked.

"Hmm?"

"Your speech for tomorrow? What's it on?"

"Speech? What speech?"

"Our big history speech? You know, the one every pilot at this event has to give?"

"I'm giving a speech tomorrow?"

"Uh oh," Yonu whispered musically.

"Since when?" Jared asked.

"Since about a month ago," Tevyr said.

"Are you kidding?"

"Nope."

"Gosh *darn* it!" Jared uttered the words with all the gusto of a curse.

Tevyr wondered why Jared never utilized his culture's rich swearing heritage. Earthers had so many good curses. It was the one place their culture had clearly advanced beyond the Aktenai.

"How about you do the Zekuut exile?" Tevyr said.

"The who?"

"The Zekuut."

Jared shook his head.

"Aktenai, Grendeni, Zekuut," Tevyr said, holding up three fingers. "You know. Forsaken, Fallen, Outcast."

"I don't know anything about them."

"Okay." Tevyr scratched his chin. "Then what about the reign of Sovereign Elexen? His story ends in patricide."

"Are you purposefully trying to confuse me?"

"No. But honestly, it's not that hard to look up."

Jared grimaced at him.

Yonu closed her d-scroll. She grabbed her tray and stood up.

"Where are you off to?" Tevyr asked.

"My quarters. I need quiet so I can concentrate."

"Oh. Sorry about that."

"No, you're fine. I'll see you tomorrow, okay?"

"Yeah. See you."

Yonu took a few steps out of the mess hall, but stopped, turned on the balls of her feet, and walked back to the table.

"Say, Tev?"

"Yeah?"

"Would you mind helping me practice my speech tonight? I just need someone to listen to it a few times."

It was hard to suppress the look of horror forming on his face, but he managed to force it into a smile. "Well, uhh, sure. I'd love to!"

"Thanks. I really appreciate it," she said. "Stop by my quarters after you're done here, okay?"

Tevyr nodded, still wearing his fake smile. This was not how he planned to spend his evening.

But, wait a second here. It's not all bad. I'm going to be alone with Yonu. In her quarters. Late into the night.

Quite a few possibilities came to mind, and he took a moment to dwell on them. Yonu had certainly developed an abundance of female qualities over the past year or so, and even the EN pilots were now calling her a "total knockout."

"Stop leering," Yonu said.

Tevyr caught himself a moment too late. "Sorry. Yeah. I'll be there."

"Good." Yonu gave him a light kiss on the cheek. "See you then."

Tevyr watched her leave. It made him feel all warm and giddy on the inside.

"Your turn," Jared said in a sinister tone.

Tevyr glanced at the chessboard. With barely a thought, he moved his queen up six squares.

"Check and mate."

The next morning, Tevyr Elexen walked bleary-eyed into the JSDC's main auditorium. The 100-occupancy room resembled a wide bowl cut in half with two large sections of desks lining its slopes. A single stairway bisected the seating, leading to unofficially segregated Aktenai and Earth Nation sections.

Tevyr spotted Jared sitting at the back of the Aktenai section. He hummed a cheerful tune while organizing his dynamic-scrolls, hologram-scrolls, and light-pens. He was one of the few pilots who didn't care which side he sat on. Tevyr walked over and slumped wearily into the desk next to him.

Jared looked up and took a light-pen out of his mouth. "So, how did it go?"

"Sixteen times, Jared. I had to hear the whole thing sixteen times."

"That bad, huh?"

"And that's just counting the complete run-throughs. She started over at least a dozen times because she either paused too long or changed a word or … or I don't even know why! It all sounded fine to me!"

"Wow. A shame I had to miss that."

Tevyr gave him a sour look.

"But hey," Jared nudged him with an elbow, "at least all your efforts were well rewarded."

"Think again."

"Really?"

Tevyr blew out a frustrated breath. "She said she was too tired."

"Wow. That's a shame."

"Tell me about it. So, Jared, what's your speech topic?"

"Jack Donolon and the formation of the Alliance."

"Are you serious?"

"Yes."

Tevyr smacked his forehead and dragged the hand down his face.

"Is something wrong?" Jared asked.

"It's the same topic Yonu picked! She'll kill you!"

"Oh." Jared slowly rolled up one of his d-scrolls. "Whoops."

"Weren't you listening yesterday?"

"Not really."

Tevyr shook his head. "I'm beginning to think we shouldn't ever let you out of your seraph."

Jared shrugged. "It's the best I could come up with on short notice."

"Can you at least make your speech worse than hers?"

"That shouldn't be hard. I basically just recount the Battle for Earth."

"At least there's that," Tevyr said. "Yonu is covering the pilot massacre, too."

Jared nodded. "Yeah, I start with your parents defecting to the Earth Nation, then move on to Jack Donolon's duel with Sovereign Elexen. I close at the merger with his seraph."

"Sounds good to me. Maybe throw in a few awkward pauses for good measure."

"Tev?"

"Yeah?"

"Was Sovereign Elexen your grandfather?"

"Sort of," Tevyr said. "There are some seriously messed up Choir politics involved."

"I'm sorry about what happened to him."

"It's cool. We were about to wipe out Earth, remember?"

"Yeah. When you think about it, it's actually amazing there's an Alliance today."

"Yep." Teyyr tugged the creases out of his uniform. "My parents were pretty awesome back in the day. They made the right call to switch sides."

"Hey, Tev!"

Tevyr turned to see Yonu hurrying over.

"Morning," he said with a wave.

Yonu stopped next to his seat and unfurled a d-scroll.

"I reordered the part where the Grendeni traitor, Dominic Haeger, infiltrates Aktenzek and sets off the nuke in the pilot concourse. It flows a lot better now. Do you think we have time for another reading before class?"

"Ahhh ..." Tevyr glanced around. Half of the pilots had already taken their seats and the other half were filing in. "Probably not."

"Good morning, Yonu," Jared said.

"Hey, Jared."

"I hope you don't mind, but I picked the same topic as you."

Yonu opened her mouth, then closed it. She put a hand on her hip and stared at Jared.

"Seriously?" Her eyes could have melted mnemonic alloy.

"I hope you're okay with that," Jared said.

"Jared?"

"Yeah?"

Yonu pointed a finger at him. "The next time our squadrons drill together, I am picking *you* as my sparring partner."

She stormed off and took her seat at the front.

"I hate sparring," Jared said. "I always end up with burns, even with the limiters on."

"Then get hit less," Tevyr said.

"Easy for you to say." Jared massaged the back of his neck. "I was so certain five of us could take you out."

"You're too passive. You need to put pressure on your opponent and force them to make mistakes."

"That's easy for you to say," Jared said. "Honestly, I never understood why Aktenai pilots spend so much time training in close combat."

"Hey, it's not my fault you Earthers suck at it. Besides, it's only a matter of time before the Grendeni come out with their own seraphs, so we need to be ready."

"Shh!" Jared hissed. "Someone's coming."

Conversations throughout the auditorium died. Seth stepped quickly down the stairway to the podium. Yonu sat on the edge of her chair clutching a d-scroll to her chest.

"Be seated," Seth said curtly.

Every pilot took his or her seat.

Seth reached the auditorium's base. He placed a hand on the podium, not bothering to stand behind it, and turned to face them.

"I know all of you were looking forward to giving your history speeches today," Seth said.

To their credit, none of the pilots said a word or even murmured something under their breath.

"And I was looking forward to listening to all of them," Seth said in a neutral tone. "For however many hours that would have taken. But then a thought came to me. Why talk about history when you can actually witness it? I look across this auditorium, and I see the gulf that still remains between us. Perhaps today we can take a small but important step towards closing that gulf."

Jared whispered through set teeth, "Does that mean I don't have to give a speech?"

"Looks like it," Tevyr whispered back.

"All pilots, to your seraphs!" Seth said crisply. "We leave immediately."

Jared's hand shot up.

"Yes, I said all pilots," Seth said. "All groundings are suspended. And, depending on your actions today, they may remain so."

Seth stepped away from the podium and climbed the steps. He exited the auditorium without another word.

When the door closed behind him, Yonu rose from her seat and flung her d-scroll to the ground.

"Curse it!" she shouted.

Chapter 4

Pilgrimage

Seth Elexen angled his wings and darted past the Alliance formation. He swept by twenty-four seraphs arranged in two squadrons. His fellow Aktenai were each clad in unique armor, their coloration and styling dictated by the whims of their pilots.

In contrast, the Earth Nation squadron used a uniform metallic gray with chaos shunts forming vents along the wings and limbs. White lettering on the wings and a sigil of a stone horsehead marked each seraph. The lettering read "KNIGHTS" in one of the more common Earther languages.

"Alpha squadron ready," Tevyr said, leading the Aktenai.

"Epsilon squadron standing by, commander," Jared said, in command of the EN seraphs.

Quennin opened a private hypercast channel with Seth, establishing a secure and untraceable connection.

"The kids are excited," she said.

"Keep an eye on Tevyr," Seth said. "Make sure he doesn't do anything too reckless."

"Always."

“Grendeni warships coming into view over the horizon,” Jared said. “They’re rising out of the planet’s gravity well.”

“I count twenty frigates,” Tevyr said. “Four dreadnoughts, too. Ouch. Several non-combat craft with them as well. Permission to engage?”

“Hold present course,” Seth said. “We’re not looking for a fight.”

Below his feet, the Seeding world turned. Tall islands of red rock pockmarked the surface, rising out of its vast ocean. Black vegetation spread across the waters, some forming kilometer-wide floating colonies. The smog of primitive civilization grayed the clouds above several islands.

Seth wondered if the humans below knew of the spaceships lifting away from their planet. And if so, did they know that these titanic vessels represented the slimmest fraction of a vast robotic armada? Could they even comprehend the scale of hostilities between the Aktenai and the Grendeni?

“What were the Grendeni doing on the surface?” Quennin asked.

“Who knows?” Seth said. “Probably looking for another source of pilots.”

“Here? They’ve searched this planet before.”

“You never know. We didn’t expect to find so many candidates on Earth.”

“Earth is different. Always has been.”

“Too true.”

“Grendeni warships altering course,” Jared said. “Now heading towards us. Epsilon squadron, rifles at the ready!”

As one, the EN seraphs reached behind their backs and retrieved their rail-rifles. They shouldered the long-barreled weapons and energized their shunts. Parallel strips along the rail-rifles began to glow with each pilot’s unique chaos frequency.

“Permission to engage?” Tevyr asked.

"Negative," Seth said.

"Our fold engines are nearly charged," Quennin said. "We will continue to the next system as planned."

"Would it help if I asked nicely?" Tevyr said.

"No," Seth said.

"Kids," Quennin chuckled privately.

"I know . . ." Seth sighed the words more than spoke them.

"Grendeni warships still on approach," Jared said. "Now entering extreme cannon range. And it looks like—"

Fusion beams shot out of the enemy warships and cut through the seraph squadrons. One hit an EN seraph in a splash of plasma, throwing her back. She righted herself and glided back into formation.

"Yes, we are definitely being shot at," Jared said.

"How about *now*?" Tevyr asked pointedly.

"Our Fallen brothers and sisters are bold today," Quennin said. "Maybe they think they can pick off a few of the kids."

"If so, they're in for a shock," Seth said. "Squadrons are free to engage."

"Alpha squadron, let's go!" Tevyr flew out in the lead. His shunts blazed with green light.

"Epsilon squadron, open fire," Jared said.

The EN seraphs unleashed a barrage of accelerated bolts from their rifles. Most of the shots missed at this range, but two solid hits breached the lead frigate's bow armor.

Aktenai seraphs swept forward. Seth followed them with Quennin at his side.

The Grendeni frigates backed off, firing their cannons in retreat. Four dreadnoughts advanced, combining their fire to unleash twelve sun-hot beams. Bulky fusion torpedoes and agile tactical seekers belched out of their massive hulls.

"Stay clear of those dreadnoughts," Seth said.

"Understood," Tevyr said. "Alpha squadron, deploy countermeasures and swing around the dreads. Jared, see if you can keep them busy."

"Confirmed. Epsilon squadron, focus fire on my target."

Twelve streams of kinetic bolts converged on the closest dreadnought. Its hull buckled under the onslaught. Dark bands of mnemonic alloy flexed and rippled, quickly repairing the damage.

Beams from the dreadnought and frigates crossed through the Aktenai squadron. Three hit, blasting seraphs momentarily out of formation.

A beam shot past Seth. He felt a tickle of heat rush over his wings.

"Fold engines nearly charged," Quennin said.

"All seraphs, stand by to fold out," Seth said.

"Requesting permission to continue the engagement," Tevyr said. "They picked this fight, and I don't believe in leaving empty-handed."

"Very well," Seth said. "Proceed."

"Alpha squadron, cover me!"

Tevyr dove towards the nearest frigate, his wings leaving a trail of green energy. Alpha squadron launched a flurry of torpedoes from their weapon pods.

"He actually asked for permission this time," Quennin said on a private channel.

"I'm as surprised as you are," Seth said.

Tevyr didn't bother with cannons or torpedoes. He snapped his arms wide. Twin emerald-hued daggers ignited from his wrists.

The Grendeni frigate descended towards the planet in a final effort to evade his attack. Beams slashed across space from every direction, all targeting his lightning-fast red seraph.

Tevyr wove and pirouetted through beams as if it were a game, ducked under the last cannon shot from the frigate, and flew underneath it. With both daggers, he slashed across the frigate's belly.

A ripple of explosions ran down the Grendeni warship's length, cracking it open.

Tevyr swung over the frigate and pumped a single beam into the center. The ship blew apart in a flash of plasma.

"Grendeni robot trash," Tevyr spat.

"Fold engines charged," Quennin said.

"All seraphs, fold now," Seth said.

Twenty-six seraphs vanished from the system.

The seraphs appeared over a dead world orbited by massive, dark artifacts. A chill fell across Seth's spine. His wings shivered. Despite how many times he'd seen it, the planet still evoked a palpable sense of horror.

"What is this place?" Jared asked.

"Imayirot," Seth said. "It means 'World of Death' in the Aktenai tongue."

Sunlight never touched the black surface of this dead world. Cadaverous cities and the skeletal remains of massive domes dotted its war-blasted surface. It was a tomb, cold and inert, devoid of life.

Above airless skies orbited an incomplete shell of reflective mirrors and canopies. A massive black shade in the form of a planet-sized disc hovered between Imayirot and its sun. It was this gargantuan device that kept the ancient world of Imayirot cold and dark, preserved at the moment of its death.

The shade was heavily armed, mounting hundreds of thousands of weapon systems around its circumference. In addition to it, thousands more orbital weapon platforms surrounded Imayirot, some surpassing dreadnoughts with their size and firepower. All of these weapons were as dead as the world they guarded, though not from decay or battle damage.

"Hey, wait a second," Jared said. "The Grendeni made some of those orbital platforms."

"That is correct," Seth said. "Both Grendeni and Aktenai weapons guard this world."

"But … well, I mean we're at war."

"We are."

An alert opened in Seth's mind. He spun around and looked up.

Twenty-three Grendeni warships flashed into existence six thousand kilometers above the seraphs. Immediately, the ships powered down their weapons and drive blades.

"They're not attacking?" Jared said.

"Of course not," Tevyr said. "Don't you know where we are?"

"Not really," Jared said.

"We'll still have to deal with them when we leave," Seth said. "But for now, they will only observe us."

"Why's that?" Jared asked.

"This is Imayirot," Tevyr said. "Violence is forbidden here."

"Okay …" Jared said. "So *why* is it forbidden?"

"You will learn this today," Seth said. "There is a tradition amongst the Aktenai. Every pilot of Aktenzek makes at least one pilgrimage to Imayirot, to witness for themselves the death of this place. Today, all of you make yours. Come now. Let us land."

Seth spread his wings and descended towards Imayirot. He cruised through the orbital swarms, weapon platforms shooting by in quick flashes of dark armor.

Two seraph squadrons followed.

"A lot of these platforms look old," Jared said. "Really old."

"That's correct, Pilot Daykin," Quennin said. "Imayirot's defenses have been erected piece by piece over thousands of years. Both Aktenai and Grendeni contribute to the orbital swarm, strengthening it, modernizing it. As you can see, it is completely inert right now. However, both factions can activate it should this world ever be threatened. No matter the differences between us and our Fallen brothers and sisters, Imayirot is something we will always come together for."

Seth approached a towering spire that showed no signs of decay. A dome sat atop its apex, ringed with dozens of docking bays. Seth picked one designed for seraphs and dropped into place. His feet touched the cold metal.

Clamps secured him at the shoulders. A pressurized tunnel extended from the dome and sealed against his chest armor. Breathable air flooded the chamber.

Seth pushed the seraph's senses away. He remembered his own limbs, his own eyes. He flexed his fingers and took a deep breath within the seraph's cockpit, once again nothing more than a human being. The cockpit walls spread out. He pushed himself out of the pilot alcove and exited the seraph.

Other seraphs began to dock. Quennin landed to his right, Tevyr to his left.

Through his neural link, his i-suit confirmed that the air was safe. Seth took off his helmet and tossed it into the cockpit. He strode through the tunnel, entered the dome, and looked around. The interior was as empty and lifeless as the planet.

Quennin exited her own tunnel and walked over.

"You have that face again," she said.

"Which one?"

"The I'm-going-to-talk-to-Tevyr face."

"Hmm. Maybe."

Tevyr jogged out of his tunnel. Already other pilots were entering the concourse and gathering at the center. He hurried over to join them.

"Tevyr," Seth said. "A moment of your time."

His son stumbled to a halt.

Seth stopped in front of him, hands clasped behind his back. "Care to explain yourself?"

"I'm not sure I understand, Father."

"I think you know what I mean," Seth said. "There was no need to engage the frigate so closely. Is your cannon not focused properly?"

"No, Father."

"Then why get in that close?"

Tevyr opened his mouth and began to form words, but quickly clapped his jaw shut. He bowed his head and said, "I have no excuse. I was trying to show off."

"For Pilot Nezrii?"

"Yes, Father."

"I *see*." Seth let that last syllable hang ominously in the air, then finally said, "Perhaps something less foolhardy next time."

"I will certainly keep that in mind, Father."

"Now go. We will join you shortly."

"Yes, Father. Mother." Tevyr bowed deeply to both pilots, then jogged over to the others.

"It wasn't that bad," Quennin said when he was out of earshot. "And he did ask first."

"Our son is brash, but I can feel the beginnings of a great pilot within him," Seth said. "We need to make sure he achieves that."

"If you restrict him too much, it may stifle the growth of his talent."

"I suppose you do have a point there."

"Besides," Quennin put her arm around Seth's waist and leaned close, "I remember you doing similar things to impress me."

"Maybe, but I wasn't as stupid about it."

Quennin laughed quietly. "Oh, is that how you remember it?"

Tevyr joined Jared and the other pilots.

"Whew! I was worried there for a moment," he said.

"So, we're heading to the core of the planet?" Jared asked.

"Yeah," Tevyr said.

"And what'll we find there?"

"The Last Death."

"Creepy." Jared brushed sandy blonde locks out of his face and craned his neck. Fragments of a broken shell orbited high overhead. Their inner surfaces could have been mirrors that had experienced eons of micrometeorite impacts. A thin web-like support structure poked out of the edges.

"And I thought Aktenzek was weird," Jared said.

"Hey now," Tevyr said. "That's my home you're talking about."

"It's not my fault your home is weird. Have you been here before?"

"Nope. It's my first pilgrimage, too."

"Quiet," Yonu whispered. "They're coming."

Seth and Quennin walked over. The EN pilots stood rigidly at attention. The Aktenai pilots bowed.

Jared pointed up. "Sirs, what's with the debris in orbit?"

"They're remnants of an attempt to save this world," Quennin said. "Imayirot, once called Ittenrashik, was the first world the Aktenai colonized after being exiled to this universe. This is where the Grendeni and Aktenai separated and where the Bane committed its greatest atrocity."

Quennin's mentioning of the Bane hushed the crowded. Aktenai pilots bowed their heads in quiet remembrance. EN pilots glanced at one another with suddenly worried expressions.

"The Bane did this?" Jared said. "A single creature destroyed this entire *world*?"

"That's right." Quennin gestured towards a group of clear discs cut into the dome's floor. "Come on. You are all pilots. It is your privilege to see this place with your own eyes."

The pilots walked onto one of the discs, which was wide enough for all of them to stand on comfortably. A guardrail rose from the edge and stopped at waist height.

Quennin moved to the center of the group.

"Ittenrashik, when our ancestors found it, was very similar to Earth," she said. "A lush planet with vast oceans and wild landmasses teeming with life. Here they began to build a civilization. It wasn't easy, but they had the leadership of the Original Eleven to guide them through any hardship."

Quennin linked a command to the disc, which then dropped down with great speed.

"Whoa!" Jared grabbed the railing.

Gravity remained normal despite the acceleration. The spire walls were transparent from the inside, affording a view of Imayirot as they descended.

"Keep it together, Jared," Tevyr whispered.

"Sorry, but we're really high up."

"You're a seraph pilot. How can you be afraid of heights?"

Seth cleared his throat. The banter ended.

"Life was difficult but not impossible," Quennin said. "And a way home had been sent with them in the form of the Gate. The Gate was theirs to use once the Bane had been killed and theirs to guard against the Bane. But, of course, the Gate also represented the Bane's path back to the Homeland, and so it was hidden.

"When the Bane finally attacked, there was no way our ancestors could harm it. How can you damage something frozen in time, something that cannot be changed? This terrible monster turned people, buildings, and even entire cities into dust in seconds, letting them feel millennia in the blink of an eye. The Bane demanded access to the Gate, but the Aktenai refused. And so, the Bane went on a rampage."

The disc descended towards the black surface of Imayirot. A large cracked dome came into view at the base of the spire.

"Where is the Gate now?" Jared asked.

"Safe," Seth said. "The Original Eleven know where it is hidden. That is enough for us to know."

"After being denied the Gate," Quennin said, "the Bane entered into a furious rage and committed the unthinkable. It pushed this entire planet into an axis of accelerated time. To Aktenai not on the planet, including the Original Eleven, the moment was barely measurable. To Ittenrashik and its inhabitants, that moment was an eternity."

The disc entered a domed city, gray and utterly lifeless. Dim lights from the spire revealed long stretches of rubble surrounding skeletal structures. Some buildings stood tall but decayed. Others had fallen over or leaned into their neighbors.

"Being pushed into another time axis had a side effect," Quennin said. "While the planet's inhabitants were still alive and capable of surviving, the planet slowly grew colder. The rest of the universe was at a standstill in their eyes. There was no sun, no stars in the sky above Ittenrashik. Only a joyless black film, a barrier that could not be crossed and that absorbed every morsel of heat and radiation that touched it. Ittenrashik grew colder, and the inhabitants fought to survive."

Tevyr nudged Jared. "That's what the shell fragments in orbit were for."

"Oh, I see."

Quennin nodded. "One of many attempts. At first there were domes like this one. Simple encapsulations to preserve thermal energy. Grander attempts were made later to prevent heat loss. Heat was also produced in a variety of methods, prolonging the inevitable. Over eons, they consumed the oceans for fusible hydrogen, leaving nothing but empty pits on the surface.

"The inhabitants made many brave attempts to combat the problems. However, entropy was always present, and the years went on for an eternity. The people of Ittenrashik began to break apart. Despite this, many banded together to build the mirror shell, hoping to enclose the entire planet. Others retreated towards the core. Each day saw the planet grow colder. Nothing could halt the remorseless advance of entropy."

Lights from the disc's edge illuminated a vast open shaft leading into Imayirot's subterranean depths. They descended rapidly through immense shafts that intersected one subterranean city after another. Some of those cities stretched on for hundreds of kilometers, their grand chambers filled with the cold remnants of dead societies.

"Wars eventually broke out," Quennin said. "How could they not? They fought over energy, food, air, and other resources. The planet's oceans shrank, and the atmosphere froze. Survivors headed towards the core as heat became more and more precious, hoping to use the planet as a buffer."

The disc passed city after city, sometimes heading at diagonals, but always moving towards the planet's core.

"How long did this go on?" Jared asked.

"Anyone?" Seth asked.

Yonu stepped forward.

"Pilot Nezrii," Seth said.

"Ittenrashik was pushed into the accelerated time axis for twenty million years," Yonu said. "The inhabitants only lasted a fraction of that time."

"Correct," Seth said.

Yonu raised an eyebrow at Tevyr.

"What?" Tevyr whispered. "I could have answered that too."

"Sure you could have," Yonu whispered.

"Ah. We're almost there," Quennin said.

"Where?" Jared asked.

"The Last Death," Quennin said.

The disc passed through a slender, roughly-cut shaft. It opened up into a small sphere much more primitive than the earlier cities. This close to the core, gravity was almost nonexistent, and the living space appeared adapted for that. The walls were lined with a honeycomb of rooms, machinery …

And bodies.

Thousands and thousands of bodies, all dried up and mummified.

"Super creepy," Jared said.

"Would anyone care to explain?" Seth asked.

Yonu stepped forward again.

"Anyone besides Pilot Nezrii? No? Go ahead then."

"The water in their bodies was extracted for fusible hydrogen," Yonu said.

"Correct."

The disc settled against an enclosed walkway and stopped. The clear tunnel led to one of many dissimilar compartments in the sphere's honeycomb. Pilots followed Quennin into a small room and gathered behind her.

Quennin pointed to two corpses, both clothed in insulated pressure suits. One was a small child. The other was a headless body with a small device in one hand.

"The last two people on Ittenrashik to die," Quennin said. "The first was the child shortly after her birth, too weak to live. The second was the mother, killing herself after losing the child."

The EN pilots crowded against the railing, taking turns gawking and pointing at the corpses. All of the Aktenai pilots kept their distance.

"The Bane did all of this," Quennin said. "It inflicted incalculable pain and suffering on our ancestors. When it finally released this world, the Bane was near death. Torturing an entire planet stretched even its limits. The monster fled into the depths of space, leaving this dead world behind. Ittenrashik had become Imayirot."

"And one creature did all of this?" Jared whispered.

"Yeah, I know," Tevyr said.

"Scary."

"The Bane cannot be permitted to exist," Seth said. "This is our Great Mission, the mission to which all Aktenai are dedicated, the mission the Grendeni abandoned long ago. And though our Earther allies may not believe in our Great Mission, your belief is not required. The Bane is real. The Great Mission is real, and one day we will be called upon to face that monster again. Let us continue to fight side by side. Let us continue to strengthen our Alliance. For together, we shall face and defeat any foe."

Chapter 5

Fallen

Assistant Administrator Dominic Haeger breathed in the fresh air from the delicatessen's balcony, two hundred stories high. Though he could take on almost any human male's appearance, he had not used the ability since returning to the Grendeni twenty years ago. With his handsome, likable face and blond ponytail, old "comrades" in the EN SpecOps would still recognize him.

From the balcony, Dominic gazed across the vast habitat cylinder within the Grendeni schism *Righteous Anger*. All around him, buildings of the northcity reached up towards the central axis of the schism's enclosed cylinder. Nothing so crude as rotation provided gravity in the habitat, and the northcity buildings could reach up and almost touch the very center of the schism.

Further north, the buildings rose until they finally met, sealing off the habitat cylinder from the northern factories and space docks. Dominic thought it resembled a giant geode, one made of metal and glass instead of crystal.

A cylindrical landscape stretched out before him, capped at the opposite end by the southcity. The interior simulated life on a planet in ways similar to the habitat discs within the fortress planet Aktenzek. Lakes, beaches, villas, gentle grassy hills, and emerald forests filled the schism with lushness and visual splendor. A long axial tube ran through the center, generating daylight.

The *Righteous Anger*, like all other schisms, glided gracefully through the voids between star systems, hidden from the Aktenai and anyone else who would dare harm them. The Grendeni were a nomadic people, constantly on the move, and schisms were their vessels. No single person knew the location of every schism, and no accurate census of the Grendeni had been produced in thousands of years.

Administrator Gurgella sat at the balcony's only table, devouring the last of the meat lathered in a tangy brown sauce. This short, bald, and rather ugly man commanded the *Righteous Anger*. The right breast of his green jacket bore the gold sigils of his rank.

"You should really try some of this." Gurgella munched sloppily on the avian meat.

"I am not hungry, administrator," Dominic said, though he knew the bones to be brittle and quite tasty.

"Come now. Even freaks like you have to eat."

Dominic said nothing, but thought: *You do realize I could rip you in two, you bloated, worthless bureaucrat.*

"Come, Dominic." Gurgella wiped at his mouth and hands with a napkin. "You are avoiding the issue."

"The archangels are not ready. I have made my opinion clear on this. It doesn't matter how many times you ask me. I will not change my mind."

Gurgella set the soiled napkin down on his empty plate. "I understand your position, Dominic, but I am receiving considerable pressure from the Executives."

A green-liveried servant came to his side, his platter ready with steaming rolled towels.

Gurgella selected one and unfurled it with a snap of his wrist. "The Executives want the archangels deployed as soon as possible."

"Where have I heard that before?" Dominic muttered.

"Excuse me?"

"They aren't ready!"

Gurgella shook his head. "I understand the desire to perfect your weapons, but we have already invested considerable time and resources into this project. The Executives are eager for payoff."

"And they'll have it, but I need more time."

"Time is something we do not have, Dominic," Gurgella said. "Every moment sees Aktenzek strengthening its seraph squadrons. Every battle sees those accursed machines tearing through our fleets. The Executives haven't launched a meaningful offensive in years, and we lost every major battle before that. Is any of this getting through that thick head of yours?"

"It doesn't change any of the facts. We should not deploy them."

"Come now, Dominic. We've produced hundreds of archangels in this schism alone."

"Yes, we have the archangels. But the *pilots*, administrator. The pilots are not ready. There are reasons why the breeders keep calling them berserkers."

"They seem stable enough."

"They're borderline psychotic!"

"As long as they're psychopaths that kill seraphs, I see no problems."

"You simply won't listen."

Gurgella stood up and tossed his towel onto the table. He tugged his jacket down, pulling out the creases. "The Executives will not wait years while you tinker with your breeding programs. Now, let's have a look at the latest batch."

"Of course, administrator." Dominic picked his jacket off the railing and pulled it over his white tunic. He was still buttoning it up when he followed Gurgella out of the delicatessen.

"Unless the pilots truly cannot perform, I see no reason not to deploy the archangels."

"Administrator, the—"

"I've heard enough of your excuses. Frankly, I'm sick of them."

Dominic followed Gurgella in silence.

Do you even realize who you're talking to? he thought. *We have our first true chance to gain the upper hand in this war, and it's all because of me. Who are you to question my decisions?*

Nearly twenty years to the day, Dominic had escaped Aktenzek with an intact seraph and the first pilot captured alive, allowing Grendeni technicians to reverse-engineer its secrets. The mechanisms within that great machine disturbed Dominic even to this day, and the ethical cost of the Archangel Project continued to be paid in the blood of innocents.

Gurgella and Dominic boarded a private tram. It floated through the northcity's vast urban sprawl and ascended. Dominic glanced back, watching the tall spires of silver and glass recede as the gravity tram accelerated diagonally towards the schism's axis. The tram's walls and ceiling were transparent, providing a spectacular view of the northcity.

They sped towards the northern factory zone.

"Are they really that unstable?" Gurgella asked.

"We end up putting down about one in five," Dominic said. "We've tried everything we can think of to stabilize them. Drugs, cranial implants, mental conditioning, and so on. Everything we do neuters their piloting talents. We simply don't understand how the ability is passed. It's hereditary, but not genetic. Clones possess none of the original's talents. Artificial insemination also doesn't work. The talent is only passed when pilots mate naturally."

"Yes, yes, yes," Gurgella said with a dismissive wave. "But one in five?"

"They have a habit of becoming uncontrollably violent towards the other pilots."

"Only other pilots?"

"Yeah. Curse it if I know why."

The tram flew along the schism's axial tube and entered the northern cap tunnel. They bypassed the tunnel's congested traffic lanes and glided into the northern factory zone. Here, the entire inner surface of the schism cylinder was one giant factory: over six hundred square kilometers of concentrated manufacturing power. The tram sped past towering mechanized edifices that almost reached the axial tube.

"Ah, there they are," Gurgella said, looking through the glass bottom.

Ten cargo haulers rose from the archangel factories. They slowed and hovered, forming a line for inspection.

The tram settled into a parallel path and stopped near the lead cargo hauler. Dominic and Gurgella occupied a small glass box next to the immense humanoid weapon.

Dominic's mouth quirked up in disgust as he recalled seraph pilot Mezen Daed's "contribution" to the Archangel Project. The man was "persuaded" to impregnate one hundred females as a precondition of his release through a prisoner exchange with Aktenzek.

These pregnancies were manipulated to have an unusually large number of fraternal and identical offspring, sometimes as many as a dozen children. The children were then surgically altered to mature in less than two years. Once capable of mating, they were interbred with each other as well as bred with suitable candidates from the general populace. The current berserkers were the tenth generation result of those experiments.

Not as good as the real thing, but plentiful and expendable. It all made Dominic sick to his stomach. Or rather, it would if he actually could become sick to his stomach.

Grendeni engineers had designed the archangels around similar principles, producing a crude, plentiful reflection of the seraph's technical mastery.

The archangels possessed no armor, relying solely on their pilots' feeble barriers for protection. Their giant bodies resembled copper skeletons packed with machinery. Only two slender wings extended from their backs. Each skull-like head contained twin scanners like large black lenses, giving them hauntingly human faces.

"What sort of trials will you be holding today, Dominic?" Gurgella asked.

"We will continue testing the newest sword variants. The last few batches have had an unacceptably high number of defects."

Unlike seraphs, archangels possessed no beam weapons. The repeatedly fatal attempts to reproduce the miniaturized fusion cannon technology had burned through too many test pilots. But this obstacle had led to an unprecedented Grendeni breakthrough: the chaos sword.

A sword was twice as expensive as the archangel wielding it and nearly as large, but the weapons elevated each archangel to their intended roles as pure, dedicated seraph-killers.

"Very well," Gurgella said. "Proceed with the test."

Dominic opened a neural link but was interrupted before he could send.

"Administrators," a schism control officer said. "We have two unscheduled vessels folding in ten thousand kilometers off the schism."

"Can you identify them?" Gurgella asked.

"One moment . . ." he said, then gasped. "Administrators, they're seraphs!"

"What?" Dominic said.

"Fold!" Gurgella shouted. "Get us out of here!"

Dominic linked to the *Righteous Anger*'s active scanners and perceived the seraphs in a small pocket of his mind. The visual distortion of their fold points made details sketchy, but there could be no mistaking the silhouettes.

Two seraphs approached rapidly, one white and one black.

The *Righteous Anger* folded space on a small standby charge, emerging five light-minutes away.

Dominic spread his mind into the *Righteous Anger*'s control network, analyzing fold engine propagator status, fold trajectory, and point of origin. But it was a pointless exercise. A craft as massive as the *Righteous Anger* could never outpace seraphs fold for fold.

We have only moments before those seraphs follow us, Dominic thought. *But why are they attacking a civilian target? Do they know about the archangels? If so, why only two seraphs?*

"Fleet has been notified," the schism control officer said. "We'll be reinforced in ten minutes."

"Fold again as soon as the engines are ready," Gurgella said.

"The two seraphs have followed our fold trajectory. They're coming in!"

Dominic shifted his primary mental focus back to the seraph visuals. The black seraph must have employed some form of stealth technology. Even under maximum resolution, he could see nothing besides its black silhouette. He shifted his focus to the white seraph.

Oh no. No-no-no-no-no. Not him*!*

Dominic's heart threatened to punch through his ribcage. How could he ever forget that terrible white seraph? Blue Aktenai letters blazed across its limbs and wings, proclaiming the litany of their false mission. Even after so many years, its silhouette evoked palpable terror in him.

"Jack …" Dominic whispered. "I'm going to die."

"One of the seraphs has latched onto the hull! It's inside our fold envelope! We can't get away!"

The white seraph walked across the *Righteous Anger*'s barren exterior. A blade of pure blue energy ignited out of its forearm.

With two deliberate strokes and a strong kick, the seraph breached the schism's outer hull and flew into the northern space dock. From within, the schism was totally defenseless.

Except for …

"Dominic." Gurgella rubbed his sweating hands together. "We don't have a choice. Launch the archangels."

"It won't matter," Dominic said, his voice quiet and unwavering. "Not against this one. Not if we had a hundred could we survive this attack."

"Curse your stubbornness! We have a seraph inside the schism! Launch the archangels!"

Dominic closed his eyes and sighed. *Well, if I'm going to die, might as well go out fighting.*

He linked to the cargo haulers. "Release pilots from stasis. Activate archangel squadron twenty-seven."

One by one, the pilots awoke from their artificial slumber. Vent-like shunts on each archangel burned with yellow inner light. Mechanical restraints snapped off their wrists and ankles. Each archangel twitched alive and climbed free of the cargo haulers. The closest one picked up a sword as long as it was tall. When its hands gripped the hilt, one edge of the blade glowed faintly and brightened.

Dominic guided the tram towards the factory surface. He didn't want to be anywhere near them.

"The seraph has broken into the factory zone!" the schism control officer said. "It's inside!"

A distant white speck flew out of a depressurization tornado. Mnemonic alloy along the schism's skin quickly closed the breach.

The seraph swung around and headed straight for them.

"Release archangel scanner blinds," Dominic linked. "Designate the white seraph as primary target."

The archangels pulled away from the cargo haulers and caught sight of their enemy. The group spread their wings and accelerated towards the seraph. One archangel lagged behind on purpose, raised its sword, and cleaved one of its comrades in two.

Dominic let out a frustrated sigh and linked a kill code to the offending craft. Devices in the cockpit liquefied the pilot. Its shunts flickered and died. The skeletal machine fell away, limbs slack at its sides. It crashed into the tiered storage warehouse below.

Eight archangels charged in.

The white seraph raised its unusually long chaos blade and met the lead archangel head on. The archangel blurred swinging its sword, even to Dominic's enhanced eyes.

But the seraph moved faster. It darted past and slashed through the archangel's waist. Two halves spun away, luminous fluid pulsing from the wound.

Three archangels dove in at once. The seraph swung wide, its blade forming a burning arc of light. Its strike bashed through two of the archangels' guards, cutting them down. The third succeeded in deflecting the attack, but its victory was short lived.

With its free arm, the seraph punched clean through that archangel's stomach. Wrecked equipment and a spray of liquid blew out the back. The seraph flung the ruined machine away.

"Curse me," Gurgella breathed. "What a monster."

"I know," Dominic said.

Only four archangels remained. Two circled behind the seraph to form a loose ring around it. The seraph waited in the center.

All four archangels swarmed in at once.

Chaos energy collected above the seraph's unarmed wrist, forming a blazing energy shield. It parried the first attack and hewed an archangel in the first swing, then turned, deflected another strike and split an archangel from head to groin.

The seraph spread its wings, climbed above the last two, then dove in again. With a diagonal slash, it cut another down. Glowing conductor fluid rained on the factories below. Coppery limbs, torsos, and wings crashed to the ground.

The white seraph stabbed the last archangel through its chest, incinerating the pilot. The archangel's barrier faded. Its shunts turned black. The seraph kicked the dead machine off its blade, then faced the tram.

"Wha-wha-what is it doing?" Gurgella stuttered.

"Coming for us," Dominic said, then whispered, "or perhaps for me."

The white seraph sped in and grabbed the glass tram in one massive fist. The jarring impact threw Gurgella and Dominic to the floor. Massive digits pressed in. Glass creaked and splintered. Cracks spread across the walls.

Dominic pushed off the floor and stood up. The seraph raised the tram to head height and looked in. He faced the seraph, back straight, head raised.

Come on, Jack. If you're going to kill me, then get it over with.

The seraph linked with the tram's audio systems. Dominic let the signal through.

"Hey, Dom. It's been a while."

"Jack," Dominic said simply.

"So those were the new Grendeni archangels. Not too bad for fake seraphs."

"How could you possibly know about them?"

The seraph shrugged its shoulders. "I have my ways."

"That's ridiculous. They're a carefully guarded secret."

"Your work?" Jack asked.

"Yes. They're our new anti-seraph weapon."

"I think you need to try harder."

"They're not designed to go against *you*."

The seraph shook as if laughing. "Fair point, Dom. Fair point."

What are you waiting for? Dominic thought.

"I can see their potential," Jack said. "This might turn out even better than I hoped. Who's your friend?"

"Administrator Gurgella. This is his schism."

"He just wet himself."

"I don't blame him. You have that effect on people."

The seraph made that laughing motion again. "Then maybe you should introduce us. You can tell him some embarrassing stories about me. Maybe pick one from our good old days back in SpecOps."

"Curse it, Jack!" Dominic growled. "If you're here to kill me, then do it. I won't beg for my life, if that's what you're waiting for."

"I'm not here to kill you."

"Then why are you here?"

"Come on. It's been so long. Aren't I allowed to look up an old friend and drop by for a beer?"

"I was never your friend. I only played the part."

"Yeah. I know. That hurt, by the way. Still does."

"Enough games, Jack. Just tell me straight. Why are you here?"

The seraph shifted its stance and angled its head forward, taking on a stern, serious air.

"It's simple," Jack said. "I have a proposal for the Grendeni."

"And why would we ever listen to you?"

"Because of what you stand to gain. The location of the Gate."

"*What*?" Dominic said. "Are you serious?"

"I am."

"You know where it is?"

"No," Jack said. "Not yet, anyway. But I know how to get it. Interested?"

"Well, of course I am. If we got our hands on the Gate, we could force the Aktenai to stop this war. We could actually win the war. They'd do anything not to see the Gate destroyed."

Cautious relief welled up in Dominic. Maybe he wasn't going to die today after all.

"An exciting possibility, isn't it?" Jack said.

"You know it is."

Jack brought the tram closer. "So, will you help me?"

"It doesn't matter what you offer. I don't trust you and neither will the Executives."

"That makes two of us. But I think you'll find we both have something to gain here."

"Prove to me this isn't some Aktenai trick."

"You want proof?" Jack said. "I'll give you proof you can't ignore."

Dominic crossed his arms. "That is something I'd very much like to see."

Chapter 6

Reunion

Seth and Quennin folded space to the solar system.

The fortress planet of Aktenzek loomed ahead. Its entire surface gleamed like a pearly sea. Ten-kilometer-thick mnemonic armor shrouded the whole planet. Forests of fusion cannon towers and mountain ranges of exodrone control pyramids covered the surface.

Just beyond Aktenzek was its younger twin, Zu'Rashik. The Earth was a swirl of blue-white in the distance, its orbit unaffected by the presence of the two foreign worlds.

From space, the fortress planets were identical. Inside, however, was a very different story.

As part of the Treaty of the Alliance, Aktenzek had remained in Earth orbit, safeguarding the vulnerable Earth Nation from Grendeni aggression. Unsatisfied with their world's new sedentary nature, the Choir had ordered the construction of a new fortress planet for operations elsewhere.

Zu'Rashik had started its life as an unremarkable airless rock. Over the past twenty years, the Aktenai had poured their immense industrial might into creating from that rock a fortress planet every bit the equal of Aktenzek.

"It's good to be home," Quennin said.

"Yes, it is. I sometimes forget how much I miss Aktenzek."

"When are the first settlers moving to Zu'Rashik?"

"This year, I think. Enough habitat caverns should be carved out by now. Perhaps we should join one of the new cities?"

"Ha! As if you could ever sit still long enough."

Seth grinned. "Too true."

"Let's not keep the Sovereign waiting."

Quennin unfurled her flame-red wings. Emerald lightning crackled within the large kite-shaped gems embedded in the side of each wing. She took off with a burst of speed. Seth diverted power to his wings and followed her descent to Aktenzek.

They fell towards the planet, passing massive arrays of robotic frigates, whole squadrons of dreadnoughts, and a pair of Aktenai seraph squadrons competing in sparring exercises. Aktenzek grew larger until its horizon was flat.

Seth and Quennin skimmed across the fortress planet's surface. Lanes of gigantic fusion towers flashed by. Drone control pyramids rose seventy kilometers into the black, airless sky. Seth and Quennin broke through the towers and climbed, cresting several large white domes each the size of a mountain. They sped past an expansive metropolis that crawled and plodded across the surface, affixing additional fusion towers as it crept along.

A vast iris of mnemonic armor opened ahead. Seth and Quennin flew up, looped over, and sped down the mammoth tunnel. They dodged around lanes of automated transports, rushed through zones of light and dark, then took a sharp turn at a T-junction. Mnemonic security shutters snapped open, permitting their entry.

Seth and Quennin shot through a coin-shaped habitat cavern several kilometers across. A simulated sun shone through a simulated sky, its light gleaming off towers of gold and glass. They arced around the spires and slipped through a square exit.

They followed the twisting network of tunnels deeper into the planet, past reinforced security checkpoints, several habitat caverns, and two industrial complexes. After several minutes, they arrived at the planet's center.

The Core of Aktenzek floated in a grand spherical chamber with no visible support: a planetoid within a planet, smooth and white. Tightly packed mechanical cylinders crammed the sky, buzzing with the colossal energies needed to power the world's gravity drives and fold engines.

A single city sprawled across the white planetoid, and in the center of that city was the Sovereign's Palace. The palace pyramid rose up from the surrounding villa with slopes like finely polished mirrors. It towered over everything else.

Seth glided across the small world's surface, past hidden doorways that led into the sensitive interiors of the Core where the seraph factories and the Choir dwelt. He skimmed across towering buildings dwarfed by the pyramid before him.

Seth spotted the landing platform: a thin strand of silver vaulting out of the pyramid's side. The platform stood large enough to accommodate scores of craft and whole squadrons of seraphs, yet it appeared insignificant next to the Palace.

The long silver arm ended in a bulbous circle equipped with all manner of docking stations. Already, dozens of vessels were moored across its circumference. Seth spotted two gleaming silver seraphs among them.

"The Renseki are here," Quennin said, slowing for the final approach.

The seraphs used by the six Renseki pilots all shared a common design. Their armor shone like sculpted silver. Ornate lines swirled, twisted, and formed delicate curlicues across their bodies and wings. One seraph stood taller than the other, its ornamental lines more prolific.

"There's Mezen's," Seth said.

"The other one must be Zo's," Quennin said. "I doubt the twins or the old guard would be called in without those two."

Seth pulled above a vacant seraph dock and eased down until his feet touched the ground. He retracted his wings behind his back.

He pushed the seraph out of his mind, wiggled his own arms, blinked his own eyes. The cockpit receded and opened. He climbed out of the pilot alcove and walked onto the landing platform.

Seth looked up, finding a perfect simulacrum of early morning sky where the planetary engines had been. To his right, Quennin's seraph dipped down, made contact with the dock and locked into place. Seth walked over to meet her.

Quennin stepped out of the seraph and glanced over at the Renseki seraphs.

"First an unexplained summons from Vorin," Quennin said. "And now the Renseki show up. Something big is going on."

"So it would seem," Seth said.

An automated aircar stopped in front of the two pilots. Low doors opened, stairs extended, and the two pilots boarded the oval, open canopy craft. A local gravity field energized around the vehicle, and it took off, swooping along the circumference of the landing platform and traveling across the long arm towards the Sovereign's Palace. Though the car accelerated harshly, Seth and Quennin felt none of it.

The aircar sped through the twenty-story archway at the far end of the connecting arm and took them into the Palace's labyrinthine interior. Other cars zipped by as short glimpses of color.

The car quickly arrived at the Sovereign's private residence, deep within the Palace. Seth and Quennin exited the automated car, which promptly took off to assist other travelers.

A great foyer opened up before them, wide and tall and supported by a dozen fluted columns. Tiny white, silver, and black tiles covered the floor with intricate curling patterns that led the eye towards three staircases.

Quennin grinned when she saw who had waited for them. A petite woman leaned against a column, possessing friendly blue eyes and long black hair woven in a complex braid. She wore the traditional long coat of the Renseki with its numerous flourishes of silver curls.

Zo Nezrii looked up. She smiled brightly and waved.

"Quennin! Seth! Good to see you two."

"Always a pleasure, Zo," Seth said. "Though I wish I knew why we're here."

"Any idea what this is all about?" Quennin asked.

Zo shook her head. "Not a clue. Vorin and the Choir wanted to wait until you two arrived."

Seth grimaced. "What would the Sovereign reserve for us that he wouldn't tell you?"

"Good question. Let's find out." Zo led the way up the central staircase.

They walked by servants and Aktenai dignitaries busying themselves with duties large and small. All of them stopped and inclined their necks until the pilots had passed. Seth noted the absence of Earth Nation citizens within the palace.

"Yonu is doing well, by the way," Quennin said.

"Oh, is she?" Zo asked.

"Top of her class in scholastics."

"That's my girl. What about combat?"

"She's in the top third," Quennin said.

"Let me guess," Zo said. "Tevyr still has the highest marks."

"Of course," Seth said.

"Well, I can't complain about that," Zo said. "I suppose I should find time to see her, but Vorin likes to keep us busy."

They proceeded upstairs and through three more doorways and checkpoints until finally coming to the Sovereign's control room. A white tiled floor gave way to black walls and a black ceiling. Two men stood with their backs to the entrance, both looking at the array of images covering the far wall. Fleets, places, and persons of interest all bore the scrutiny of the Sovereign and his chief lieutenant.

Sovereign Vorin Daelus and Renseki Mezen Daed faced the three pilots entering the control room.

Vorin clasped his hands in the small of his back. He was tall and gaunt, with ghost white hair and dark eyes. Though two centuries of service had taken their toll, his face remained unravaged by time. He wore a uniform similar to the Renseki, but with gold instead of silver highlights.

Mezen Daed stood like a slab of muscle to the Sovereign's left. With his grim demeanor, Mezen made Vorin look cuddly. Just below the edges of his cuffs and above his uniform collar, Seth could make out the jagged lines of scars: souvenirs from his Grendeni captors.

Seth could remember Mezen as a loud-mouthed braggart, back when they were both young and impulsive pilots trying to earn names for themselves. Now, Mezen rarely spoke, and when he did speak it was almost always to either Zo or Vorin.

Seth, Quennin, and Zo dropped to one knee and bowed their heads.

"Please rise, pilots," Vorin said. "We have much to go over and little time."

"How may we be of service, Sovereign?" Seth asked, standing. It may have been his imagination, but Mezen's and Vorin's expressions seemed darker than normal.

Vorin cleared his throat and gestured to the arrayed images behind him. Screens flickered to new shapes. At first Seth thought the images showed crippled seraphs or perhaps seraphs under construction. However, he soon realized these flayed copper skeletons deviated too heavily from existing seraph designs.

"We all know the Grendeni have reverse-engineered parts of seraphs recovered in battle," Vorin said. "We also know that the Grendeni managed to capture one seraph nearly intact."

One of the screens showed images of a ferocious battle within the atmosphere of a gas giant. Seth, Quennin, and a powerful white seraph fought against four hostile seraphs, their systems corrupted by a Grendeni agent. Three were recovered during the battle, and the fourth pilot was eventually returned to Aktenzek through a prisoner exchange.

"It was inevitable that the Grendeni would duplicate seraph technology," Vorin said. "But we had hoped they would find our pilots more difficult to match. Despite the odds, our Fallen brothers and sisters have jumpstarted their own pilot breeding program."

Seth glanced over at Mezen. The man's stoic expression was unreadable.

"Behold the Grendeni archangel," Vorin said. Several screens merged, revealing a strange seraph-like machine in crisp detail. The edge of its long sword blazed with light.

Seth stepped closer and took in the image. "No armor. No weapon pods. Only two drive shunts. This is very different from our seraphs. Is that sword acting as a chaos energy conductor?"

"That's correct," Vorin said. "It appears the Grendeni have made an advance we lack. We're still analyzing its capabilities, but it could make these archangels very dangerous in close combat."

The display flicked to a new image showing the vast cylindrical girth of a Grendeni colonial schism. Several small specks of copper light maneuvered in the space around it.

"The Grendeni schism *Righteous Anger*." Vorin let out a disdainful snort at the name. "This schism appears to be the base of operations for the archangel field tests."

"Is one of our exodrones tracking the schism?" Quennin asked.

"No. I will elaborate on that point in a moment," Vorin said. The single external feed switched to what had to be an industrial area within the schism. Row after row of archangels were lined up outside a factory that curved with the schism's inner wall.

"How did we ever get images from *inside* the schism?" Seth asked.

"That is why I have requested your presence here," Vorin said. "Pilot Elexen. Pilot S'Kev. The source of these images is Pilot Jack Donolon."

"*WHAT*?" Quennin exclaimed. "I beg your pardon, Sovereign, but did I hear you correctly?"

"Yes, Pilot S'Kev. After all this time, we have received our first contact with Pilot Donolon."

Quennin clasped Seth's hand tightly. Their eyes met. "Jack's back," she whispered, smiling excitedly.

Seth didn't know what he felt. Joy, of course. The three of them had grown close in the years before Jack's departure. But Seth had long given up hope of seeing him again. He felt numb with emotions he had buried long ago and forgotten.

"It would be good to see him again," Seth whispered, then said aloud, "What is he doing on a Grendeni schism?"

"Apparently, he convinced them he has defected over to their forces," Vorin said. "Pilot Donolon used his relationship with the traitor Dominic Haeger to gain their trust."

Zo smirked. "Now that is clever. And rather typical of the Grendeni. So quick to betray. So quick to assume betrayal in others."

"Is it possible he really has defected?" Seth asked. Out the corner of his eye he saw Quennin shaking her head. True, Seth found it almost impossible to suspect Jack of treachery. However, circumstances warranted an explanation.

"I do admit this behavior upon his return is unusual," Vorin said. "The Choir suspects he has a personal goal in this. After all, none of us know why he originally left. But at this time the Choir can see no possible motives for treachery."

Vorin looked to Seth and Quennin expectantly, but the two pilots merely shook their heads.

"We have been separated for too long, Sovereign," Seth said. "I can offer no insight."

"Of course. Regardless, his actions have proven quite advantageous to us. We now possess considerable data on the archangel program. In fact, he is scheduled to give us an update momentarily."

Quennin squeezed Seth's hand. Seth knit his fingers with hers and squeezed back.

"Could these messages be faked?" Zo asked.

"Doubtful," Vorin said. "Hypercast codes match Pilot Donolon's personal seraph. To fake these transmissions, the Grendeni would have to capture his seraph intact. A daunting task indeed."

Quennin leaned over and whispered into Seth's ear. "We're going to see Jack again."

Seth smiled, letting some of his own excitement leak through. Indeed, he was probably happier than Quennin to hear he'd returned. Seventeen years had passed since Jack's sudden and unexplained departure from the solar system.

Seth recalled his last conversation with Jack aboard the *Scion of Aktenzek*. Jack had seemed distraught, perhaps even frightened. The three previous years had been painful for Jack. Psychological scars from the merger with his seraph ran deep, but Seth and Quennin had supported him every step of the way. Those trials had brought the three of them amazingly close together.

And so it was a shock when Jack departed on his sabbatical without explanation and forbade his friends from following. Though it pained them to see him go, Seth and Quennin had honored that request. Seth had long suspected it was more a quest of self-discovery for Jack than a search for something tangible.

What did you go searching for? he wondered. *What did you find that brought you back?*

The complex eye of screens merged into an image of Jack in his pilot uniform.

"Sovereign Daelus, I ..." Jack realized who else was in the room. A thousand emotions played across his face.

Seth dipped his head slightly. "It is good to see you again."

"Very good to see you again, Jack," Quennin said.

Jack grinned tentatively. "Seth? Quennin? Wow, look at you two! Look at you guys, all grown up. It took me a moment to recognize you. Hell, it's fantastic to see you two again! I wish I had time to say more, but I must be brief. The Grendeni will get suspicious if I take too long."

"Of course, we understand," Quennin said. "There will be other chances to catch up."

"Sovereign, the archangels are being readied for deployment. I think around twenty pilots are here on the *Righteous Anger*, but more will arrive in three days. There could be enough to crew all three hundred archangels."

"A formidable threat indeed," Vorin said.

"If you strike now, you could set their program back years, though I'm afraid you can't stop their progress. The *Righteous Anger* is just a staging point. From what I understand, the factories and breeding centers are well distributed throughout the schisms."

At the mention of "breeding centers," Mezen clenched his fists until his knuckles were white. His face remained unmoved.

"I'm transmitting what little data I have," Jack said. "Use it as best you can."

"Jack?" Quennin asked.

"Yeah?"

"Did you find what you were looking for?"

Jack grinned sadly. "Yes, unfortunately I did. I need to go. I wish you all well."

The screen turned black.

Quennin and Seth exchanged puzzled looks. Just what had Jack meant by that statement?

"We should act upon this information, Sovereign," Mezen said, his deep, gravelly voice filling the silence.

Vorin nodded. "Yes, I have to agree. This is an unexpected opportunity. Choir, your thoughts?"

A personality rose to dominance within the Choir's cacophony of thought. The hologram shimmered into existing next to Vorin, taking the form of a young woman clad in the grey and gold of a sovereign from Aktenzek's past. When she spoke, her voice was ancient and devoid of mercy.

"We concur, Sovereign Daelus," the Choir's representative said. "Attack. Make our Fallen brethren pay for their crimes."

"Then it is settled," Vorin said. "Pilot Elexen. Pilot S'Kev. Let us plan the attack."

Jack pushed away from the console. He blew out a frustrated breath and rubbed his face, feeling dirty and disgusted. Both sides were in motion now, heading towards an inevitable collision. It had to be done, but that didn't make the task any more appealing.

"Well, here we go," he said quietly.

Jack leaned back in the chair and stared at the ceiling. He wanted to focus on the now, to cleanse himself of these past attachments, but seeing those two again opened old wounds and dragged out forgotten memories. He tried to clear his mind of them, but it didn't work.

"I thought this would be easier."

The seraph did not respond.

"I know, you're right. I wouldn't be here if it wasn't for them."

Jack sighed and closed his eyes, letting the memories play out. His mind gravitated towards one particular event twenty years ago, the first of many times Seth and Quennin helped him battle his inner demons. It had happened shortly after they drove back the Grendeni at the Battle for Earth, amidst the jubilation of a great victory.

And in the pit of his personal despair …

Jack sidled up to the edge of the seraph bay's catapult pit. His giant white-skinned machine filled the chamber. He looked down at the twenty-five-meter drop to the pit's first shutter, his seraph's feet resting on the armored pane below.

"Shouldn't feel a thing. Or, if I do, it'll be brief."

The seraph said nothing.

"For the last time, get out of my head!" His voice echoed in the cavernous bay. "Damn it, I am so sick of you! It's your fault I'm doing this!"

The seraph didn't speak.

"You know what? Forget it. I don't have to put up with your garbage. Not anymore. I'm going to solve this problem very shortly."

A lift opened.

"Oh, crap!" Jack quickly hid his hands behind his back.

Seth and Quennin stepped out, both dressed in storm-gray shorts and T-shirts. Jack still couldn't help thinking of them as kids. Seth was, what? Sixteen? Quennin was barely older than that. They should have been in school having fun and making awkward mistakes. Not fighting someone else's war.

"What's going on, Jack?" Seth asked, rubbing the sleep from an eye with his fist. "Equipment alarms keep going off in this bay."

"Jack?" Quennin asked.

Her urgent, worried tone seemed to wake up Seth.

"What are you doing?" Seth asked. "What's going on here?"

"Umm …" Jack wore a faux-perplexed face. "What does it look like I'm doing?"

Quennin glanced from Jack to the edge and back. Realization dawned on her face. "Now, wait a second. Don't be hasty."

"You're going to kill yourself?" Seth asked, walking slowly forward.

"You make that sound like such a bad thing."

"By jumping?"

Jack shrugged his shoulders. "Guess so."

Seth dismissed him with a wave. "Go ahead then. The safety fields will catch you."

"Yeah. About that." Jack took a deep breath to steel himself. He opened his neural link and sent the buffered command.

Lights in the bay switched off, casting them into total darkness. A distant humming vanished, only audible when it was no longer there. Backup lights switched on, painting the bay with a dim red glow.

"What just happened?" Quennin asked.

"I cut primary power to this bay," Jack said. "The safety fields won't work."

"You might still survive the fall." Seth said, creeping forward.

"Yeah, thought of that too." Jack unclasped the hands behind his back and brought one of them slowly up. He put the barrel of the gun against his temple. "I figure why settle for one method of killing myself when I can be doubly sure? I shoot myself in the head, then fall into the pit. Bang, then splat. If you're going to do something, go all the way. Besides, you Aktenai are just way too good at putting people back together."

"Just step away from the ledge," Quennin asked. "It'll be okay."

"Look, you've caught me at a really awkward moment here," Jack said. "I've been trying to work up the courage to do this, okay? And the two of you being here are *not* helping."

"How inconsiderate of us." Seth edged closer.

"Stop this," Quennin said. "This is insane!"

"Yes, it is. And that's the problem. Now, Seth, that's close enough. Why don't you stop right there? My trigger finger is feeling itchy, and

I'd hate to blow my brains out where you can see it. How about you both turn around so you don't have to see the mess?"

Seth started walking to the side, circling Jack at a set distance.

"Okay, fine," Jack said. "Watch the brains splatter out of my head. I won't care at that point, anyway."

"Jack, please don't do this!" Quennin pleaded.

"Look, I'm not killing myself because I want to die. Believe me, I'd rather not. But the truth of the matter is my thoughts are no longer my own. This *thing*—" Jack pointed the gun at the seraph. "—is in my head. I've got voices bouncing around in me, and some of them are *angry*. Some of them want blood, and I don't think I can control them forever. I'm a danger to you and everyone else. And so, before I have a chance to hurt someone I care about, I'm ending this. It's as simple as that. Really, it's for your own good."

Seth stopped next to the catapult pit's edge. He looked down as if inspecting the drop.

"Jack?" he asked.

"Yeah?"

Seth broke into a sprint. He charged straight at Jack, running along the pit's edge.

"Stay back!" Jack shouted.

Seth leaped and tackled him. They crashed to the ground next to the edge. Jack's gun smacked against the decking and went off. The bolt ricocheted around the bay until it flattened against the seraph's armor.

Jack shoved Seth's face back and tried to put the gun to his own head, but Quennin grabbed the barrel with both hands. She forced it to the ground and pinned his forearm under her knee.

"No, you don't!" Quennin shouted.

"Get off of me!"

"This is what I think of your plan!" Seth shouted.

He straddled Jack's chest and punched him in the face, breaking his nose with a wet crack.

"This is for your own good!"

Seth pounded Jack's face again. Teeth cut the inside of Jack's lips.

"This is to protect you from yourself!"

Seth swung into the side of Jack's jaw and connected in a shower of spit and blood. He stopped and sat back on Jack's stomach, panting.

"Ouch …" Jack whimpered.

"Don't ever do that again," Seth said. Tears began streaming down his cheeks. "If you do, I swear I will kill you myself!"

"You know, that's not much of a disincentive."

Seth snarled. He raised his arm and pounded Jack in the face over and over again. Stars filled Jack's vision, and then everything went dark.

Chapter 7

Seraph Assault

Two days after speaking with the Sovereign, seraph pilots prepared for combat aboard the *Resolute.*

Quennin pulled her arm through the i-suit sleeve. With both arms in, she began locking the waist seals.

The formfitting interface suit was thicker than a standard pressure suit. Its highly textured skin provided a massive amount of surface area for its size, aiding in the connection between pilot and seraph. For feedback damage, the spongy mesh underneath could extrude fibrous threads into her body to perform emergency surgery.

She gripped the neck ring and fed her long red hair in so the helmet would fit.

"Shouldn't you be off by now?" Quennin asked.

Zo leaned against the wall of Quennin's spacious quarters. The wall screen displayed the robot fleet amassed near the *Resolute.* Two dreadnoughts, six frigates, and a negator hovered in formation. The negator was a stubby cylinder nearly as large as the dreadnoughts, its hull dotted with formidable close-in defenses.

"I still have time before the carrier makes its final fold." Zo fiddled with the cuffs of her Renseki coat.

"Yonu will be fine, I assure you." Quennin slipped her sidearm into its holster.

Zo continued playing with her cuffs.

"Tevyr will be with her," Quennin said, grabbing her gloves.

"I know, but Vorin should have permitted the Renseki to handle this. They're just so young."

"We were both younger when we first went into battle," Quennin said.

"But we had experienced pilots backing us up."

"Seth and I aren't experienced?"

"I didn't mean that," Zo said. "None of us know what to expect from those archangels."

"She'll be in good company," Quennin said.

Two full squadrons of good company, to be precise: twelve Aktenai and twelve Earth Nation pilots with Seth and Quennin in overall command. The carrier, negator, dreadnoughts, frigates, and tens of exodrone squadrons would support this already formidable strike force.

"I know," Zo said. "Still …" She tapped her foot nervously.

Quennin pulled her gloves tight and sealed them. She walked over.

"Come on. There's no point worrying about it. Let's go."

Zo gave Quennin a weak smile. "Yeah, you're right."

They exited Quennin's quarters, turned down a long hall of pilot accommodations, and entered the lift at the end.

"They do make a nice couple," Zo said.

"Hmm?"

"Yonu and Tevyr."

"Oh, I quite agree," Quennin said. "I'm surprised they haven't bonded yet."

"Me too." Zo folded her arms. "Maybe those EN pilots are to blame."

"Oh?"

"They can be a really bad influence. Have you seen some of the things they do to themselves?"

"Like what?"

"They *self-mutilate.*" Zo shivered in disgust. "They have these strange rites where they pierce themselves and hang ornaments from the holes."

Quennin grabbed her right forearm with her left hand. This had the effect of covering her unseen bellybutton. "You mean, like earrings?"

"Yeah, I think that's what they're called. Revolting."

"Yes, quite a deplorable practice," Quennin muttered. She idly scratched her bellybutton.

"And Yonu has two of these *disfigurements*," Zo said. "I told her to have them repaired, and you know what? She ignored me!"

"Well, they are quite attractive on her," Quennin said, avoiding eye contact.

Zo stared at Quennin. "Just whose side are you on?"

"Well ..." Quennin mumbled, still avoiding eye contact.

Thankfully, the lift arrived. Quennin walked into the seraph bays.

"Good luck," Zo said. "I'll see you when you get back."

Quennin nodded a farewell. The lift closed and took Zo directly to her seraph in an adjoining bay.

Quennin turned and gazed upon the familiar scarred lines of Seth's black seraph. A thin gray scar existed for every hit that breached his barrier. For a pilot with such an extensive combat history, there were very few marks.

Seth stood near a gangplank that extended from the ledge to the seraph's torso cockpit. Conformal weapon pods lowered from the ceiling. Slender robotic arms attached them to his seraph's limbs.

Seth turned as she approached.

"Quennin, do you have any idea what 'hooah' means?"

"Huh?"

"It's something I heard the EN pilots shout." Seth looked in the direction of the next bay down. "Pilot Daykin had all of them together in a circle. They put one arm in the center of the circle and yelled 'hooah' at the same time. My neural link was unable to translate the word."

"I don't think it means anything."

"Strange," Seth said. "But certainly not the strangest thing our allies do."

Quennin gave Seth an emphatic nod.

They walked down the long row of self-contained bays, past Quennin's seraph, and stopped at Tevyr's seraph. Not unexpectedly, Tevyr and Jared were making wagers on who would get the most kills. When they finished their acts of youthful bravado, Tevyr joined his parents.

"Father, Mother," he said, bowing. "Thank you for reassigning the squadron to my command. I will not fail you."

"The Sovereign's command was for our best pilots," Seth said. "How could I not include my own son?"

Tevyr beamed with pride. "I will be cautious, Father. We don't know what to expect from the archangels."

"Good. I am glad to hear that." Seth gestured towards Tevyr's seraph. "We'll be launching soon."

"Of course, Father." Tevyr bowed once more and went to board his seraph.

When their son was out of earshot, Quennin said, "A part of me is thinking the same way Zo is right now."

"She's worried about Yonu?"

"Naturally."

"Pilots belong on the battlefield." Seth rested a hand on Quennin's shoulder.

Quennin nodded. "I must be getting soft."

"Nonsense. I am every bit as concerned for our son as you are. Fear not. He will do us proud."

The starry void flashed alive as thirty-five fold points snapped open. A vast intermingling field of distortion rings expanded across space like rippling water. Twenty-six seraphs, six frigates, two dreadnoughts, and a single negator appeared near the Grendeni schism *Righteous Anger.*

"Negator field is coming on-line," Jared said. "Looks like we have a single Grendeni dreadnought running escort."

Seth mentally keyed the command hypercast channel. "Maintain formation. The fleet will handle this."

Aktenai dreadnoughts and frigates came about and accelerated, bringing their main cannons to bear on the lone Grendeni target. A frigate lined up on the Grendeni dreadnought and fired its centerline cannon. The white beam pierced through space and slammed into the dreadnought with terrific force. Mnemonic armor heated and expanded, becoming a jagged glowing boil across the surface.

The Grendeni dreadnought brought its own weapons to bear and returned fire. Three parallel beams cut through space. Two hit the negator, leaving twin superheated scars on the surface.

The target choice made sense, Seth noted. Until the Aktenai negator was destroyed, no Grendeni vessel could successfully engage its fold engines and leave the conflict. The negator effectively pinned down all opposing craft, forcing them to stand and fight.

Twelve beams lanced from the Aktenai formation in unison, focusing as if through a lens down to a single point. The beam carved across the Grendeni dreadnought's surface, leaving a patchwork of crisscrossing, white-hot lacerations.

"Alpha squadron, stand by to recon the schism," Seth said.

Aktenai frigates closed rapidly and fired salvos of torpedoes at the Grendeni dreadnought. The lasers and railguns in its interception grid lashed out but destroyed only a fraction of the incoming torpedoes.

Titanic explosions wracked the Grendeni dreadnought and ruptured its outer hull. Still it fought on.

Seth tried to raise Jack via hypercast but received no response. Even if Seth knew for certain Jack wasn't on the schism, he wouldn't order its destruction. Only the most radical elements of the Choir would countenance the destruction of a schism without great need.

Another round of fusion beams carved a gash through the Grendeni dreadnought's midsection. It continued to fight back.

Seth turned his chaos scanner up to full gain. The other twenty-five seraphs were bright lights in a black world devoid of other signals. He permitted himself a shallow grin. No active archangels in flight.

Another salvo of torpedoes detonated across the Grendeni dreadnought's tortured hull. It shattered into three uneven sections, yet still it fought, each piece firing whatever functional weapons remained. Torpedoes continued to launch while lasers sliced through space, but the main threat of its beam cannons had been neutralized.

"Epsilon squadron," Seth said, "clean up that mess, then form a perimeter around the schism's northern dock."

"Confirmed, sir," Jared said. Twelve identical EN seraphs broke off and sped towards the dying dreadnought's wreckage.

"Alpha squadron, recon the schism interior."

"Understood," Tevyr said. Twelve Aktenai seraphs, each as fanciful or mundane as its pilot desired, approached the northern space dock on the *Righteous Anger*. Tevyr, along with Yonu in her sleek blue seraph, led the formation.

Seth and Quennin flew past the Aktenai fleet elements. Jared's squadron assumed tactical positions above the northern space dock.

Lights flashed along the perimeter of the schism's northern cap. Massive berthing arms reached into space. In the center of the docks were a set of heavy kilometer-wide doors designed for admitting whole ships as large as dreadnoughts into the schism interior.

With a mental command from Seth, the Aktenai fleet opened fire.

Twelve fusion beams struck the door simultaneously. Alloys heated, cracked, and shattered. The Aktenai squadron dove into the dark interior of the Grendeni space dock.

Visual feeds from the twelve Aktenai seraphs played in Seth's mind.

"Proceed cautiously," Seth said. "Find the archangels and destroy them."

"Understood," Tevyr said. "But something's not right."

"Elaborate."

"There's very little activity here in the dock. It could be they buttoned up as soon as they saw us coming, but it doesn't feel like that."

Seth studied the images coming in from the Grendeni space dock. Granted, he had no reference for normal operations in a Grendeni schism, but it did seem strangely dormant. A few automated machines went about their work, repairing and servicing the collection of transports and military vessels. However, he saw no evidence of people within the ships or berthing structures.

"The factory zone should be just beyond the space dock," Seth said. "Inform me once you've broken through."

"Understood."

"Could they have discovered what Jack was up to?" Quennin asked privately. "If so, would they abandon the schism?"

"Doubtful. They would have folded away or brought in a heavy fleet presence to defend the schism."

"Perhaps he engaged them from inside the schism and they fled," Quennin said.

"If so, why hasn't he contacted us?"

"And, for that matter, why have a dreadnought guarding an empty schism?"

"We're in the factory zone," Tevyr said. "Still no sign of archangels. Some activity here, but it's all automated. Wait a second ..."

"What is it?"

"I don't think this is the *Righteous Anger*. It's close, but the layout of the factory zone doesn't match what Pilot Donolon sent us. The towers here don't reach as close to the axial tube, and there're fewer of them."

Seth opened the archive imagery in his mind. The exterior matched perfectly, but Tevyr was right. When the true interior was compared to the archive imagery, the differences became frighteningly apparent.

This is the wrong schism!

"Alpha squadron, get out of there!"

The Aktenai seraphs made a break for the schism space dock. Seth's chaos scanner lit up with new contacts. None were as strong as a seraph, but they had weight of numbers on their side, and they came alive between the Aktenai squadron and their escape.

"Power ups! Multiple archangel power ups!" Tevyr shouted. "There must be over a hundred in here!"

"Punch through," Seth said. "We'll secure your exit from this side."

"Multiple fold points opening up," Jared said. "Hostile negator field coming on-line. Look sharp! Here they come!"

Six Grendeni archangels folded in less than a kilometer from Seth's position. They swiveled their skull-like heads and caught sight of him. Coppery skeletal wings flared out and ignited with yellow light. The archangels dove in, long swords powered and ready.

"Quennin, behind us!"

Seth aligned his fusion cannon on the lead archangel and fired. A white beam shot out of the conformal pod on his right arm, piercing the space between him and his target. The beam was every bit as powerful as a dreadnought's main guns, and it hit dead on.

The archangel's yellow barrier flashed opaque and died. Scorching plasma incinerated the upper half of its skeletal frame. The remainder tumbled wildly, falling back from the other five archangels.

Quennin opened fire a split second later. Six tactical seekers snapped out of her leg pods and rocketed into the approaching archangels. The warheads exploded in brilliant blue flashes of light, throwing the lead archangel back and severing its left arm. It spun away, righted itself, and retrieved the sword from its severed limb.

Quennin shot a fusion beam into its torso and blasted it to atoms.

"They can't take much punishment," she said.

"But they're coming in like death is meaningless," Seth spat.

Without time to get off a second shot, he flew out to meet them. Twin blades of purple luminescent energy snapped out of his forearms. He shot straight in at the lead and ducked down at the last moment.

The archangel flew above him, sluggishly trying to turn around.

Seth climbed sharply and pierced the archangel's feeble barrier with ease. His blade cut through the chest cockpit. Yellow energy shunts across the archangel died. Black fluid spurted out of the ruined body.

Seth had no time to relish the kill. He whirled around and raised his daggers in an X to block the oncoming attack. The closest archangel swung down, its sword meeting his daggers.

The collision released a short snap-flash of chaos energy. Painful heat rippled down Seth's arms.

The strength of these swords! he thought.

Seth pushed up and threw the archangel off balance. He followed that with a quick swing, slicing cleanly through the archangel's torso. Another foe slain.

The last two came in, their swords more than capable of cutting Seth down in a single stroke. But Quennin was at his side now, her single dagger active, her kite-crystal shunts burning with emerald fire. She dodged the archangel's stroke, pulled behind it, and thrust deeply into the small of its back.

Her blade penetrated through the archangel's barrier and burst out the center of its chest. Energized fluid wept from the wound. The impaled archangel writhed about, its limbs spasming erratically. Quennin drew the blade down, slicing through the enemy's cockpit.

The spasms stopped. Leaking fluid turned stagnant and black.

Seth rushed the last archangel, bashed its sword aside with one dagger and stabbed through its cockpit with the other. He kicked the dead archangel contemptuously off his dagger and turned to the greater battle erupting around them.

Horrifically vast numbers of archangels and Grendeni warships continued to fold in. Escape was their only option.

Too far away to help, Seth watched a wave of thirty archangels swoop down onto the EN seraphs in epsilon squadron. Many of the archangels died from the barrage of fusion beams, rail-rifle bolts, and tactical seekers the Earth Nation pilots threw out.

From this first wave, only fifteen archangels broke through and engaged in close combat. Though the EN pilots were just as capable as their Aktenai brethren, their training focused heavily on ranged weaponry. Only three seraphs ignited their daggers before the two formations crashed together.

Archangels brutally hewed two seraphs in the first exchange. Their swords carved through barrier and armor with terrible ease, but the EN seraphs quickly recovered. With rail-rifles slung and daggers ignited, the remaining seraphs fell in on their assailants, vengefully cutting them down.

Eight EN seraphs remained functional in the end, with the ninth bleeding fluid from a deep torso cut. The survivors fell into formation. Half retrieved their rifles while the rest stood ready with daggers active.

Another archangel wave folded in and dove at the EN seraphs. Seth spotted Jared Daykin's seraph with its command bars leading the defense, his blood red dagger burning brightly. He slashed through the first archangel to reach him.

Seth linked with the Aktenai ships and ordered everything poured into the Grendeni negator. As long as that ship existed, there was no escape. The Aktenai warships, now receiving fire from their Grendeni counterparts, lumbered about with their new orders.

"We need to join up with epsilon," Seth said.

"I'm with you," Quennin said.

Seth could hear the faith in her voice. Even as their plans fell to ruins and their comrades died around them, his beloved's support did not waver.

A wing of four archangels stood between Seth and the EN seraphs. They turned about, apparently deciding that two isolated seraphs were easier prey than nine.

How wrong you are, Seth thought.

He and Quennin fired twin fusion beams into the archangel formation. Both hit their marks, but only one of the archangels blew apart. The other spun in space, the yellow aura of its barrier crackling wildly before it righted itself and flew on.

Seth met the three archangels head on. The first attacker swung wide with its blade, but Seth darted above it and fired his fusion cannon. The beam penetrated the torso of the archangel, shattered the chest, and flung its limbs and wings into space.

The last two archangels were now on either side of him, hoping to pincer him between their swords.

They didn't even see Quennin coming.

The two pilots were so familiar with each other that their target selection was almost subconscious. Seth immediately knew which archangel to strike and which to ignore. His trust in Quennin was absolute.

And she did not let him down. Her dagger cut through the left archangel's torso just as Seth disarmed the archangel to his right. With its sword arm lazily spinning away, he thrust in for the kill.

Seth and Quennin rejoined epsilon squadron, which had been pushed away from the schism and the northern space dock. That area ran thick with archangels trying to bottle up and overwhelm the Aktenai seraphs inside.

Seth accessed alpha squadron's status. A pearl of thought gleamed in his mind, displaying the vitals of the seraphs trapped within the schism. Alpha squadron had suffered two casualties, but the rest held out within the factory zone.

"Alpha squadron, report."

"We're holed up on the southern edge of the factory zone, near the northcity," Tevyr said. "We're not getting out the way we came in."

"Try looking for alternate routes out. In the meantime, I'll move epsilon squadron in to clear the space dock."

"Understood."

Seth broke the link. He was about to contact Jared when two new seraphs folded in.

The first seraph unmistakably belonged to Jack Donolon. The tremendous power output could be produced by no other pilot. The second seraph was a featureless black presence. No light reflected off it; no seams appeared on it. It was the black of a shadow or silhouette without form or feature. Seth couldn't detect the slightest trickle of chaos influx.

Wonderment and hopefulness quickly turned to despair. Seth watched the two new seraphs fall into formation with ten archangels. The entire formation ducked into the schism's northern space dock.

"We have been betrayed," Quennin said, her voice dark and cold.

Seth linked to Tevyr. "Do not attempt to break through the northern space dock. Overwhelming enemy forces present."

"Understood. I think we've found another way out. Looks like there are archangel launch catapults built into the outer hull of the schism. We're going to make a break for one. Relaying coordinates now."

Seth received the location and laid it on top of the Grendeni schism's image. The catapult was nearby, but several groups of archangels congregated around it.

"Epsilon squadron, we need to occupy this position!" Seth transmitted coordinates. "Our trapped seraphs are going to break out of the schism at this point!"

"Confirmed, sir," Jared said. "Epsilon, new target!"

The entire formation moved as one, flying down to meet the waiting archangels.

Seth, Quennin, Jared, and three other EN pilots slammed into the archangel swarm. Behind them, five EN seraphs drove salvo after salvo into the skeletal machines. Together, they pushed through the Grendeni archangels, cutting and blasting and killing in a desperate bid to save their comrades.

Just before they reached the catapult, the exterior hatch reddened and bulged outward. A moment later, the hatch blew into space. Seven Aktenai seraphs shot through the breach with archangels close behind.

"Where are the rest?"

Seth quickly retrieved the squadron status. Seven seraphs outside the schism, two confirmed dead, three still inside. His son and Yonu were among the pilots trapped with the schism.

"Tevyr, report!"

"Ah! Little busy right now!" Tevyr shouted. "Curse it! I can't get to the catapult! We're cut off!"

Tevyr's and Yonu's indicators showed all green. The third pilot, a young woman named V'Zen, was critically injured but still alive.

"Pilot Daykin, take command of both squadrons and secure this catapult," Seth said. "Quennin, follow me!" He flew over the catapult and looked down its warped, blasted length.

"Sir, the interior is swarming with archangels!" Jared said.

"And our comrades are trapped with them." Quennin joined Seth at the catapult. Without hesitation, they flew into the schism.

Chapter 8
Destroyer

Tevyr perched atop a manufacturing tower along the southern edge of the factory zone. The axial tube in this zone, or what was left of it, had shattered during the battle and crashed into the factories below.

Archangels continued to pour through the space dock. Over thirty were already positioned between him and the catapult on the far end of the zone.

Tevyr glanced at Yonu. Her lithe blue seraph landed on the next tower.

"We need to rescue V'Zen," Tevyr said.

"It's not going to be easy," Yonu said.

Bleeding wreckage from V'Zen's seraph had impacted near the center of the factory zone. Archangels had lopped off almost her entire upper torso, but thankfully had missed her cockpit.

"V'Zen, what's your status?" Tevyr asked.

"The burns ..." she wheezed. "Curses, they hurt ..."

"Give yourself another painkiller hit," Tevyr said. "We're coming to get you."

"I'm not going anywhere ..."

“It’s a miracle she can even talk,” Yonu said privately. “Her i-suit is the only thing keeping her alive.”

Tevyr nodded. The influx feedback from those swords was tremendous, more than enough to cause actual physical injury to a pilot that mirrored the seraph’s damage. And with V’Zen suffering a cut to the upper torso …

He didn’t want think about it.

An ugly swarm of archangels buzzed around the launch catapult. Six broke off and headed for Tevyr.

“Okay, let’s go!” he said.

“Right behind you.”

Tevyr levitated off the tower, his great wings flaring out. Angular runes in the form of the Litany ignited with green fire. His wing edges blurred brightly, almost white with sudden power.

Tevyr rocketed forward, skimming deftly across the cluttered factory-scape between him and V’Zen’s downed seraph. Six archangels dove at him.

Yeah, right! Tevyr thought. He pulled up, twin chaos daggers bursting out of his forearms.

Yonu fired. Her fusion beam snapped across the factory zone like a solid shaft of lightning. She struck one archangel and flash-vaporized a wing and an arm. The archangel rolled out of control, its altitude dropping. It slammed into the ground, then bounced and careened through the factories.

The lead archangel swung its oversized sword sluggishly at Tevyr. The differences in speed, agility, and performance between Tevyr and this Grendeni imitation were vast.

Before the archangel completed its attack, Tevyr pulled in to the side, sheared off the sword arm, spun rapidly, and cut through its torso.

Pressurized fluid burst from every wound, darkening as the imbued chaos energy dissipated. The archangel's yellow shunts died with its pilot. Severed parts of the lifeless machine rained down on the factories below.

Tevyr reoriented himself on the other four archangels. Yonu hit the archangel directly in front of Tevyr with another beam. Ribbons of energy splashed off the impact point, but its barrier held.

"Watch it!" she said. "Some of these things are stronger than others!"

Despite surviving the beam attack, the archangel's shunts flickered and the edge of its sword fizzled completely. Tevyr flew in and cut across the archangel. Two severed halves plummeted away.

Another archangel rushed in, its sword forming a killing arc of light. Tevyr blocked quickly. The archangel's sword and his dagger met in a violent flash of green and yellow light.

Tevyr angled his dagger and dodged to the left. The archangel overshot him, swinging through empty space. Tevyr cut deep into its undefended side.

One archangel remained, and despite the hopelessness of this contest, it charged them with suicidal fervor. A normal pilot, indeed any *sane* pilot, would have fallen back and regrouped, especially with so many allies nearby. But not these *things*. Not once had Tevyr seen them break from losses and retreat.

The archangel pulled its sword above its head and swung down.

Tevyr blocked with both daggers. The impact sent a wave of scorching pain down his arms.

"Argh! Curse it!"

Tevyr sliced the archangel's arm off at the wrist, then hewed through its torso with a quick horizontal stroke. He spotted another group on approach.

"Keep moving!" he shouted. "Get V'Zen out of there!"

Yonu landed amongst the toppled buildings where V'Zen had fallen. Gently, she slipped her arms underneath the seraph's headless body and lifted away from the crash site.

"Okay, I've got her! Where to?"

"We need to …"

Tevyr trailed off. His wings shuddered with fear.

A white seraph flew through the axial gateway and surveyed the battle-wracked factories before it. A black seraph followed, cloaked by impenetrable shadow. Even though Tevyr was physically cut off from his allies, hypercast signals kept his tactical data current. He knew exactly who piloted the white seraph and which side he fought on.

"We need to get out of here," Yonu said. "*Now*!"

"I know, but …"

The northern space dock or the archangel catapult were their only means of escape, unless…

Tevyr turned around and faced the southern cap of the factory zone. The cap reminded Tevyr of geode crystalline deposites, except instead of crystals these were buildings, all rising up and meshing as they approached the central axial tube.

But there was a gap near the axial tube for traffic and commerce, a gap large enough for seraphs.

"There." Tevyr transmitted the coordinates to Yonu. "We'll retreat through that point."

"That takes us even further into the schism!"

"We'll make a break for the southern space dock. If we need to punch through, we've got the fleet and both squadrons outside ready to help us."

Parts of two squadrons, Tevyr thought grimly.

"All right," he said. "No point wasting time here. Let's go!"

Yonu shot towards the gap with V'Zen's broken seraph in her arms. Tevyr trailed behind, escorting the other two pilots. He spun around and sighted another fifteen archangels approaching.

Tevyr reached the axial gap shortly after Yonu. He landed just inside the lip, aimed his arm cannon at the closest archangel, and fired. The fusion beam burned through the archangel. It fell away and crashed, headless and wingless.

The other archangels came in.

Tevyr crash-launched his remaining inventory of tactical seekers: all forty-two warheads. The seekers deployed from weapon pods along his legs, spread out in front of him, and ignited their powerful drives.

Individually, the warheads didn't stand a chance against even an archangel's barrier. Against a seraph, the best the warheads could do was unbalance an opponent. However, Tevyr's neural targeting commands singled out three archangels.

They made no attempts at evasion. Barriers collapsed beneath the glare of short-lived blue-white suns. There was no debris.

"I'm through," Yonu said. "Interior is clear."

The white and black seraphs rushed towards them.

Tevyr turned away and sped into the schism's habitat cylinder. The undamaged axial tube illuminated a serene landscape of lakes, grassy hills, and small towns. He flew through the northcity, its towering structures of metal and glass receding towards the ground the further he traveled.

The southcity was at the far end, along with a gap leading to the southern factories.

They had a way out!

"Make a break for it!" Tevyr shouted. "Move!"

Hostiles flooded into the northcity before Tevyr and Yonu were halfway across. Several archangels slowed, taking up positions in the northcity. They couldn't catch up, but those slow machines weren't what concerned him.

A flash of white blurred past Tevyr and Yonu. It stopped, spun in space and dropped down directly in front of them. The white seraph leisurely ignited a single massive energy blade from its left arm.

The shadowy seraph approached from behind. They were cut off.

Tevyr and Yonu halted their advance above a mountain range that bisected the habitat cylinder's interior. Tevyr floated between Yonu and the white seraph, his twin chaos daggers buzzing to life.

Yonu fired her fusion cannon, the beam bright even against the lit axial tube. The thin strand of superheated plasma struck the white seraph's barrier and splashed off harmlessly.

"What do we do now?" she asked.

"Head for the southcity. I'll distract him."

"You can't take him on alone!"

"We don't have any options!"

Jack Donolon dashed in.

Tevyr's senses and reflexes were infinitely enhanced by the chaos energy surging through him. Even so, he barely responded in time. The traitor's giant luminescent blade slashed down. Their blades met with a violent flash, and Tevyr was thrown back by the force of the blow. He recovered, wings flaring, shunts burning, and he charged at Jack.

The two danced and dodged and attacked around the sun-bright axial tube. Tevyr found he could not meet that blade head on. Instead he tried to deflect it and get within the traitor's defenses.

It almost worked. Tevyr blocked the next attack with an angled dagger. The massive energy blade crackled across his dagger and continued past. For a mere fraction of a second, Tevyr was inside Jack's defenses. He pulled his off-hand dagger up for a killing blow.

But Jack dodged back before Tevyr struck, turned quickly, and rushed Yonu and V'Zen.

"No!"

Tevyr had been too intent on distracting this foe. Too late, he realized Jack had led *him* away, and Yonu was now alone and vulnerable.

"YONU, BEHIND YOU!"

Jack slashed down with terrible force, sheering through Yonu's arm and cutting clean through V'Zen's torso. The wounded pilot died instantly, and Yonu screamed from the feedback.

Tevyr rushed to her aid. He thrust with a dagger, but Jack juked upward with maddening agility. Tevyr found himself dangerously overextended with Jack directly above. Jack dove at him.

At the last moment, Tevyr raised and crossed his daggers. Their blades clashed. Hot chaos energies crackled, competed, and finally exploded. Tevyr flew back from the explosion and crashed into the schism's mountain range. Rock and dirt blew out from the impact crater.

"Gah!" Tevyr's barrier shimmered around him. He pulled himself free of the rocks.

Jack charged in. Tevyr stood up and reignited his daggers.

"Yonu, get out of here!"

"We can take him together," Yonu said, her voice shaky with pain.

"Stay back!"

Jack thrust with the tip of his blade. Tevyr flew back, gliding up the mountain's craggy slopes. Jack followed.

"I'm ordering you to get out of here!"

Yonu charged Jack from the side.

The black seraph chose this moment to attack. In an eye blink it flew out of the northcity and crossed half the habitat cylinder. He'd never seen a seraph move so fast! Yonu blocked at the last moment. Their blades met, Yonu's shattered into a thousand snaps of energy, and the black seraph's blade sliced up through her torso.

Its attack exited at the neck, severing an arm, wing cluster, and the head from the rest of the body. Lambent blue fluid poured from the seraph's wounds, and Yonu's scream chilled Tevyr to the bone. Her blue seraph fell and crashed limply against the rocks below, remaining shunts sputtering weakly.

Jack flew down for the deathblow.

"YONU!" Tevyr charged in wildly.

Jack spun around and met Tevyr's charge head on. Their blades clashed and ground against each other, sparks scintillating. Tevyr managed to redirect the attack and get inside his opponent's defenses. With his second dagger, he thrust for the white seraph's cockpit.

Only it never reached his opponent. Jack raised his weaponless right arm. In that fraction of a second before Tevyr's dagger struck, blue energy crackled to life and coalesced into a blue kite shield.

Tevyr's attack rebounded off the shield, unbalancing him. Jack slashed up with the point of his shield, cutting through Tevyr's shoulder.

"Ahhh!"

Tevyr's arm fell away. Green, chaos-imbued fluid geysered from the wound. His mnemonic skin expanded over the amputation, sealing the breach.

Scorching pain shot through him. Medical reports for his true body spiked red at the shoulder, his flesh cooked from the inside out. Nano-cilia extended from his i-suit and dug into the wounded shoulder.

Tevyr pulled away, tasting burnt meat and blood in his true mouth. He fought through the pain, raised his remaining arm, and readied his dagger.

Jack slashed across and slammed into Tevyr's defenses. His dagger wavered against his opponent's seemingly infinite power. Finally, the dagger shattered into a million green shards, and Jack's blade cut in.

Tevyr screamed as his other arm fell from his torso. His shunts gave out, and he fell, crashing into the mountain. He struggled to his feet and forced the flows of chaos energy to reestablish. His barrier reconstituted. His wings spread out and activated.

But he was too slow.

Jack rushed him, massive chaos blade held above his head.

Strangely, calmly, Tevyr's last thought was that it couldn't possibly end like this.

Seth decapitated the last archangels guarding the axial gap and flew into the habitat cylinder. He and Quennin had cut a vicious path through the archangel squadrons in the factory zone. At last, they reached the northcity.

But they were too late.

Seth watched in helpless horror as Jack cut his son down.

Tevyr's barrier flickered and died. Jack cleaved Tevyr's head in half and pulled the blade through his entire body. Armor melted and vaporized. Twin halves fell to each side, their shunts fading from green to black.

"CURSE YOU!"

Seth energized his wings and swooped in, all his thoughts running dark with the need for vengeance.

"Seth, I can't keep up!" Quennin shouted.

"Get Yonu!" Seth shouted. "I'll handle this!"

Behind him, Quennin dove after Yonu's stricken seraph.

Seth shot straight in and met Jack head on. He slashed down and jarred against Jack's sword as if it was a stone wall. Seth thrust his free dagger in, only to clash with Jack's shield.

Their two seraphs turned slowly above the schism's mountain range. Sparks of chaos energy showered out from their grinding, locked weapons. They stared at each other, weapons unable to strike. Seth pushed with all his might and willed his weapons to burn brighter. His daggers blazed with renewed fury.

But Jack was no ordinary opponent, and he countered Seth with equal resolve. Neither pilot's blades moved.

"I have Yonu!" Quennin said. "We need to get out of here!"

In a flash of motion, Jack pulled his blade free. Seth dodged back hard and the blade sliced up through empty air. Seth fell away, placing his seraph between Quennin and Jack. But Jack held his position near the mountain peak where Tevyr had died.

Seth's mind boiled with thoughts of vengeance, but he refused to succumb to rage and grief. Even if somehow he could defeat such an opponent, there were countless archangels and the other mysterious seraph to contend with. He knew he was outmatched and outnumbered.

"Pilot Daykin, report your status," Seth said.

"We're holding on, sir," Jared said, his voice strained and distracted. "The fleet almost has that Grendeni negator beat."

"Move the fleet to the south space dock and blast an escape route for us. We'll exit there."

"Confirmed, sir. We'll clear the way for you."

Quennin retreated along the lit axial tube with Yonu's broken seraph over her shoulder. Seth backed away from the mountain range and joined her. He watched Jack for any sign of movement.

The black seraph hovered slowly into position next to Jack. Then in a startling blur of speed, it dashed towards him. Seth pulled hastily to the side and let it by. Even at close range, he couldn't see any details on the seraph. The axial tube glowed like a noon sun, but the seraph showed no features besides a thin blurry aura around its black, shadowed body.

The seraph activated a black dagger and lunged with startling speed. Seth barely had time to raise his daggers. The attack hit with such incredible force that the endoskeletal supports in his arm fractured in two places.

"Gnh!" Seth grunted. But despite this opponent's fantastic speed, its technique was not without flaws. He spotted an opening and stabbed in.

His dagger ricocheted off the black seraph's barrier. Impossible! No one could generate a barrier that strong! Seth dodged upward, barely evading the enemy's counterstroke.

"Come on!" Quennin shouted. "We're almost out!"

Seth couldn't let Jack and the black seraph overwhelm him. He fled back to the southcity and joined Quennin. Both enemies could easily have overtaken them, but they did not give chase.

Seth and Quennin flew into the southcity axial gap and across the southern factory zone. Vast armored shutters impeded their exit to the southern space dock.

Those shutters suddenly glowed red, bulged, whitened, then finally exploded. Seven EN seraphs standing in a loose gun-line had breached the door with their beam cannons. Another six Aktenai seraph hovered watchfully over the southern exterior.

These thirteen seraphs, along with Seth, Quennin, and Yonu, were the only survivors.

Seth sped through the congested debris of the space dock and into open space. All Alliance seraphs followed.

"Commander, the fleet just finished off that negator," Jared said. "Requesting permission to get the heck out of here!"

"All forces, withdraw!" Seth said.

He turned his seraph around, watching for a moment as the other seraphs folded space and escaped. The Grendeni schism, now a tomb for his son, stood out against the raging fleet battle. Archangel squadrons, like swarms of copper insects, swirled around the Grendeni colony ship.

With one last look, Seth Elexen engaged his fold engine and disappeared in a brief flash of light.

Chapter 9

Until One Falls

Jack exited the schism's southern space dock and landed on the illuminated outer ring. He gazed up at the Alliance seraphs and watched them vanish with tense satisfaction. Seth and Quennin had survived, despite his betrayal.

He thought back to his years spent with those two. The merger with the seraph had left him scarred, haunted by constant nightmares and phantom voices. The only two people who had truly been there for him, to whom he confided the whole story, were Seth and Quennin.

And now I return their kindness with betrayal and murder, he thought. *What a pathetic wretch I've become.*

The corpses of blasted warships, broken archangels, and hewn seraphs choked space around the schism *Dauntless Purpose*. Wreckage from the negator, dozens of frigates, and three dreadnoughts floated serenely in space.

Vierj flew out of the southern space dock. She glided down and landed gracefully next to him. The lifeless black of her barrier painted a shadow against the stars.

"You held back," Vierj said.

"Those two," Jack said. "They were the comrades I spoke of."

"Ah. I see," Vierj said. "We will probably face them again. If it bothers you, I can be the one to eliminate them."

"No. They were my friends. They're mine to deal with."

"As you wish. I won't interfere if you feel that strongly."

"Thank you, Vierj."

"Though I will kill them if they become too great a threat."

"Of course."

Jack glanced at Vierj's silhouette. Once again, he wondered if all this killing was worth it. Did he really have the right to condemn so many people to death?

If I fail, this will all be for nothing, he thought, looking away.

A message came in from the *Valiant Artisan*. Jack accepted.

"Hello, Dominic."

"Jack, that was incredible! We slaughtered them!"

"A slaughter, huh?" Jack said. "We must be talking about two different battles."

"It's true our fleet took more losses than I would have liked. But, Jack, we have ten confirmed seraph kills. Ten of them! We've never killed that many at once. Not ever!"

"How many archangels did you lose?"

"Only seventy-nine," Dominic said.

"*Only*?" Jack asked.

"Excluding your two kills, that gives the archangels a ten-to-one loss ratio."

"That doesn't seem very good to me."

"You have to understand the economics of the situation. Our raw materials may be substandard, but they're far more plentiful. We can afford to throw archangels into a seraph meat grinder. Even if we lose all of them and only kill a few seraphs, we will because we're keeping those accursed things away from our fleet. Losses of twelve to one and above are acceptable in the big picture."

"You had surprise and numbers on your side. You won't always have that."

"What are you getting at, Jack?"

"I'm just not very impressed with your new toys."

Jack sent a hypercast command to the now poorly named *Scion of Aktenzek*. The seraph carrier folded space and came into position two thousand kilometers beyond the *Dauntless Purpose*. Jack and Vierj lifted off to meet it.

"I have to disagree," Dominic said pointedly.

Jack smirked. "Sounds like someone has a case of wounded pride."

"This is nothing of the sort. The archangels performed well beyond my expectations. We've clearly proven the theory behind our archangel tactics and now know how effective they can be, even against seraph elites. The Executives needed proof before they would commit archangels to larger fleet engagements, and now they have it."

"I need those archangels as a distraction. It's either that or fight every seraph in the legion."

"Now, don't be hasty," Dominic said. "We haven't committed to moving against Aktenzek."

"Then you'd better make up your minds. Vierj and I aren't going to wait forever."

"Hold on a second, Jack."

"I've gone out of my way to prove we're not some Aktenai plot. Now it's time for you to step up. Either you help us get inside Aktenzek or we try it on our own. Together we both get what we want. Alone, whether Vierj and I succeed or fail, the Grendeni get nothing. Are you hearing this?"

"All right, Jack. You've made your point."

"Hell, you have a good chance of ending this war outright if you seize the Gate. You should be begging me to help you."

"Look, Gurgella and I have a meeting with the Executives in an hour. We'll bring up your assault plans again. Will that make you happy?"

"It'll make me happy when they say yes. Other than that, your words don't really matter."

"Damn it, Jack. There's only so much I can do."

"Then you and your Executives should be ready for disappointment. Are we free to fold yet?"

"Yeah," Dominic said. "The fleet's finished clearing the area for stealth exodrones. You can fold to *Valiant Artisan* whenever you're ready. Look, how about we try this? I'll meet up with you after our meeting and fill you in over a drink or two. Hell, I might even bring good news. The stuff these Grendeni get sloshed with is pretty good, though it'll never beat a cold refreshing beer."

Jack grinned despite himself.

"Just like old times, huh?" he asked.

"Well, except neither of us have our EN dress blues anymore. Besides, I don't think the ladies here would be impressed in the least."

Jack chuckled. "Sounds interesting, Dom. All right. I'll join you for a drink, but you had better work those Executives over hard."

"Thanks. I'll be sure to press them in our meeting and stress your needs."

Dominic closed the link.

Jack slowed along his final approach to the carrier and pulled up through one of several catapults along the *Scion*'s underside. Catapult mechanisms locked onto his wings and raised him into the seraph bays.

Jack ascended into the brightly lit interior. Clamps latched onto his shoulders and secured his position. Insectoid arms deployed from the ceiling and pulled his conformal weapon pods off.

Jack weakened the bond with the seraph and became aware of his true body once again. The cockpit chamber widened and opened. Light filtered in, banishing the gloom. He crossed the gangplank and headed for the adjacent seraph bay.

Catapult rails lifted Vierj's seraph into the adjacent bay. She let her barrier dissipate, revealing the seraph beneath. She had ordered the *Scion of Aktenzek* to create a black design with long silver ovals across the arms, legs, and wings. A diagonal cross-hatch of vent-like shunts provided energy exhaust on the limbs and sides of the chest.

Vierj stepped out of the seraph once it came to a halt. She walked across the gangplank, looking young, beautiful, and dangerously alert. She appraised him with her unique, silver eyes.

"Well spoken, Jack Donolon," she said.

"You were listening in?"

"I find your negotiations with these peasants fascinating."

"We just need to remind them who's in charge."

"There are other options available to us," Vierj said carefully. She tilted her head to the side. "If you think they need more persuading."

"Oh, God, I hope it doesn't come to that."

The last thing we need is you splitting schisms open, Jack thought. *Or worse.*

"Well, it is an option if your more cautious methods fail."

Vierj walked up to him. She traced her fingers down his chest.

"You are a very talented pilot," she said with a sly grin.

"You've seen me fight in the past."

"I've never seen you battle our kind's lesser forms before. You were quite magnificent."

Jack gave her a sad smile. "You think I enjoy facing my old comrades?"

"I think they are no longer your comrades. Do you disagree?"

"No." Jack shook his head. "You're right, of course."

“Do we really need this Grendeni rabble?”

“It’s too risky for us to attack Aktenzek alone.”

“I believe I am up to the challenge.”

“Well, too risky for me at least. Come on. We’re about to fold.”

The two pilots entered the bay’s lift and took it to the ship’s main concourse. The lift opened to a long hallway lined with empty quarters. They entered the first room on the right.

Jack’s quarters had changed little in the past two years. He’d placed his Litany d-scroll, a gift from Seth and Quennin, in storage. Vierj found the words quite comical, though she had never asked him to change the Litany on his seraph.

Jack linked a command to the display covering the far wall. Local tactical data, Grendeni fleet deployments, known and suspected Aktenai fleet positions, and their own current location compressed into the upper left quarter. A live visual feed took up the remaining space.

A few seconds passed, and the *Scion of Aktenzek* folded space to the *Valiant Artisan*. A black sunless void wavered as if submerged beneath turbulent water, then cleared.

Thick curtains of sky-blue nebula stretched to infinity in every direction. Small wisps of lighter and darker colors swirled about them. But here, in the center, was the eye of the storm. Far beneath them shone a white dwarf star roughly the size of Earth.

Stretching up from the star was a million-kilometer-long conduit of rings, each ring one kilometer in diameter and protected by powerful gravitic field generators. The rings pulled at the star, coaxing and goading it into a hot channel of stellar matter that rode up within the ring conduit.

At the top of the ring conduit, the hot matter split into hundreds of thin strands, each flying off at forty-five degree angles through thinner conduits. It looked like the fiery edges of a conical hundred-faced diamond.

Most of the strands passed through a ring of factories, where they were further manipulated for power, material, and various manufacturing processes. The strands thinned noticeably wherever they passed through a Grendeni structure.

The *Scion of Aktenzek* approached the hundreds of structures that made up the factory ring. The nearest one produced archangels and stored them on a large plate protruding from its boxy center. Others fabricated frigates or dreadnoughts or even whole schisms.

And not all of the strands were used by factories. A dozen satellites refracted their strands back in towards the broken remains of a lifeless planet above the ring. The Grendeni used the focused strands to carve chunks off the planet, which robot tenders then moved to factories as raw materials.

"Welcome to the *Valiant Artisan*, Vierj."

Aboard the seraph carrier *Resolute*, Seth crossed the gangplank and held out his i-suit helmet. The waiting technician accepted it and bowed in wordless respect for his grief.

They knew. They all knew.

Seth turned around and looked at his seraph in silence, wondering where he'd gone wrong, what he could have done. Should he have flown in with his son's squadron? Could they have secured a retreat through the northern dock? Maybe he should have sent the EN squadron in first instead.

Or perhaps he should have seen this trap for what it was long before the mission launched.

Seth looked away and proceeded wordlessly through the seraph bay. Technicians and other pilots avoided his gaze.

My son is dead.

Even now, the fact refused to settle. Dark denial swirled in his mind. How could this even be possible? How could Jack have betrayed them and killed his son? *Why* had he betrayed them?

Try as he might, Seth couldn't figure it out. For what possible reason would a hero of Earth and forger of the Alliance side with the Grendeni? Seth thought back to Jack's great journey, his sabbatical into the unknown, and his long search.

What were his words?

"Did you find what you were looking for?" Quennin had asked.

"Yes, unfortunately I did."

What had Jack found? Why was it so unfortunate? Why did it drive him towards such treachery? Seth couldn't solve the riddles behind Jack's actions and soon found he no longer cared.

My son is dead, and Jack killed him.

Seth walked down the long line of seraphs. Many of the machines were damaged, their pilots shaken. He watched a medical team pull a wounded EN pilot out of his cockpit and placed him on a float pallet. The pilot clutched at his chest in pain, smoke rising from a blackened scar on his i-suit. Looking up, Seth noted the nasty diagonal gash across the seraph's torso.

He walked by Yonu's seraph. The skin of the blue machine was slick with black fluid that leaked and dribbled from multiple torso wounds. The right arm, right wing cluster, and head were completely gone. The chest had been cut open by maintenance arms, allowing a medical team to retrieve the wounded pilot.

Seth finally came to his son's empty hangar. Quennin stood near the bay's edge, staring into the empty space. She had a helmet in a gloved hand. Smoke fumed from the helmet's interior, and the material was blistered around the neck and chin. Small runic letters spelled "YONU" on the surface.

Seth walked up to her, afraid of the answer to his unasked question. He looked at his beloved's face and saw one as hard and emotionless as his own.

"She has a good chance of living," Quennin finally said, still staring into the empty hangar. "We got her out fast enough, but her burns are severe."

Seth glanced once more at the smoke rising from Yonu's helmet.

"The i-suit did what it could," Quennin said. "But her skin fell away like ash. I could see part of her jawbone."

Seth didn't know what to say, was fearful that whatever words he used would only make matters worse. He wasn't the only one bottling up his rage and grief.

"I ..." Quennin's mouth wavered on the edge of words, but no sound came out. Suddenly with a yell, she flung the helmet with all her strength. The helmet clapped against the far wall and fell into the catapult pit.

"I'm sorry," Seth said.

Quennin shook her head. "Don't blame yourself."

Seth draped an arm over Quennin's shoulders. She put her hand over his and squeezed. Her eyes moistened, but she fought the tears back.

"The Choir will want a report," she said. "We lost so many."

"I'll take care of that."

Finally, Quennin broke down. She fell to her knees, tears streaming from her clenched eyes. She put her hands to her face. "Why? Why did he do it?" She began sobbing uncontrollably.

Seth knelt beside her and pulled her close. She buried her face in his chest and wept.

The Choir requested Seth's presence through his neural link. He ignored them. After several minutes, their polite requests turned into stern orders. Seth switched his neural link completely off.

“I’ll be okay,” she said. “Go talk to the Choir. They’re being persistent.”

“Are you sure?”

“Yeah.” She rubbed her eyes. “Yeah, go ahead. I … I’ll go see how Yonu is doing.”

“Okay.”

Despite not wanting to leave Quennin’s side, Seth knew they were both warriors. They understood their unending responsibilities. And with his duty foremost in mind, Seth headed up the bay’s lift to the pilot concourse, then followed it to his quarters.

For a pilot of such seniority and importance, his quarters were quite mundane. It was a single room in the common Aktenai fashion, combining sleeping, eating, and relaxation areas without the need for Earther walls in the way. It was clean and utilitarian. D-scrolls proclaiming the Litany hung above the door and the futon.

Only one object seemed out of place. A roughly made model seraph floated above the dinner table, displayed with the prominence of a treasured possession. The purple runes along its black limbs were painted by a clumsy hand, the letters uneven and blotchy.

An eight year old Quennin had given it to him.

Seth linked to his wall screen. He opened the feed from a pebble-sized probe left at the Grendeni schism. Its hypercast link was still active.

Good. The Grendeni didn’t find it, Seth thought.

The schism was still present, but several ships had folded out. The probe had relayed those fold coordinates to a waiting squadron of stealth exodrones.

Grendeni warships rejoined other known fleet elements, but the archangels folded space to a vast nebular facility near a white dwarf star. One exodrone spotted a carrier fold in near the nebular facility and two seraphs launch from it.

Seth watched the archived visual. Jack and that mysterious black seraph flew up to one factory among a vast ring of hundreds. Seeing Jack once again made him realize, with absolute clarity, what he had to do.

Jack, I'm going to kill you.

Seth reactivated his neural link and informed the Choir he was ready to be debriefed. Normally, the Choir spoke in a tossing cacophony of voices. Sometimes a single voice would fight to the top and become dominant. Even more rarely would the individual manifest before Seth in person.

So it surprised him when two holograms appeared, a man and a woman. Seth recognized both as members of the Original Eleven. He immediately fell to one knee and bowed his head before the dead founders of the Aktenai.

Every child of Aktenzek memorized the names of the Original Eleven, and Seth could put faces to those names. The tall man possessed handsome, chiseled features with neatly trimmed black hair. He wore a white suit with black heraldry that looped around his waist and ran up his arms. The heraldry consisted of an interlocking pattern of circles, semi-circles, and arches.

His name was Veketon: architect of the Choir and First among the Eleven.

The woman was fair-skinned with short, white hair and unusual silver irises. Her dress was split down the middle, half white and half black, with gloves of the opposite color. She was Dendolet: the scientist who created the Bane and chief executor of the Great Mission to destroy that abomination.

The Original Eleven only appeared when the Great Mission was in peril, and his mind searched for the trigger that brought these personalities to the Choir's forefront.

Seth kept his eyes downcast. "Venerable masters, how may I serve you?"

“Rise, pilot,” Veketon intoned.

“We wish to discuss certain elements of the ambush with you,” Dendolet said.

Both founders spoke in the Aktenai tongue, but their unusual accents were full of harsh consonants. Seth had to focus to understand some of their words.

“Of course, venerable masters,” he said, rising. “What in particular do you wish me to elaborate on?”

Veketon walked across Seth’s quarters and gazed at the wall screen. He gestured to the image of the Grendeni nebular facility. “An interesting find. A pity we cannot bring the drone any closer.”

“Resolution is poor,” Dendolet said, “but evidence suggests at least some of the archangels were produced here.”

Veketon snorted. “Pathetic imitations of a truer weapon.”

“They are quite formidable in numbers, venerable masters,” Seth said.

“No matter,” Veketon said, his back to Seth. “It was inevitable the Fallen would eventually learn our secrets. In fact, their efforts seem to have produced unanticipated rewards.”

“Your pardon, venerable master?”

Veketon turned to face Seth. “Those swords. The technology is quite impressive. I’m disappointed you didn’t claim at least one for our study. There were certainly enough floating around during the battle.”

“The few of us that escaped were fortunate to do so.”

“And what is the purpose of your life,” Dendolet said, “if you do not serve the Great Mission?”

“Yes, of course, venerable masters.” Seth bowed his head. “My apologies.”

“There will be other opportunities to claim the sword technology,” Veketon said. “But enough of these mundane matters. It is the black seraph that concerns us.”

"Did you notice anything unusual about her?" Dendolet asked.

Veketon shot her a sharp look.

"About *her*, venerable master?" Seth asked.

"Or him, I suppose." Veketon made a dismissive wave. "It's an easy conclusion to mistakenly jump to. We're so used to dealing with pilots in male-female pairings."

"Ah," Seth said.

"For now, let us call this one Azeal until we know more," Veketon said. "Hmm, yes. I think that will be an appropriate name."

Seth had to use his neural link to pick up the reference. Azeal was a very old Aktenai word for darkness.

"But the question remains," Dendolet said. "Did you notice anything unusual?"

"The pilot, Azeal, was incredibly powerful, venerable masters. Perhaps even stronger than Pilot Donolon, though I have no way of being sure. I could not accurately measure Azeal's coefficient. Also, Azeal's seraph appeared featureless, but I believe this is a result of an extremely intense barrier."

"Pilot, do you think we are blind?" Veketon sighed and shook his head. "All this we already know."

"Then what, venerable master, should I elaborate on?"

"You came into contact with Azeal," Veketon said. "Your blade touched that seraph's barrier. There is no way to quantify the data you felt, that you alone experienced. So I ask again, did you notice anything unusual?"

"I … I don't know." Seth tried to recall the actual strike. With death and destruction all around him, how did they expect him to remember a single blow? And why the focus on only one pilot? Was the Choir not even concerned about Jack's betrayal?

"Think harder, pilot," Veketon said. "Was it any different? Yes or no?"

"It was …" Seth raised his arm. He looked at his open hand, clenched it, then relaxed his fingers. "It felt … cold, I think. But only for a moment."

"Did you hear anything?" Dendolet asked.

Seth gave the founder a confused look. "No, venerable master."

Dendolet leaned next to Veketon and whispered in his ear. "It may not be her."

Veketon held up a hand. "Let us not jump to conclusions."

"Venerable masters, do you know who this pilot might be?" Seth asked.

"It would be unwise of us to voice a mere theory at this point," Veketon said. "We will wait for more data."

"But even a theory may help us face this new enemy," Seth said. "Surely you must share it."

"It is not your place as a mere soldier to question us," Veketon said firmly.

Seth bowed his head. "Of course, venerable master. Please forgive my rudeness."

"We can leave the mystery behind this Azeal for another time," Veketon said. He gestured to the image of the nebular facility. "For now, we will send your forces back into combat. One of these factories may be a source of archangels and their swords. You will claim examples of both."

"Such a base would have extensive defenses, and we have taken heavy losses."

"We will dispatch the Renseki to reinforce your depleted strength," Veketon said, "and give you command over a larger fleet element."

"Is it wise to have the Renseki leave Aktenzek unprotected, venerable masters? Has Sovereign Daelus approved their deployment?"

Veketon grinned ever so slightly. "The Sovereign and the Choir will obey our wishes."

"But the Sovereign—"

"Will do as he is told," Veketon interrupted.

The statement gave Seth great pause, but he bowed his head and said, "My apologies, venerable masters."

"You have much work ahead of you. See to it."

The two holograms flickered and vanished. Seth found himself alone with many disturbing thoughts and more questions than before.

Seth stayed in his quarters and brooded over what Veketon and Dendolet had said. It wasn't unusual for elements of the Choir to hold secrets. Naturally, some information was too sensitive to be discussed outside the ruling circle of the Choir and the Sovereign. But why would the Original Eleven hold secrets in the face of such an obvious threat?

He agonized over the situation so intensely that he completely forgot his other obligations.

Quennin walked into the quarters.

Seth looked up apologetically, the passage of time suddenly registering. "Oh, I'm sorry."

Quennin waved away the apology, her eyes red from tears. She collapsed next to him on the couch. Her hand found his, and she squeezed.

"Yonu will live," she said, her voice steadier than before.

"That's good."

"She was lucky," Quennin leaned her head against his shoulder. "There wasn't any permanent damage."

Seth nodded thoughtfully. Aktenai medical science could repair almost any physical damage and extend human life until it was measured in centuries, but pilots who suffered head injuries often lost their talents permanently.

"The Choir questioned me," Quennin said. "Probably after they questioned you."

"Veketon and Dendolet?"

"Yeah."

"They should not have bothered you," Seth said.

"They are the Original Eleven. They can do whatever they want."

"I don't care who they are. They should have waited."

Quennin closed her eyes and nestled against his neck. "Veketon kept asking me questions about that black seraph we're calling Azeal. He kept pushing and searching, like there was a particular answer he wanted me to give."

"I had a similar experience with him."

"I don't *care* about that other seraph. What about Jack? Why did he turn?"

Quennin took a deep halting breath.

Seth squeezed her hand tighter. "Before he left, there was no one in this cursed universe who knew him better than we did. If we don't know, no one does."

"Maybe he finally snapped," Quennin said. "He was always close to the edge after … after he merged with his seraph. We should never have let him go. We should have gone with him."

"He asked us not to follow."

"We should have gone anyway."

"But we couldn't do that, Quennin. The Alliance needed us back then."

"Well, we should have done *something*," Quennin said, tears returning.

"Perhaps, but the opportunity has passed us. He has chosen his allegiance. All we can do now is face and defeat him in battle."

"Seth, please don't say things like that." Quennin leaned into him. "I don't want to lose you, too."

The two pilots sat in silence holding each other, sharing their grief and pain.

The Choir chose that moment to request another audience.

"Not again," Seth said. "We should just ignore them."

Quennin sat up on the couch. She rubbed her eyes and stood up.

"We have our duties, Seth," she said.

"Yes, of course." He stood up and linked an acknowledgement to the Choir.

A familiar hologram appeared before Seth and Quennin. The young man stood tall and slim with an oval face, prominent nose, and dark brown hair. But despite this appearance, a certain sparkle in his hazel eyes betrayed the depth of his age and experience. Though the man had been a withered shell when he died, his elevated existence within the Choir allowed him to take on this youthful visage.

He wore the uniform of a sovereign: storm-gray with gold trim and the white-stitched hawks of a full seraph pilot. The man was Taen Elexen, adoptive father of Seth Elexen, biological father of Jack Donolon, and former Sovereign of Aktenzek.

Seth and Quennin kneeled before him.

Taen motioned to the couch. "Please be at ease. Sit. There's no need to be so formal."

Seth and Quennin sat on the couch. Taen dropped into the chair opposite them. His hologram sank back into cushions that did not give.

"What brings you here, Father?" Seth asked.

"First, I would like to offer my most sincere condolences for your loss. I followed Tevyr's career with great interest, especially after he chose our shared surname upon coming of age. It saddens me to see such a bright star snuffed out like that."

Seth bottled up his grief and nodded. Quennin rubbed her eyes.

Taen leaned forward in his seat. "Now, I know you two have much on your minds right now, but I felt I must warn someone."

"Warn us of what, Father?"

"The Original Eleven are hiding critical knowledge from the rest of the Choir."

"Is that even possible?" Quennin asked.

Taen smiled grimly. "They designed and created the Choir. Anything is possible to them. Now, we may be overreacting. The Original Eleven do love to horde their secrets, and it may be nothing more than that. Everyone in the Choir hides something, even me."

"They know something about Azeal, don't they?" Seth said.

"Yes, I'm certain they know who this pilot is, but they have refused to share his or her identity with us."

"Why would the Original Eleven want to hide anything?" Quennin asked.

Taen gave her a sly grin. "Don't be too trusting of the official histories. After all, the Original Eleven are only human. I am sure they've many mistakes they do not wish the masses to know."

"And Azeal could be one of them," Seth said.

"Precisely."

"What about Jack?" Quennin asked. "Do they know anything about him?"

"Yes, but they won't share that either," Taen said. "Did you know that Veketon was the last person Jack spoke to before he decided to leave?"

"No, I didn't," Seth said. "Jack never shared his reason for leaving."

"Veketon refuses to divulge the contents of that discussion," Taen said. "But I do know it was the Original Eleven who gave him the carrier. I think they wanted rid of him. Perhaps they even feared him."

"But why?" Seth asked.

"I do not know. More is afoot than has been revealed. Be alert. Use your instincts. I fear our venerable masters' whims will place all of you in great peril."

Chapter 10

Honor Guard

Seth walked through an open emergency airlock into the *Resolute*'s recreation center. The room had started as dead space for future upgrades or additional cargo. EN pilots had found and commandeered it three years ago, and the resulting center bore many strange Earth Nation touches.

The wide room contained several clusters of round tables, each ringed with metal chairs and illuminated by a clumsy fixture suspended from a cable. Various automated kitchenettes and one manual kitchen lined the right side. Seth couldn't fathom why EN pilots insisted someone manually prepare their meals. Such a waste of time.

The chef saw him entering and greeted him with his typical "Hello, Seth!" and a sharp wave of his arm. Seth returned the gesture awkwardly, not for the first time wondering why Earthers greeted each other by flailing an arm about. Still, despite the room's foreign nature, he had to admit the open kitchen aroma was quite pleasant.

Various games could be played at the tables, involving cards, playing pieces, or relying on holographic imagery. Seth had tried a few of them over the years but found most of them totally nonsensical.

He walked down a row of tables. The left wall was transparent and tilted outwards, revealing below what the EN pilots called a basketball court. A polished wood floor with numerous colored lines stretched out between two suspended baskets. Two teams of three currently competed for the orange ball.

Seth recalled the one time, at Tevyr's behest, he had tried the game. The memory brought back a flutter of grief that he tried to ignore.

Out on the court, three Aktenai pilots did their best to keep up with three EN pilots. Everyone dealt with the loss of comrades and the stress of future battle in different ways. These young men and women buried it with physical exertion.

Seth checked the holographic scoreboard and grinned. The Aktenai pilots were doing quite well for a change.

He walked further into the rec center, rounded a corner into the second chamber, and found Jared and Yonu sitting at a table. Yonu had recently left the medical ward with her injuries fully repaired, but the young pilot still seemed shaken by her near-death experience.

She and Jared sat picking at their manually prepared Earth Nation meals. Yonu fussed with the raw pink flesh around her neck.

Normally Yonu wore a blue ribbon twined through her braid of raven black hair. Now she wore a black ribbon with one side edged in bright green, perfectly matching Tevyr's chaos frequency. It was a common mourning ritual amongst Aktenai pilots to display the color of a lost partner.

The Choir paired most pilots at very early ages. Yonu and Tevyr had grown up, fought, and matured together. Often the pairs would conceive children as had both Yonu's and Tevyr's parents. In the end, Seth wondered if Yonu's grief ran deeper than his own.

Jared looked up from his meal and hastily brushed aside locks of disheveled sandy blonde hair.

“Commander Elexen,” Jared said, standing abruptly. “Please, join us.”

Seth pulled out a chair and sat. “Thank you.” He turned to Yonu. “Good to see you up and about, Pilot Nezrii.”

Yonu looked up from her barely touched food and offered Seth a joyless smile.

“Morale is up, sir,” Jared said, sitting down. “Everyone I talk to is glad we’re going back in. They’re looking forward to the upcoming mission.”

“That’s good to hear.” Seth glanced at Yonu, who continued to poke at her food.

“We took a beating from those archangels, no mistake,” Jared said. “But epsilon’s pilots have been working on counter tactics day and night. We’ll be ready for them this time. They’re all rather keen to get some payback. For everyone, sir.”

Seth nodded. “Thank you. I appreciate the sentiment.”

“I even have them taking turns drilling short-ranged combat outside the *Resolute*. I hope you don’t mind me asking the Aktenai pilots for assistance. You guys are a lot better in close than we are.”

“Not at all. In fact, I wanted to discuss that with you.”

“Sir?”

“I’m combining our remaining seraphs into epsilon squadron,” Seth said. “And I’m placing you in command.”

Jared’s eyes widened. “Me, sir?”

“And that’s not all.” Seth nodded towards Yonu. “As you know, Aktenai pilots operate in pairs. Even when we group together for a squadron, it’s still comprised of closely knit partnerships.”

“Yes, sir. I know how you Aktenai operate.” Jared shrugged. “Sort of.”

“Well, we currently have an odd number of Aktenai pilots,” Seth watched Yonu for any sort of reaction. “And I want you to stay close to Yonu.”

"Me, sir? But I'm from the Earth Nation."

"You two seem to share some familiarity. And you've more than proven yourself in battle."

"Well . . ." Jared muttered.

Seth waited for Yonu's reaction. She looked up, met their eyes in turn, and nodded her approval.

"Excellent," Seth said.

"Pardon the question, Commander," Jared said. "But since the Renseki will be joining us, wouldn't it make more sense for alpha squadron to join them?"

"No. The Renseki always work alone. They will deploy independently in the coming battle."

"Hmm, I see." Jared glanced at the basketball court. "A few of my pilots are quite eager to meet the Renseki. Me too, in fact."

"You haven't met them before?" Seth asked.

"Not the current group. I guess we EN pilots don't get exposed to them like you Aktenai do. I've met one, but it was from the back of a classroom during the last joint deployment exercise. Even then, he was retired. I understand that four of the six current Renseki are very young for the position."

Seth nodded, the names coming to mind: Mezen Daed, Zo Nezrii, Kevik Torvulus, and Kiro Torvulus. "Yes, they were accepted into the Renseki shortly after the Alliance formed."

"Well, together we'll show those archangels what the Alliance can do. Those two traitor seraphs won't stand a chance."

Seth grimaced. "The reason the Alliance exists is because Pilot Donolon forced the Choir to stop its attack on Earth. He is the man most responsible for the peace between Earth and Aktenzek, which makes his betrayal all the more troubling."

"I know, sir. But his actions in the past cannot forgive what he did at the schism," Jared said. In his eyes Seth glimpsed carefully suppressed anger.

"I do not suggest forgiveness, Pilot Daykin, but caution. He and this Azeal should not be underestimated."

In a weak raspy voice, Yonu spoke for the first time since Seth's arrival. "Will Pilot Donolon be at the nebular facility?"

"Almost certainly. We have a confirmed sighting of his seraph at the facility."

Yonu reached back and tugged at her braid and mourning ribbon.

"Sir, why do you think he turned traitor?" Jared asked.

"I have been struggling with that question ever since we returned. Perhaps the chaos slaves finally overwhelmed him."

"The chaos slaves? I'm sorry, sir. I don't understand."

"I'm sorry. I shouldn't have said anything. Please continue your meal."

Seth rose from his seat.

"Sir," Jared said firmly. "If you know something, we have a right to hear it."

Seth opened his mouth to make another excuse, but stopped. He thought back to his debriefing with the Original Eleven and realized the parallels in what he was doing. He actually chuckled quietly at the comparison.

"Sir?" Jared asked.

"It's so easy to demand secrets when they're not yours."

"I'm sorry, but I feel I have a right to know."

"No, it's all right." Seth sat back down. "I'll tell you what I know."

"Thank you, sir."

Seth settled into his chair. "Jack Donolon was not born on Earth, nor is that his original name. His parents were Pilot Zonri Len and

Sovereign Taen Elexen, the man who would one day adopt me as his son and who Jack would kill to save Earth."

Jared's eyes bugged out. "*What*? You're *related*?"

"I suppose from your perspective it could seem like that, but we share neither blood nor a surname. Shall I continue?"

"Please, sir."

Seth cleared his throat. "Jack's birth created a critical problem for the Choir. For over two thousand years, every sovereign has also been a seraph pilot. Jack's lineage made him the most obvious candidate, but at birth his chaos coefficient was zero. He would never be a pilot and therefore could disrupt the smooth transition of power. Seeing no worth in Jack, but rather a future problem, the Choir and his father exiled him to Earth under the stewardship of observers like the traitor Dominic Haeger, never to be heard from again."

"But, sir, a coefficient of *zero*?" Jared said.

"Strange, is it not? A near-death experience awakened his talents, but at that point he was already thirty years old and immersed in Earth culture. They could not retract their mistake. And so my father and the Choir conceived a plan to bring him back. The Earth Nation wanted to capture a seraph, and my father allowed them to succeed. Jack entered Aktenzek under my father's watchful eye and eventually commandeered a seraph built specifically for him.

"My father planned to draw Jack into our way of life, to show him the technological marvels of our world and the adulation its people lavish upon seraph pilots. But that all fell apart when the Grendeni struck Aktenzek itself.

"Sovereign Elexen manipulated even these events, preventing Jack's escape. He forced him into an uneasy alliance with me and Quennin, and together we hunted Dominic Haeger and his four captured seraphs.

Jack fought alongside us and eventually learned of his true lineage. He even saw Imayirot and there came to understand the core motivation behind our whole culture.

"But my father and the Choir underestimated one thing. Jack was still an outsider looking in, and it was he, *not* an Aktenai pilot, who discovered the chilling nature of the original seraphs. Over a hundred slave minds had to be pooled together to create the influx amplifiers, each in constant unbearable agony, each unable to die. The terrible price of our power had been revealed."

"Well, it's a good thing you people don't do that anymore," Jared said. "Didn't failed seraph trainees get chopped up and used for influx amplifiers, too?"

Seth sighed and nodded. "Regrettably, yes. When other sources of chaos-adept minds were unavailable, we did do that."

"You guys take your Great Mission a bit too seriously. You know that, right?"

"Perhaps there is some truth to what you say, Pilot Daykin. Understandably, Jack left immediately after his discovery, and Quennin and I followed him. The Grendeni, now in possession of a captured seraph, knew this secret as well, and both Aktenai and Grendeni fleets converged on Earth: the richest source of chaos-adept minds in the universe. Both forces planned to strip-mine Earth of all sentient life, with the Aktenai fleet arriving first. Together the three of us fought against them and won, but the cost to Jack was terrible.

"While the Renseki battled against me and Quennin, Jack faced his own father: one of the most powerful seraph pilots ever. Jack could not win, and so in a desperate bid to strengthen his seraph, he removed the limiters repressing its chaos slaves. The gamble worked. As Jack's mind expanded out into the seraph, his power increased phenomenally.

"But the experience shredded his sanity. In an instant Jack experienced over a hundred human lives, each ending in days of indescribable torment. The bloodlust of the chaos slaves took over, and he killed his own father.

"Slowly, the intense fury of the chaos slaves faded, but his newfound strength remained. Still barely grasping his sanity, Jack ordered the massive Aktenai armada to stop. And they obeyed, so frightening was his power and state of mind.

"The Grendeni fleet attacked Earth shortly after this, but with Jack, a handful of seraphs, our combined forces, and Aktenzek itself, we turned them away."

"What was he like afterwards?" Yonu asked quietly.

"A broken man," Seth said. "Often, he'd wake up in the dead of night, screaming and sweating from horrible nightmares. His mind slowly healed, but he was never the same. Quennin and I helped him through this trial of his, and we grew very close during that time. It pained me to see him go."

"Hmm," Jared said. "I still don't have any idea why he turned traitor."

"Neither do I," Seth said.

"But let me get this straight, sir. We're up against a mildly insane, super-powerful seraph pilot that your government let gallivant around the galaxy instead of keeping a watchful eye on him. And now he's back with *another* super-powerful seraph pilot that no one seems to know anything about."

"Yes, Pilot Daykin, you put the matter into perspective quite well. We are all puzzled by the actions of the Choir and the Original Eleven." Seth stood up. "Well, the Renseki will be arriving in a few minutes. I should be present to welcome them onboard."

The three pilots said their goodbyes, and Seth left for the *Resolute*'s seraph bays.

Jared Daykin fidgeted in his seat, the pervading silence starting to eat at him. He was almost finished with his meal, but Yonu had hardly touched her food.

He rapped his fingers on the table. Awkwardness set in, and he tried to figure out what to say to Yonu.

"Come on, Yonu," he said. "Eat up. It'll make you feel better."

Yonu poked at her food a little more vigorously, but his comments had no further effect.

What to do? he thought. *What to say?*

"Maybe some exercise will feel good," he said. "How about you let me teach you how to play basketball? It's not as bad as the other Aktenai say."

Yonu skewered a baked potato with her fork.

Okay, wrong thing to say.

Jared rapped both sets of fingers on the table. He scanned the floors, walls, and ceiling around him in a quest for inspirational material.

"I think some of the pilots are outside right now. I bet they've got some close quarters training going on. Want to join in?"

Yonu massaged the side of her neck as if it were cramped or sore.

"I know. How about a game of chess? I bet you'll like ... ahh ... chess?"

The look she gave him froze him in place. She leaned towards him and stopped in front of his face.

"Shut. Up."

Jared shut his mouth and inched his seat back from Yonu.

Yonu sighed. "Do you understand what an Aktenai pilot does when he or she loses a partner?"

"Uh, no. Not really. Actually not at all. Was this in one of those classes I didn't pay attention to?"

Yonu shook her head. "It's a matter of tradition, really. Kind of an unwritten code. We are supposed to seek revenge in battle. In my case, I suppose I'm expected to go after Pilot Donolon."

Jared rapped his fingers on the table, contemplating the enormity of Yonu's task.

"Well, look at it this way," he said. "We know what to expect this time, and we'll have the Renseki with us. He might be powerful, but with enough numbers we can take him down. No doubt in my mind."

Yonu rubbed at her neck. "I wish I shared your confidence."

"May we join you?"

Yonu and Jared both looked up at the new arrivals.

Twin pilots stood at the edge of the table, holding trays of food from the automated Aktenai kitchenettes. The two men wore long Renseki coats and were tall and slim with neatly combed sandy blonde hair.

Yonu immediately stood up. "Of course, Renseki Torvulus," she said with a curt bow.

Jared found himself the only person sitting, but not out of rudeness. The intricacies of how Aktenai greeted each other and who bowed to whom always seemed to elude him. And just when was it permissible to use a person's first name instead of a formal title? That part always got him into trouble.

However, Yonu had other ideas. She grabbed his arm and attempted to haul him out of his seat.

"Hey!" Jared exclaimed.

Yonu leaned over and hissed through clenched teeth, "Come on, Jared. Stand up and bow."

Jared grimaced, not seeing why a soldier of Earth had to bow to some Aktenai pilot, but he rose out of politeness and followed Yonu's lead. They stood straight, faced the twins, and bowed their heads.

The two Renseki set their trays down and seated themselves. Then and only then did Yonu release her grip on Jared's arm and allow him to sit.

"We could not help but overhear your conversation," one of the twins said. He motioned to his identical brother. "We ourselves had the unfortunate duty of facing Pilot Donolon in battle. He was powerful even before his merger with the seraph. His presence amongst the Grendeni is quite troubling."

Jared leaned over to Yonu, still maintaining eye contact with the two Renseki. "Which Renseki are these, again?"

One of the twins smiled. "Ahh yes, perhaps some introductions are in order." He gestured in turn to each person at the table. "Lieutenant Jared Daykin. Pilot Yonu Nezrii. Renseki Kiro Torvulus. Renseki Kevik Torvulus. There, now we know each other."

Jared was surprised and a little embarrassed. "You know my name?"

"Of course," Kiro said. "We have been following your career with some interest."

"Really? Why would that be?"

"Because your talent is quite unique," Kevik said. "All pilots have heightened reflexes in their seraphs, but you also possess enhanced intelligence."

"That's the only way an idiot like him would get a squadron," Yonu said.

"Oh, hah hah. Very funny," Jared said.

Yonu gave Jared a jab with her elbow. "I'm only kidding. Still, it's hard to imagine the Renseki interested in a guy like you."

"We have wondered if his talent might be linked to our own condition," Kiro said. "The mental boundary between the two of us has always been murky. Perhaps learning more about Pilot Daykin's talent will help us understand it."

"Hmm," Yonu studied the three pilots in turn. "But wouldn't you have to be related for there to be a connection?"

"Actually, we are half-brothers with Pilot Daykin here."

Unfortunately, Jared had chosen that moment to take a sip of water. The drink made a rapid exit through his mouth and nostrils. He coughed loudly, grabbed a napkin, and pressed it against his face.

Yonu stared wide-eyed at the twins with her mouth hanging open.

"It is true," Kiro said. "That is why we came here after landing, so that we might meet our estranged kin."

"But you're Aktenai!" Jared said.

"Actually that's only partially correct," Kevik said. "Many Aktenai pilots were born on Earth before the Alliance was formalized. No one knows why, but all seraph pilots can trace their lineage back to Earth, be it a hundred generations or one."

"The Aktenai actually did that?" Jared asked. "Abduct kids from Earth?"

"Uhh." Yonu shook her head. "Don't you know anything? It's one of the chief articles found in the Treaty of the Alliance. You know, the one where Aktenzek pledged to stop its mistreatment of Seedings like Earth."

"I know that. But I guess I didn't really believe it. It just seems so farfetched."

"No, it was actually quite common," Kiro said. "For example, Pilot Elexen was born on Earth, though he does not remember it."

"Well, I guess you guys know what you're talking about," Jared said. "So, did you two just find this out? About the three of us, I mean."

"Oh, not at all," Kiro said. "We've known our origins for almost twenty years. But openly acknowledging such crimes is a touchy subject for pilots in our positions. We relegated ourselves to simply watching your progress from afar."

Kevik nodded. "Though, it pleases us to finally have the opportunity to meet in person. The Choir can hardly object to us working closely with you under current circumstances."

Jared swirled the water in his glass with a straw. "I think I need a drink." He started to get up.

Kevik took a glass off his tray, placed it on the table, and slid it over to Jared. "I believe that this is your preferred beverage."

Jared eyed the dark beer with suspicion. "You do know I'm not allowed to drink that for another year?"

Kiro wore a bemused smile. "A curious Earth Nation tradition. For something you are not allowed to drink, you seem to consume it quite often."

"Well …" Jared gave the twins a guarded smile. He accepted the glass and took a deep gulp. It was going to be a long day.

Chapter 11

The Valiant Artisan

Seth folded into the sky-blue nebula. Eddies and currents swirled around him, carrying wisps of lighter and darker shades. Ahead and down from his orientation was the gauze-enwrapped glow of the white dwarf star. The nebular facility was directly ahead, shrouded behind thick clouds of blue and blue-green.

"I'm not detecting any Grendeni craft," Seth said.

"Same here," Quennin said. "There could be stealth exodrones this far out, though."

"We'll just have to take the risk." Seth linked with the rest of the Aktenai fleet. "No enemy vessels detected. We'll proceed in. Stand by to reinforce on my command."

"Confirmed, sir," Jared Daykin said, leading epsilon squadron's fourteen seraphs.

"Understood," Zo Nezrii said, in command of the six Renseki. All seraphs, along with a formidable fleet of Aktenai frigates and dreadnoughts, waited one light-year beyond the nebular boundary.

Seth checked his loadout one last time. He'd equipped a compact eighteen-shot fusion cannon in the right forearm pod and a multipurpose railgun in the left. However, in order to carry out this mission, he'd dispensed with the leg-mounted weapon pods, wing-mounted countermeasures, and extended scanner array pods.

Instead, he carried four evasion pods that tapped into his barrier and generated an active stealth field. In theory, he was almost undetectable at long range, even by high-powered active scanners. However, the evasion pods were temperamental due to the human mind that powered the barrier. Loss of concentration, fast movement, weapon firing, dagger activation, or anything else from a long list could spoil the effect.

Seth and Quennin had used the pods five times before and were the *Resolute*'s best qualified pilots to reconnoiter the nebular facility.

"Okay, Quennin. Time to head in," Seth said, activating his evasion pods.

"Understood. Engaging active stealth."

Quennin's seraph vanished completely from Seth's passive scanners, but data continued to flow between them through a hypercast link. In a small section of his mind, a tactical plot showed two seraphs beside one another, their positions continuously updated.

Seth accelerated forward, fast for a frigate or dreadnought, but painfully slow for a seraph. He and Quennin plunged into thick nebular clouds.

"I'm detecting something ahead and to our left," Quennin said after almost half a hour. "It's big."

Seth turned to look. A large ribbon of darker blue passed by. He zoomed in on a giant silhouette behind it and enhanced the image.

"It doesn't appear to be a ship," Seth said. "Nor is it moving."

"One of the factories?"

"Perhaps, but our data shows all the factories in a ring above the star. This is too far out."

"More objects. Three directly ahead."

"Change course. Fifteen degrees down," Seth said.

"Understood."

Seth passed underneath a trio of massive objects shrouded by dense clouds. Dark bands of gas billowed aside, revealing the object in the center.

"A derelict?" Quennin asked. "Out here?"

A warship every bit as large as a schism lumbered by above them. Leprous patches of decay dotted the leviathan, revealing jagged teeth of armor and keel bars. Other sections had been neatly cut away, inner mechanisms removed.

"Ship class confirmed," Quennin said. "It's a Grendeni dreadnought, probably over three thousand years old. We might be passing through a refuse field of some sort for the nebular facility."

"Which would make this facility at least as old."

"You could be right. I can see where they cut away and salvaged some sections. That wasn't done recently."

Seth and Quennin flew past the ancient warships and pushed deeper into the nebula. They pressed on, passing mined-out asteroids, abandoned factories, blasted frigates, and structures Seth could not identify.

"Do the Grendeni pitch all their junk out here?" Quennin asked.

"Who can possibly understand our Fallen brothers and sisters?" Seth said. "Slow down. We're almost through."

The white dwarf star burned brightly within an opening in the blue nebular expanse. A long cord of hot matter rose from the star, focused through a conduit of giant rings. The cord split and shot off at angles into the waiting ring of factories. Most of the strands passed through the factories, but some refracted up into the carved remains of a dead planet.

"That's a lot of ships," Quennin said.

Seth passively scanned the hundreds of ships along the facility-ring. About one in ten had a complete outer hull.

"At least they're only under construction," Seth said. "We need to get closer to those factories and find one that produces archangels."

"I'll follow you in."

Seth and Quennin descended, skirting the nebular wall as they approached the facility-ring from above. Seth devoted all of his passive scanners to searching the factories but could only make out details on the closest ones. Most of the installations were devoted to frigate or dreadnought construction, though a few were fabricating new schisms.

"One of those factories with the plates coming out of the sides could be producing archangels," Seth said.

"Exodrones approaching from below," Quennin said.

Seth spotted the formation of sixteen exodrones. The drones maneuvered in teams of four carrying cube containers. He didn't think mere cargo haulers would carry precision scanners, but he also didn't believe in taking chances.

"Follow me." Seth descended down to the facility-ring's outer edge. The drones flew above them.

"I'm detecting several negators under construction," Quennin said. "Three near our position. Maybe more on the far side of the facility-ring."

Seth grimaced. He focused his passive scanners on the new coordinates. Two had open patches in the outer hull. One was nothing more than a row of keel rings. But no matter how incomplete the hulls were, their fold-preventing field generators might be functional. Seth marked every negator as a priority target and sent the list to Jared and Zo.

"We'll need to take these out before moving on the archangels," Seth said.

"Confirmed, sir," Jared said. "But if we engage the negators first, we'll lose the element of surprise against the archangels."

"I am aware of that, Pilot Daykin. My orders stand."

"Yes, sir."

So where are the archangels? Seth thought. *They folded here. That indicates they're at least based nearby.*

"Take a look above us," Quennin said. "We've got trouble."

Two Grendeni frigates and several combat exodrone squadrons prowled the nebular wall where Seth and Quennin had emerged. The exodrone squadrons glided about in tight formations, crisscrossing at diagonals as they searched. Two frigates hovered close to the nebular wall.

"They haven't found us yet," Seth said. "Continue as planned."

"We can't stay hidden for long."

"Then let's find that factory."

Seth and Quennin stopped above the facility-ring and followed its circumference clockwise.

"I've got another four frigates in motion," Quennin said. "And a dreadnought. They're approaching the facility-ring from above."

"There's nothing we can do about that. Continue as planned."

"If there even is one. The Choir could be wrong."

"I don't think—"

"Fold signatures!"

Two Grendeni frigates and forty-eight exodrones folded space directly above them. Wide rings of distorted light expanded out from their dark, streamlined hulls. The frigates aimed their main guns straight at him.

"Move!" Seth shouted.

Seth drove raw power into his wings. His stealth field collapsed. Drive shunts flared up to full power, and tiny snaps of chaotic energy crackled around his black armored body. He sped across the curving line of factories.

Twin beams of searing light bored down from the Grendeni frigates, missing by a few meters.

"At least four negator fields coming on-line!" Quennin said.

Seth looped above a half-finished dreadnought skeleton and aimed his fusion cannon on the lead frigate. He and Quennin fired as one. Seth's beam punched into, through, and out of the vessel. Explosions snapped across its length, joined moments later by a second frigate's death spasms.

The exodrones flew down at them, robotic and suicidal. Seth and Quennin fired their railguns, sending volleys of kinetic shells into their ranks. The shells exploded just before reaching the exodrone formations. Thick clouds of high velocity flechettes vomited out, ripping the exodrones apart like so much tissue paper. Staggered pin-prick explosions marked each kill.

"Come on. We need to move!" Seth said.

Every active Grendeni warship turned about and began lumbering towards them.

"Right behind you!"

Seth and Quennin flew underneath the facility-ring's huge circumference, using the factories as shields. Beams lanced past them every time they darted from cover to cover.

"Epsilon! Renseki!" Seth said. "Begin your attack runs! Take out those negators! If we don't find the factory soon, we're aborting!"

"Confirmed, sir," Jared said. "We're on our way."

"Understood," Zo said.

Twenty fold points snapped open. Six seraphs materialized at the far end of the facility-ring, their fold points nothing more than momentary white specks. The silver Renseki seraphs pounced on a half-completed negator. They ignited their chaos daggers and sliced it apart from the inside.

Fourteen seraphs under Jared's command swarmed a separate target. Beams exchanged, and Grendeni warships began to die in titanic eruptions.

"Seth, I think I found the factory." Quennin relayed the coordinate data.

Visually, the factory looked no different than any other. Its boxy main body wrapped around the star strand, but the large plate extending from its side was packed with tight rows of archangels. Even at this extreme range, Seth could make out hundreds of those machines crouching like so many winged skeletons.

Two shapes broke off from the archangel factory. They ducked underneath the ring of factories and flew out at incredible speed. Far faster than any archangel, and faster than almost any seraph in existence.

Their course led them straight to Seth and Quennin.

"Quennin, we have incoming."

"Yes, I see them …"

The two enemy seraphs closed. Seth received their request for a direct hypercast link. Hesitantly, he opened the channel.

"Seth, this is Jack. We need to talk."

Jack had to wait almost half a minute before receiving a reply.

"I have nothing to say to you," Seth said.

"Look, I understand you're upset," Jack said. "But we don't have to fight."

Seth and Quennin stopped beneath one of the *Valiant Artisan*'s factories. Jack slowed, remaining in the open. He had nothing to fear from the Grendeni warships above.

"Shall we kill them together?" Vierj asked, halting next to him.

"Not yet," Jack said privately.

“Your compassion for your former comrades is sweet, but misplaced.”

“It is mine to misplace,” Jack said. With a mental flick, he toggled back to his channel with Seth. “There is no need for us to fight, Seth. Call off your attack, and I will order the negators to stand down.”

“That is not an option,” Seth said. “Our battle will not end until one of us is dead.”

“Come on. Be reasonable, Seth. Neither of us wants to—”

“YOU KILLED MY SON!”

Jack opened his mouth to reply, but words failed him. The true price of his actions slammed home in his mind. He'd only been concerned with not harming Seth or Quennin. The possibility of a son or daughter among the pilots had never occurred to him.

Damn it! How could I have been so stupid? Jack thought. *That flame-red seraph. Was he in that one? Oh God, what have I done?*

“I didn't know. Please believe me, Seth. I didn't know.”

“It doesn't matter if you knew,” Seth said. “My son is dead because of your treachery.”

“I … I swear I didn't know.”

“There is no shame in fighting to win, Pilot Donolon,” Quennin said coldly. “But you have chosen your side, and it is not ours.”

“I only have one question for you,” Seth said. “Why have you betrayed us?”

“I …” Jack felt sick to his stomach. Seth's son was dead by his hand. How could he have been so careless? He knew that this was a small sacrifice in the greater scheme of his plan, but the thought brought him no comfort.

“I did it because—” Jack stopped. Vierj would be listening. Even within the untraceable security of hypercast, Vierj could listen. He dared not risk exposure now.

And even without Vierj listening, how could he tell Seth the truth? How could even *that* justify his actions? He doubted Seth would actually believe him, and the truth would only serve to forewarn the Choir and the Eleven.

No, silence was his only option.

"If you will not answer, then we have nothing further to say."

Twin purple daggers exploded out of Seth's forearms.

I knew this moment would come, Jack thought. *Deep down I knew it, even if I thought I could plan my way out of it. It was inevitable that I would face Seth and Quennin in battle from the moment I set down this path.*

Jack found his gaze drawn to Vierj's shadowy seraph. *So be it. I will be neck deep in corpses before this horrid business is over and will have only myself to blame.*

Jack summoned his chaos sword. It snapped vividly into existence and solidified as a bar of blue light.

"Stay out of this, Vierj. This is personal."

"As you wish."

Vierj pulled up and away. She landed one factory back along the ring and crouched like a vicious bird of prey.

Jack took a deep faltering breath, then expanded his blade-wings. Their edges blurred and ignited with blue fire. He swept in with deadly intent.

Seth flew up to meet him.

Jack swung in, and the two clashed in the snap-flash of meeting blades. Their energy weapons ground against each other, spewing showers of purple and blue sparks. Jack pushed forward, threw Seth off balance, and swung upward with the edge of his shield.

Seth blocked the attack. He dashed away and curved around to Jack's side. Jack dodged back and raised his sword. Their weapons connected once again. Seth pushed in and tried to stab a dagger past Jack's defenses.

Jack grabbed the incoming forearm. He pulled Seth along his intended path and threw him into the factory.

Seth spun wildly. He crashed into the factory's outer hull and knocked it out of alignment. The star strand passing within the factory wavered for a moment before fountaining outward in a wild cone.

Seth tore himself free of the wreckage, pushed off, and flew out.

All the while, Jack had lost track of Quennin.

She looped behind him and fired her fusion cannon squarely into his back. The beam struck his barrier and exploded into a spray of energy.

"Gah!" Jack grunted.

Seth dove at him.

Jack dashed to the side, making Seth overshoot him. Jack thrust down, trying to skewer the black seraph's back, but Seth spun around and knocked the blow aside with calculated ease.

Seth fell away with the white dwarf at his back and regrouped with Quennin along the closest factory's star strand.

Jack flew down after them.

Seth and Quennin fired their fusion cannons, but Jack dodged out of the way. Both beams punched into the factory above and bored through, vaporizing metal and machinery. The factory listed uncontrollably, allowing the star strand to cut effortlessly through its side.

Jack approached along the star strand, flying by guiding rings that kept the plasma stream tame. Seth and Quennin fired once more, but not at Jack.

At first, Jack wondered if the archangel squadrons had activated, but he quickly he realized the true target. Both beams made precise hits on a guide ring halfway between Jack and the two seraphs. The beams weren't strong enough to destroy the ring, but they did knock it out of alignment.

The thick cord of plasma changed directions as it passed through the maladjusted ring. A wild cord cut through the space, obliterating anything it touched.

Jack dodged frantically to the side. The nimbus of his arm's barrier touched the the passing cord, and the short contact sent hot needles of pain dancing up his arm.

"Gnh!"

The seraph said nothing.

"I know! I know!"

Seth gave him no time to recover and charged along the undamaged portion of the star strand's guides. He slashed in, and Jack was forced to block with his weakened shield. Its edges lost definition and wavered, but Jack forced it to hold. His arm burned with pain. In a sense, it actually was on fire. His barrier was not some piece of technology but rather a part of him magnified by the seraph's influx amplifier.

However, as wounded and stunned as he was, Jack's abilities dwarfed even Seth's. His shield held, and he threw Seth's attack back and thrust in with his sword.

Sword met dagger in a powerful flash of light. Jack pressed in. Seth dodged back sharply, and Jack's blade stabbed through empty space. Seth and Quennin regrouped at a distance.

"Six seraphs are approaching our position," Vierj said. "They are making a circuit of the facility-ring destroying negators along the way."

"Nothing I can do about that, Vierj."

"But I can. Do you need assistance?"

"No, I've got this."

"Then I think I will have a little fun. These fake seraphs should provide ample amusement."

"Don't give anything away."

"Naturally. I will restrict myself to basic attacks. Let us see how they fare."

Vierj took off from her factory perch, spun slowly around, and sped towards the Renseki.

Seth and Quennin flew in. Jack accelerated and met their attacks.

Jared Daykin surveyed the archangel factory's defenses with a vastly accelerated mind. Chaos energy circulated through his body, greatly enhancing his reflexes and intelligence.

Unlike other facilities in the nebula, the archangel factory possessed considerable defenses in the form of thick mnemonic plating, dozens of seeker ports, and hundreds of laser blisters and railgun turrets.

But none of these stood a chance against the fourteen seraphs bearing down on it.

Like most EN seraphs, Jared's was configured for maximum ranged firepower. He carried an eighteen-shot fusion cannon on his arm and three tactical seeker pods, one on the other arm and two on his wings. This gave him a total of ninety archangel-killing tactical seekers. His two leg conformal pods were stocked with sixty ship-killing fusion torpedoes, half of which he'd already pumped into three now-dead negators.

In addition to this already massive arsenal, every EN seraph carried an MR2-X rail-rifle into battle. Back when the Alliance first formed, Earth Nation scientists and engineers had provided a fresh perspective on seraphs and their miniaturized fusion cannons, and they wondered what really limited a device connected to a seraph's barrier.

A seraph's power output always equaled "as high as required" within the pilot's individual limitations. So theoretically, a device connected to a seraph's barrier could draw almost limitless power. Development and experimentation between combined corps of Aktenai and Earth Nation engineers led to the development of evasion pods and rail-rifles.

Jared leveled his rail-rifle at the closest weapon blister and fired. Armor superheated and vaporized in the exchange of kinetic force. White-hot debris exploded from the defensive railgun battery.

The rest of epsilon squadron rained kinetic bolts and fusion beams upon the archangel factory. Its defenses withered under the fusillade, and the main body cracked open. The star strand blew out of the factory in an ugly cone of white-hot plasma. Grendeni guns fell silent.

"Recon the factory," Jared said. Six Aktenai seraphs swept towards the factory's large rectangular plate. Eight seraphs waited, rifles and cannons ready. Yonu held formation with Jared.

This close to the factory, Jared detected a transit system running through the plate's topside that connected to each of the archangels.

That must be how they get pilots to the archangels, Jared thought. If pilots were in the factory, they didn't have a lot of time.

Before the Aktenai seraphs reached the factory, twenty archangels powered up on Jared's chaos scanner. The archangels pushed off from the cargo plate and faced oncoming seraphs. Long swords ignited with yellow fire, and they flew out to meet their foes.

"Open fire," Jared said.

The EN gun-line unleashed a round of rifle fire. Seven kinetic bolts slammed into the archangels. One exploded when a bolt tore through its stomach, but the rest shrugged off the impacts.

Another salvo hit home, splattering five into clouds of broken metal and yellow goo. The surviving archangels approached without fear or hesitation. Only six seraphs met them, but these were some of the best pilots in all of Aktenzek, and they were ready.

The Aktenai seraphs lit their daggers. They charged in, parried the archangel swords, and cut them down with killing strokes.

Another group of archangels began to power up.

Jared spotted an archangel tumbling out of the melee. He lined up his rail-rifle and fired. The kinetic bolt struck the archangel's shoulder, flared briefly yellow against its chaos barrier, and punched through. The archangel blew apart, its appendages spinning away.

More archangels launched from the factory plate, glowing red in Jared's thoughts. His accelerated mind played the battle out to its conclusion.

Act quickly or be overwhelmed, he thought grimly.

"Gun-line, keep up the pressure," Jared said, flying out of formation. "Yonu, cover me."

"Following!" Yonu pulled in behind him.

Jared looped around the growing melee. Aktenai seraphs continued to cut through the archangels, and EN seraphs poured volley after volley into them. But the archangels kept coming.

Jared stopped with his line of fire perpendicular to the next archangel swarm. He selected six targets and flushed his conformal ordnance pods, launching all ninety tactical seekers in a single volley. The cloud of munitions refined into six tightly packed arrows of death.

Fifteen tactical seekers slammed into each archangel. Flashes of heat and radiation erupted like short-lived suns. Of the six targets, a single archangel survived. Yonu blasted it to pieces with a fusion shot.

Three archangels broke from the swarm, heading for Jared and Yonu.

Jared drew down his rail-rifle on the leader and fired once, twice, three times before its barrier gave out. The final bolt punched through the abdomen with such force that its torso burst apart.

Two archangels left.

Jared stowed the rail-rifle on his back as the final two archangels came in. He ignited his deep red chaos dagger and awaited their attack. The first archangel raised its sword over its head and slashed down. Jared met the sword in a short flash of chaos energy, pushed the sword up, and slashed his dagger through its armpit.

The archangel's sword arm tumbled away, thick fluid pulsing from the wound. Though stunned and defenseless, the archangel clearly had no concept of self-preservation. It rushed in and tackled him.

"No!"

The second archangel flew above them, sword held high, ready to cut him in half. Jared tried to jerk his arm free but couldn't pull out in time.

The second archangel swung down. Yonu sped across, her dagger cutting through its chest. Pressurized fluid gushed from the wound. The second archangel's sword struck Jared and rebounded harmlessly off his barrier.

The sword's edge, along with the pilot, was dead.

Jared freed his arm and stabbed through the first archangel's cockpit. He kicked the dead machine off.

"That ... was close," Jared said. "Thanks, Yonu."

"No problem."

"Renseki, we're at the archangel factory. What's your status?"

"Two negators left," Zo said. "We'll fold to you once their fields are down."

"Confirmed."

Jared and Yonu approached the factory from the side, avoiding the worst of the seraph-versus-archangel action. Epsilon squadron was holding out, but archangels kept activating in droves. They wouldn't hold out much longer.

Jared retrieved his rail-rifle and hovered at the edge of the factory. Most of the factory plate was covered by dormant ranks of archangels, but he spotted long crates at the ends of each row, just the right size for storing archangel swords lengthwise.

"There." Jared linked coordinate data. "Those crates at the end of each row."

"I see them," Yonu said.

"Crack one open," Jared scanned the ranks of crouching archangels with his rail-rifle. "I'll provide cover."

"Moving in."

Yonu landed on the edge of the cargo plate, ignited her dagger, and cut through the exterior of the closest crate. She jammed her fingers into the glowing rent and pried it open.

"Archangel swords," she said. "About forty to each of these crates."

"Grab the crate. I'm coming down to pick up one of the inactive archangels."

"Understood."

Jared descended towards the nearest row of archangels.

A group of fourteen archangels activated and took off. One took its sword and backstabbed another. Both shut down and drifted away. The other twelve came at him.

"Watch out!" Yonu said.

"Last negator down," Zo Nezrii said. "Redeploying to assist."

Six Renseki seraphs flashed into existence above the factory. Fold points expanded outwards.

The Renseki dove at the archangels. They moved in a precise and deadly ballet, as if each seraph was simply one cog in a larger machine. They fired their cannons, launched seeker volleys, and finally ignited their daggers. In seconds, not a single archangel remained.

Jared had never seen anything like it.

"Moving to assist epsilon," Zo said. The Renseki streaked into the melee.

"I've got the crate," Yonu said.

Jared selected an archangel and landed next to it. The archangel was locked into position with heavy clamps on its limbs and wings, but these stood no chance against a seraph's strength. Jared grabbed the archangel's torso with both hands and pulled. He ripped the torso free, but the limbs stayed in place.

"Ahh, crud. This is harder than it looks," Jared said. He flung the torso aside and flew over to the next archangel. This time, he tore the clamps open one by one, grabbed the archangel underneath its arms, and hefted it up.

"We have what we came for!" he said.

"Fall into formation with us," Zo said. "We'll hold this position until all units are ready to fold."

"Where's the commander?"

"Pilot Elexen is currently engaged."

Jared and Yonu pulled into formation with the Renseki. The fighting around the factory grew increasingly intense. Whole squadrons of archangels began folding in, but the Renseki demonstrated just how far the archangels had to go before they could match seraphs. Wave after wave fell to their tightly coordinated attacks.

Amidst the onslaught of archangels, Jared spotted a single fold point. At first, he thought it was a lone archangel folding in behind its squadron. But as the distortion passed, Jared discovered who this new foe was.

"Azeal's here!" Jared shouted. "Gun-line, new target!"

EN seraphs brought rail-rifles to bear on the featureless black seraph. Jared slung the archangel limply under one arm and retrieved his own rifle. Every EN pilot poured fire into the enemy, but shots that would have torn an archangel to pieces only ricocheted off Azeal.

The black seraph sped past the latest wave of archangels. Renseki and Aktenai beams fired, but it didn't bother dodging. Every hit splashed harmlessly off its barrier.

Azeal crashed shoulder-first into one of the Aktenai, slashed across the seraph's belly, then grabbed hold and ripped it in two. The pilot's vitals flatlined.

The Renseki flew out, Mezen's command seraph in the lead. He thrust in with his bright yellow dagger and struck Azeal's shadowy blade. The two exploded against each other in a nova of light and darkness. Chaos energy threw the Renseki back.

Two more Renseki dove in, their twin orange daggers ready, but Azeal moved impossibly fast and their strokes found nothing but empty space.

Jared received Seth's squadron-wide fallback signal, authorizing him to leave the area of engagement.

The Renseki and epsilon survivors folded space back to the *Resolute* near the edge of the nebular expanse. Alongside the carrier hovered four dreadnoughts and a negator, along with full squadrons of exodrones and frigates.

Seth and Quennin folded in and headed towards the carrier.

"Everyone land!" Seth shouted. The Alliance seraphs dropped directly onto the carrier's exterior, not bothering with the time-consuming processes of docking internally.

Hundreds of fold points disgorged Grendeni warships, drones, and archangels. The Aktenai dreadnoughts and frigates moved in to protect the carrier, exchanging beams and torpedoes with the Grendeni ships.

Two winged shapes folded in, one white and one black.

Jared landed on the carrier last, careful not to damage his captured archangel. Every Alliance seraph was now within the carrier's fold envelope.

"Fold!" Seth shouted.

The *Resolute* engaged its fold engines and slipped away. Less than a nanosecond later, the Aktenai negator switched on its field. Unable to fold space and pursue, the Grendeni fleet continued to pound the Aktenai warships.

The Alliance seraphs had escaped.

Chapter 12

Before the Storm

They never expected the attack on Valiant Artisan, Jack thought, hurrying through the *Righteous Anger*'s northcity streets. The Grendeni Executives were finally ready to launch an attack on Aktenzek itself.

That tipped things in my favor. I finally have the leverage I need.

Even though Aktenzek and the Grendeni schisms were powerful industrial centers, their civilian populations shielded them from military aggression. Attacks against Aktenzek were often followed by retaliatory strikes against schisms and vice versa. Millions of Grendeni lives could hinge on the decision to assault Aktenzek.

Cars zipped by or took off for the northcity heights. The axial tube dimmed and reddened, simulating dusk.

Jack stepped off the street and entered the five-hundred-floor residential tower. He walked across the foyer and took a lift to his suite. Dominic had arranged the accommodations as one of many small gestures meant to placate him and buy time.

Jack preferred staying on the *Scion*, but living with the Grendeni was an important gesture of trust. Besides, the less time he spent near his seraph, the less nervous he made the Grendeni.

Though it doesn't stop them from prying, Jack thought. He knew what the Grendeni had tried to do to his seraph, and how his seraph had responded.

On the top floor, Jack walked by a group of four Grendeni civilians who ignored him completely. He now wore the attire of a Grendeni administrator: black trousers, white tunic, and dark green jacket adorned with the gold sigils of rank. The clothes and honorary title were yet another gift from Dominic.

Hell, Dom, I'd wear a clown suit if it made you attack sooner.

Jack stepped into a wide room subdivided by white curtains. Most were pulled back against narrow fluted columns that met a high ceiling. He joined Vierj and collapsed into a couch with a weary exhale.

"Did it not go well?" Vierj asked, leaning against a column, appraising him with her silver eyes. Dominic had provided her with a selection of popular Grendeni fashions, and she'd selected a light cream ensemble with dark-red trim that hugged her youthful curves.

"No, it went fine," Jack said. "I'm just tired."

"Does his death bother you that much?"

Observant of her, he thought. *Dangerously observant of her. I need to be careful.*

Jack sighed. "Yeah, it bothers me."

Vierj sat next to him and placed her hand on his. "The boy was nothing more than a lesser form. Why does his death matter?"

"Vierj, he was Seth's son. I should have expected someone like him would be out there. I screwed up."

"If we are to find the Gate, such deaths are to be expected. You should not dwell on them."

Jack shook his head. "It's not that easy."

"I used to think like you do."

"Yeah?"

"A long time ago." Vierj squeezed his hand. "You are not the only one who has faced allies in battle."

"How did you deal with it?"

"I harden my heart. I refuse to feel sympathy for those who oppose us."

"Yeah, that's not working too well for me."

"Fighting Zophiel was a million times more painful," Vierj said. A specter of dark emotions passed over her face and then was gone.

"Zophiel?"

"A name best left forgotten."

"Comrade?" Jack asked.

"My son."

"Oh."

"And one of my worst mistakes. He was a failure without equal."

"That had to hurt."

"It did …" Vierj smiled suddenly, but the gesture held no warmth. "Perhaps I should not judge. You may deal with your comrades as you see fit."

"Thank you, Vierj."

"Enough about the past. Please tell me how your meeting with the Executives went."

"Sure," Jack said. "It actually went surprisingly well, though it took us seven hours to get there. How anyone could be so in love with their own voice, I will never understand."

"Did they consent to the attack?"

"Yes. Even with the losses at *Valiant Artisan*, they have enough for the assault. They'll get us to the planet and cover our withdrawal."

"And so we shall return to Aktenzek with a powerful fleet," Vierj said. "Initially, I had my doubts, but the results of your cunning are undeniable."

Jack shrugged. "I do what I can."

Vierj turned around, suddenly distant.

"What is it?" he asked.

"These Grendeni peasants are trying to listen to us again." Vierj closed her eyes and inhaled slowly. "There. The problem has been dealt with."

"Did they hear anything?"

"Of course not. These primitives are not as clever as they think."

Hypercast transceivers, Jack thought. *Just how can Vierj sense them?* It was an incomprehensible talent, much like Vierj's other abilities, and one Jack had learned about almost too late during their return.

"If you think they might break through, we could return to the *Scion*," Jack said.

"You underestimate my abilities. That is not necessary."

He laughed. "Underestimating you is the last thing I'd ever do!"

"I am glad to hear that. However, perhaps your caution has its merits."

"What do you mean?"

"Have you considered that these Grendeni might be becoming suspicious? Perhaps this spying game they play has given them a clue."

"I know it's risky being here," Jack said. "But they've agreed to the attack. It was a worthwhile risk. And besides, once we reach Aktenzek who cares if they find out?"

"And if they realize we have fooled them?"

"The Aktenai and the Grendeni will keep each other busy while we claim the prize. I'll still give them the location."

"Why not withhold it?"

Jack shrugged. "Well, if only the Aktenai know where the Gate is, they'll try to stop us. If *both* the Aktenai and the Grendeni know, they'll fight over it."

"And we will slip in while they occupy each other."

“Exactly,” Jack said. The best lies were a mix of truth and omissions, after all.

“The Gate is so close.”

“And the Homeland beyond it. I’m excited to finally see what all the fuss is about.”

“Oh, Jack Donolon, it is paradise compared to this stunted and accursed universe. When you experience it for yourself, you will understand. It is where humans originated and where we are destined to return.”

“Looking forward to that.”

Vierj clasped her hands and sighed, grinning. It was perhaps the happiest Jack had ever seen her. “I will enjoy these coming battles. It has been a long time since I used the full scope of my talent.”

“I don’t like this, Dominic. I don’t like this at all.” Administrator Gurgella paced across the *Righteous Anger*’s dimly lit control room. An array of visual feeds from throughout the schism gave the room a ghostly glow. Around the administrator, a dozen technicians analyzed the few scraps of data they’d obtained so far.

“I do not understand your reluctance, administrator,” Dominic said. “We have two individuals who, by all estimates, are the most powerful seraph pilots in existence. They are willing to assault Aktenzek and even retrieve the Gate’s location for us.”

Gurgella tossed his jacket aside and began fussing with his sweat-soaked collar.

“There are too many questions,” he said. “And the Executives are not asking enough of them.”

“Administrator, everyone has secrets.”

"But not ones like these!" Gurgella charged up to a screen and plastering his hand over the center. The screen's visual feed came straight from Jack Donolon's northcity residence.

It was completely black. Seven bead-size transmitters communicated with the control center via secure hypercast channels. There was no physical way the signals could be interrupted.

And yet those signals had been blocked with incredible precision.

Dominic shrugged. "So Jack and his girlfriend want a little privacy. Is that so unusual?"

"That is beside the point." Gurgella slapped the empty screen. "This is not physically possible!"

"Administrator, with all due respect, I agree that this is impossible from our perspective. But remember, our understanding of chaos physics is based on far less empirical data than Aktenzek's. And furthermore, these are two extremely powerful pilots. Does it not make sense that they are capable of feats other pilots are not?"

One of the technicians cleared her throat and stepped forward, awaiting permission to speak. She was short and slender, with prim black hair and a calculating look in her dark eyes.

Chief Technician Shollin, Dominic thought, recalling the data from an archived portion of his mind. He found his eyes drawn to the light pen twirling between her fingers. She stopped the nervous habit and clasped her hands tightly behind her back.

"Go ahead," Gurgella said. "Speak your mind."

"Administrators, if I may offer my humble opinion," Shollin said. "We have an extensive library of battlefield encounters with seraphs. We also have the direct experimental data from the seraph pilot Mezen Daed and his reverse-engineered craft. Never in all those encounters have we seen a seraph pilot interfere with hypercast transmissions."

"So noted," Gurgella said. "Well, Dominic? What do you say to that?"

"What can interfere with hypercast transmissions?" Dominic asked.

"A few extreme circumstance sets exist," Shollin said. "Fold engines can briefly introduce mild static onto a signal at the source or destination, though this is quite rare. Also, close proximity to a black hole can interfere or even block the transmission."

"And we know one of those isn't inside the schism." Gurgella faced the blank screen and shook his head. "Well, if you find out anything let me know."

"Of course, administrator."

"Pull up the seraphs," Gurgella said. The visual feeds switched to live images of the two seraphs stored in the *Righteous Anger*'s archangel catapults. "Analysis."

Shollin gestured to the black shadow of Vierj's seraph.

"We have made one hundred two attempts to breach the black seraph's barrier and analyze its interior. All one hundred two attempts have failed. As far as we can tell, its barrier is impervious."

"Seraph barriers are almost invincible normally," Gurgella said. "Are you sure there's something special about this one?"

"Yes, administrator. Even across a very powerful barrier, it only fully manifests when needed. For example, at the impact point of a beam weapon. Under such circumstances, a barrier will momentarily become opaque, and only near the impact point. This barrier has maintained complete opacity since we first began observation. And it's done that without the pilot physically in the seraph, which we didn't even know was possible.

"Also, a normal barrier radiates waste energy through light," Shollin continued. "Each pilot's frequency is unique and serves as an absolute form of identification even if they change the seraph's frame. However, this barrier has no frequency. All waveforms impacting on the barrier are not returned."

"Sort of like the room," Dominic said quietly.

"Eh? You say something?" Gurgella asked, turning around.

"No, administrator. Just mumbling to myself."

"Well don't mumble so loudly," Gurgella said. "Continue with your analysis, technician."

"We do have one important exception to report," Shollin said. "During one test, we fired hypercast transmissions at the seraph. As expected, the hypercast transmissions passed through … most of the time. Signals had a failure rate of less than one percent, but I believe this suggests controllable permeability to hypercast signals, which of course is imposs—"

"Yes, impossible. That must be why we keep seeing it happen," Gurgella said. "Do you have anything useful to add from your analysis?"

"Ahh, useful? No, not really."

"Then, to paraphrase your long-winded oratory, you don't have a clue."

"I suppose that's one way to put it, administrator." Shollin frowned, looking wounded.

Gurgella shook his head. He wiped the sweat from his reddened brow. "And your analysis of the white seraph? Have you made any better progress with it?"

"Sadly, no, administrator. Our one attempt to study the white seraph's interior ended in failure, and we decided to discontinue the analysis."

"Why?"

"Because the seraph moved without a pilot," Shollin said.

Gurgella and Dominic shot her disbelieving looks.

"And not a little, either," Shollin said. "The seraph made it quite clear it was not to be tampered with."

"What? Did it ask you not to touch it?" Gurgella asked.

"No, administrator. Please observe." Shollin linked to the nearest screen and brought up the archived imagery.

Jack's seraph stood motionless in a cramped bay, shoulder to shoulder with ranks of archangels. A mobile trolley accelerated across a track running the length of the bays, then stopped directly above the seraph. Its maintenance arms folded and reached for one of the seraph's wing clusters.

The seraph twisted around, too fast even for Dominic's enhanced vision. It grabbed the maintenance trolley, ripped it from its moorings, and crumpled it in a fist. The seraph dropped the mechanical carcass, turned, and looked directly at the camera.

A moment later, the seraph's fist filled the screen, and then the screen went blank.

"I hope you will bear with the repetition," Shollin said. "But what you just observed is impossible."

Gurgella blew out a frustrated breath. "Too many accursed questions."

Dominic found the behavior of Jack's seraph curious, but not impossible to explain. Seraph pilots did not require actual physical contact with their machines to supply power, though proximity improved performance. Add to this Jack's unique experiences with his seraph, and Dominic saw no deep mystery.

It was the other seraph and its female pilot that drew Dominic's attention. Something nagged at the back of his mind, as if filed away long ago and forgotten until now. The seraph's barrier and their failure to see into the room seemed strangely familiar.

A barrier capable of preventing anything from passing through it, capable of defying science with its impossibility. Why does this feel so familiar?

Dominic knew he'd seen this before. He walked past Gurgella and Shollin, who had meandered into some irrelevant topic, and stepped in front of the screen showing Jack's residence.

A completely black screen. Nothing got through. Not light, nor heat, nor even hypercast. Nothing came out either, as if the room didn't even exist.

But it had to exist. Dominic could walk into that room any time he wanted to …

Any time I want to …

Dominic lingered on this last thought, tantalized by the sentence for some reason. He pondered the words, rolling them around in his mind, playing with them, but nothing came of the exercise.

And so Dominic tried a different tactic. *If I could command the laws of physics to change, how would I do this? These are not just seraph chaos barriers. There is something else here, something different.*

So, in order to prevent anything from getting through, how would I do that?

Or perhaps I'm not looking at this right. There doesn't have to be a physical barrier. All I have to do is stop anything coming in. Stop it dead in its tracks.

But how to do that?

…

Hell, that's easy! I'd just freeze it in time!

In that instance, Dominic had the answer in totality. A shiver of fear washed over him. He staggered back from the screens and looked at the black seraph again. There it stood beneath its impervious cocoon. He wondered if anything in this accursed universe could stop it.

"Dominic? What's the matter with you?" Gurgella asked.

"Oh, nothing." Dominic collected himself and stood straighter. "I was just wondering if we've taken adequate precautions."

"We already have assassin squads standing by. What more do we need?"

Could something so mundane stop such a being? I doubt it.

“Administrator, I suggest we make arrangements for something more drastic. We should equip the assassin squads with antimatter charges.”

Shollin gasped.

An explosion of that magnitude could rip the whole schism apart, Dominic thought. *Would even that work? Yes, that would surely do it. Even if she can’t die, she would float helplessly through space for the rest of eternity.*

“That seems a bit extreme,” Gurgella said.

“I merely suggest we prepare for the worst.”

“Are you sure, Dominic?”

“Yes, administrator. Quite sure.”

“But didn’t you just telling me I was overreacting? Are you all right? Has something unnerved you?”

“No, administrator. I am quite fine. I’ve simply come to appreciate the large number of unknowns we’re dealing with. These two pilots are extremely dangerous, as you have often pointed out.”

“Hmm, very well,” Gurgella said. “Yes, perhaps we should take another look at our termination options.”

The meeting dragged on, but Dominic paid it little mind.

Jack, he wondered. *Just what is it you’re after?*

Finding somewhere he and Jack could have a private conversation was not easy, but both had worked in EN SpecOps. Dominic in particular knew everything about the *Righteous Anger*’s surveillance network, including the best ways to defeat it. Finding a place he and Jack could meet secretly other than Jack’s carrier wasn’t too difficult.

Like many Grendeni cities, the *Righteous Anger*’s northcity had existed for centuries. This meant that layers of construction, demolition, refurbishment, and revitalization lay piled one atop of the other. Beneath the gleaming exterior of silver, metal, and glass was a labyrinthine underground of dark tunnels and old buildings filled with the underclass.

Dominic walked along one such tunnel, still wearing his administrator uniform. Even in these parts of the schism, rank had its advantages, and people took steps not to be around him or even to notice him.

Light strips ran the length of the gently curving tunnel. Shops and dwellings grew out of the walls in three levels. Dominic leaned against a shop façade on the second level and waited for Jack to arrive.

Jack descended in a lift from the third level. He stepped off and walked over.

"Okay, Dominic. What's so important?"

"Is *she* with you?" Dominic glanced at the balcony behind Jack.

"No, Vierj went back to the *Scion*. I should be over there as well. The *Scion* is supposed to rendezvous with your fleet before we make the final push for the solar system."

"I know, but this is important." Dominic scanned the area for surveillance devices. Nothing.

"And you don't want Administrator Gurgella or any of the Executives involved in this?"

"This isn't about what I want. This is about what *you* don't want people to know about that woman."

Jack folded his arms across his chest. "All right. You have my attention."

Dominic bobbed his head towards a small corridor that broke off from the main tunnel. Jack followed Dominic into the corridor, which snaked left then down, passing dormant machinery the size of buildings.

"Where are we?"

"This used to be part of the northern factory zone," Dominic said. "Back when the northcity was a lot smaller. It's all been decommissioned, but some people still live down here."

"Wonderful."

Dominic stopped at a dimly lit cul-de-sac. Black passages led to the old unseen factories.

"Okay, Dom. Talk."

"Let's cut to the chase. I've got only one question for you. Who is Vierj?"

Jack gave him an insufferable smirk. "Like I told you before, she's an exiled pilot."

"Don't mess with me. That woman is dangerous, and you know it."

"Being dangerous doesn't make her special."

"You know what I'm talking about," Dominic said. "I'll ask you again, who is she?"

"She—" Jack stopped and shook his head. "I'm sorry, I can't tell you. You'll just have to trust me."

"I'm finding that hard to do, Jack. Her seraph is *invincible*! Nothing gets through her barrier. If she turned on us, she could kill every last person on this schism, and there's nothing we could do about it."

"So could I, if you want to be picky about it."

"Yes, but you can't manipulate time," Dominic said.

"What is that supposed to mean?"

"Damn it, Jack, just tell me what I want to hear."

Jack wore a carefree grin. "And what exactly do you want to hear?"

"You're not going to tell me, are you?"

"Nope."

Dominic let out a frustrated sigh. "If that's how you want to play this, then so be it." He pulled off his jacket and tossed it aside.

Jack raised an eyebrow.

"Let me explain something to you," Dominic said. "I want answers, I don't care how I get them, and we are all alone out here."

"Dom, I love you, too, but not in that way."

"Shut up. You may be a remarkable pilot, but outside your seraph you are just a man like any other."

"Oh, my mistake. I thought you were going to try to seduce me."

"No, Jack. I'm going to give you one last chance to tell me the truth before I beat it out of you."

Jack crossed his arms. "You do realize I could have my seraph here in less than a minute."

"And I can kill you in seconds," Dominic said, his posture unchanged and unthreatening. "Remember, for a human my size, I'm ten times as strong, twice as fast, and far more durable. The Aktenai didn't hold back when they made me."

Jack sighed. "Well, if you want to try, I won't stop you."

"Last chance."

Jack shook his head.

Dominic shot forward with inhuman speed. But instead of punching Jack in the stomach, he suddenly found himself staring at an approaching knee.

Jack had grabbed Dominic by the hair and then slammed the observer's face straight into his rising knee. Dominic staggered back, momentarily stunned. He shook his head and raised two fingers to his mouth, gently touching it. Blood oozed from his cracked lip.

"What the hell?"

Jack shrugged. "Maybe I got lucky that time. Would you like to try again?"

Dominic dashed forward, made a brief feint to the left, and swung a fist into Jack's right side.

The punch should have landed, but Jack suddenly wasn't there. Something hit Dominic's leg. He flew off his feet and landed hard on his hands and knees.

"Again?" Jack asked, hands in his pockets.

Dominic sprang to his feet and snarled. He may have been a construct, but his emotions were all too human. Rage boiled hot inside him, purging any semblance of rational thought. He rushed in again. With Jack just standing there mocking him, surely he could land a hit.

Dominic threw an uppercut that would kill an unprotected human on impact, shattering bones and pulverizing organs. But his efforts weren't enough. Jack caught the punch and locked onto Dominic's arm with both of his.

"How?" Dominic gasped, struggling to free his arm.

Jack replied with a sly grin and shifted his stance. He picked Dominic up and threw him over his shoulder. Dominic rocketed through the air and smacked hard against the wall. The force of the impact cracked the wall's tiled plastics. He fell to the ground and landed painfully on his back.

Dominic struggled to his feet. He coughed, tasting blood in his mouth.

"Do we really need to keep doing this?" Jack asked.

Dominic pointed at Jack. "You should not be able to do that!"

"Let me tell you something. What makes a seraph work? It's a pilot's instincts drawing on that vast chaotic sea of energy in order to stay alive. Even Aktenai and Grendeni science has trouble detecting that small spark of energy unamplified in a normal pilot."

Jack held his hand out, palm up. "But as you know, I'm no ordinary pilot." A small pin-prick of blue light ignited above his palm. The pin of light blazed and grew until it was the size of a fist, making Dominic squint.

Jack let the ball of light disappear.

Dominic backed half a step away. "How did you do that?"

Jack shrugged. He reached down, retrieved Dominic's jacket, and brushed the dust off it. "Vierj is the real expert. She taught me how to channel this power even without a seraph."

Dominic accepted his coat back.

"So, as you can see, I'm quite capable of defending myself," Jack said. "I know what you think is going on. I know you think Vierj is dangerous, and you would be right. She is a very dangerous woman. However, please trust me. I know what I'm doing, and when I'm done the universe will be a better place."

"For whom?"

Jack grinned sadly. "For everyone but me."

Chapter 13

Forged in Chaos

From a balcony above the seraph bay, Seth gazed down at the dissected Grendeni archangel. With its internal systems spread out below, the archangel looked even more like a grotesque metal skeleton. Spindly maintenance arms moved in blurs of motion, prying into its systems at Zo Nezrii's neural commands.

Quennin and Jared both watched the dissection with rapt attention. Once finished, the arms folded into cradles along the bay ceiling.

"So what are we dealing with, Zo?" Seth asked.

"A lot of sloppy engineering, courtesy of our Fallen brothers and sisters," she said.

Jared pointed at a flexible column pulled from the archangel's back. Over one hundred spheres wrapped around the column in a rising coil.

"Is that what I think it is?" he asked.

"Yes, unfortunately," Zo said. "Like pre-Alliance seraphs, the archangels need live neural material for their amplifiers rather than the synthetic mass we currently use. We were able to overcome that requirement by studying Pilot Donolon's merger and partially replicating it for all seraphs. I can only imagine what we'd be up against if the Grendeni could duplicate current seraph tech."

"The Grendeni must have a vastly accelerated breeding program," Seth said. "Given the numbers we've faced."

"Agreed," Zo said. "Genetic analysis of the, shall we say, unwilling donors leads us to the following conclusions. One, the archangel pilots and amplifier donors are indeed descended from Mezen Daed by roughly ten generations. Two, those generations have repeatedly interbred to produce the desired chaos coefficients."

"Disgusting," Quennin breathed.

"The archangels employ several radical design choices," Zo said. "The pilots actually share a direct physical link to the amplifier. While this increases performance, it also makes buffering out the chaos slaves extremely difficult. This may have contributed to the violent behavior we've witnessed."

"We should destroy this amplifier," Quennin said.

"Agreed," Seth said. "Find out what you can, Zo, then let those minds rest in peace."

"Of course." Zo pointed to a pile of coiled tubing next to the archangel. "There's another item I'd like to review first. The archangels' circulatory system actually floods the cockpit with conductor fluid. We abandoned that method long ago because it's highly detrimental to pilot health."

"Grendeni concern for their pilots seems rather lacking," Seth said.

"True," Zo said. "But while pilot life expectancy is severely diminished, performance is increased."

"Sort of like burning a candle at both ends," Jared said. "Twice as bright, half as long."

The three Aktenai pilots turned to Jared. Their neural links looked up the obscure Earth culture reference.

"Oh!" Zo said. "A candle. So that's what you meant. Yes, something like that." She tilted her head to the side. "But wouldn't that be difficult?"

"What do you mean?"

"Burning a candle at both ends," Zo said. "Wouldn't you drip wax all over the place?"

"Umm, actually I never thought of it like that." Jared shrugged an apology. "It's just a saying. I didn't make it up."

"But if you're going to use a vague cultural reference, shouldn't you pick one that makes sense?"

"Well, I, uhh …"

"In fact, aren't you that strange Earth Nation pilot who's been hanging around my daughter?"

"Umm …"

"You better not be the one who suggested she pierce her ears."

"What? No! I had nothing to do with that!"

Seth cleared his throat. "Zo, the archangel swords?"

"Oh, very well," Zo said. "Pilot Daykin, you and I will continue our discussion later." She linked a command to the bay.

Ordnance hatches opened along the ceiling. A massive sword descended next to the archangel, stopping when its grip touched the bottom of the bay and its tip just barely cleared the ceiling ordnance chamber.

"We recovered forty-eight intact swords," Zo said. "Unlike the archangels, these are simply amazing."

"At cutting us down," Seth said darkly.

"How do they work?" Quennin asked.

"They're chaos energy conductors similar to the fluidic conductors in our seraphs, but with a dramatically lower decay rate. The conducting polymer is solid and runs from the tip of the blade down a single edge to the grip. Contacts on the archangel's hand allow chaos energy to be transferred through a standard fluidic exchange inside the archangel's arm."

"So, instead of projecting chaos energy into dead space," Seth said, "they generate a blade along a solid conducting edge."

"Precisely," Zo said. "That gives them a huge advantage in close combat."

"Can we adapt this technology for our seraphs?" Seth asked.

"Well, the polymer is extremely complex," Zo said. "Special facilities will need to be constructed in Aktenzek to replicate it."

"No, I mean *us* here with *these* swords." Seth pointed out the balcony window.

Quennin smiled and shook her head. "I can't believe I didn't think of this."

Seth gave her a warm smile.

"You're on to something, Seth." Zo nodded thoughtfully. "Yes, I think we can. In fact, the Earth Nation seraphs already have a similar connection with their rail-rifles. Our seraphs' arms will have to be redesigned and modified to accommodate the connection. We'll need to wait for Aktenzek to produce replacements, but yes, we should be able to use these swords."

"Zo, why don't we keep enough swords here to equip the Renseki and Epsilon squadron," Seth said. "We can forward the rest to Aktenzek for further study. We have enough of them for both, right?"

"Oh, yes. More than enough."

Seth took another look at the sword and pondered what he could do with one or even two of the Grendeni devices.

Could this give me the edge I needed to defeat Jack? he wondered.

"Have we learned anything about Azeal?" Quennin asked.

"No," Zo said. "But here's something strange. Immediately after we got back to the *Resolute*, the Choir demanded an audience. And you won't believe who the representatives were!"

"Veketon and Dendolet?" Seth asked.

"No fair," Zo said. "You already knew."

"Just a lucky guess," Quennin said. "Seth and I were approached after fighting Azeal. Our venerable masters seemed very concerned about that pilot."

"Yeah, I got that impression, too," Zo said.

"They know who Azeal is," Seth said flatly.

"Seth, they would tell us if they did," Quennin said.

"I don't know," Zo said. "You could be right, Seth. I talked to Vorin shortly after Veketon wrung what he could from us. He and the rest of the Choir are completely in the dark. Can you imagine that? The Original Eleven keeping secrets from the Sovereign *and* the Choir?"

"What does the Sovereign plan to do?" Quennin asked.

Zo shook her head. "He didn't say."

Sovereign Vorin Daelus stepped into the Great Hall. In truth, the Great Hall was nothing more than a small dark room within the Sovereign's Palace. However, as Vorin entered the room, the walls came alive with sweeping images of a vast bowl-shaped auditorium that rose high above him on all sides. A midday sun within a cloudless sky warmed his face.

Dead sovereigns of Aktenzek filled the auditorium's tightly packed stands: row after row of men and women in strange uniforms or modern attire, some famous and others forgotten. But each of them had been a leader of the Aktenai. Vorin felt tiny and humbled in such esteemed company.

Taen Elexen waited for Vorin as he entered. Vorin always found it disconcerting to see Taen so young and full of energy. Towards the end, he had been a shriveled old man hardly able to move on his own.

A future I will face all too soon, Vorin thought grimly.

Taen gave him a polite nod. "Sovereign."

"Have the Original Eleven made a decision?" Vorin asked.

"Not yet," he said, facing the Great Hall's center.

Six men and five women stood far apart from everyone else, shrouded behind a privacy screen. They clustered together in a tight circle as if fearful their conversations could still be heard. Each of the Eleven wore a variant of the black-and-white dress they favored: one completely black with white gloves, another all white with layers of black zigzags up the arms, and most with an even mix.

Their visual ages also varied. Each of them was over twenty thousand years old, present at the moment of Exile and firsthand witnesses of Imayirot's destruction. Most assumed youthful guises, though a few had chosen the look of dignified age.

"What could possibly make this so complicated?" Vorin said. "Their silence only adds to our unease."

"Our venerable masters are not accustomed to defiance," Taen said. "Pressing this issue may have dangerous consequences."

"Regardless, the sovereigns and I require all available information on this Azeal. A seraph that is impervious to our weapons? Surely the Original Eleven see the reason behind our need."

"Agreed, but I advise caution," Taen said. "The Original Eleven are as ancient as they are powerful. They must not be trifled with."

Vorin took several steps into the auditorium. Polished flagstones ranged in circles from the center, eventually rising to form the ring of surrounding stands. The din of thousands of conversations hung heavy in the air.

"Venerable masters!" Vorin's voice echoed across the Great Hall. The din of conversation died quickly as the decisive moment drew near. "Venerable masters, have you decided?"

The Original Eleven continued to debate among themselves, though two of the founders glanced in Vorin's direction.

"I ask again, venerable masters, that you share with us your knowledge of the pilot Azeal. Or, if you cannot, please impart upon your humble servants why you must keep this secret."

Still the Original Eleven refused to speak.

"Venerable masters, if the pilot Azeal is a threat to Aktenzek, we must know. Please, at the very least, share with us your reasons for silence. It is unprecedented that you would deny us knowledge we need."

Vorin let the words hang in the air. A ripple of activity spread through the auditorium's stands. Groups of past sovereigns were becoming restless and even angry at the Original Eleven's refusal to share.

But there was nothing they could do beyond wait for the Original Eleven's deliberations to end.

Veketon took one long look at this upstart sovereign and the stands full of irritating rabble before turning back to his ten colleagues.

"They're a restless bunch of peasants, aren't they?"

"We must salvage this situation," Dendolet said.

"Yes, but how?" asked Balezuur, appearing as an old bearded man with diagonal stepping patterns of white and black across his cloak.

"What right do they have to demand information from us?" Veketon said. "We should send them on their way and be done with it."

"That would only deepen their resolve," Dendolet said.

Veketon glanced at Dendolet, then at the other nine faces looking at him expectantly, for he was their leader and had set them down this path all those eons ago.

"Hmm. Yes, you are correct," Veketon said. "This rabble is now driven by fear of the unknown, and that fear must be redirected somewhere constructive. But how best to do it?"

"Do you mean to reveal our secrets?" asked Xixek, a woman clad in a flowing white gown with thorn-like patterns of black at her cuffs and hem.

"Perhaps." Veketon tapped his lips with a finger. "Naturally, we must continue to hide as much as possible. If we reveal too much, then our other manipulations will begin to unravel. We shall deal with this matter carefully."

"Perhaps a measured bit of fact is in order," Dendolet said. "I see no reason to believe these peasants know anything about the Great Mission or the Grendeni origins. Even if we reveal the truth about Vierj, I doubt they will see the connections."

"Do not be overconfident," Veketon said. "Our web of lies is dangerously close to crumbling. If we reveal anything to this rabble about Vierj, it could set them searching along unexpected paths. It is foolhardy to reveal our manipulations, especially when our experiments are so close to success."

"Your fears are somewhat premature," Dendolet said. "Even if someone suspects we created the Grendeni, how would they prove such a radical claim? The war has gone on for so long that its genesis is lost to all but us."

"True," Veketon said. "And though we have had difficult moments in this long war, the rationale for creating an enemy remains just as true. Creating the Grendeni and sustaining the war provided an ideal environment for us to continue our research. But, all our struggling means nothing if we do not complete our work before these peasants find out."

"We have long known this moment would come," Dendolet said. "Vierj's return was inevitable. Though the timing is ... most inconvenient, especially when the products of this false Mission are so near fruition."

Veketon shook his head. "To think that we would actually succeed in creating another one, only to make the same critical error."

"We did not foresee the consequences of removing the seraph's limiters," Dendolet said. "We thought no one was capable of surviving such an ordeal, since all our previous attempts had failed."

"At the time, Pilot Donolon's strength nearly exceeded our own when we lived," Balezuur said. "We should have anticipated he'd survive the merger."

"Regardless, we have failed to foresee much," Veketon said. "To think that both those failures would unite. We chased Jack Donolon away too quickly."

"We could not control him, as we could not control Vierj," Dendolet said.

"Veketon, what do you believe those two are planning?" Xixek asked.

"We've known what Vierj wanted ever since Ittenrashik fell and became Imayirot," Veketon said. "Is it not obvious those two seek the Homeland Gate?"

"But what possible motivation could Jack Donolon have for seeking the Homeland Gate?" Dendolet asked.

"Unknown. Perhaps he seeks it for Vierj's sake." Veketon shook his head, unsatisfied with his own answer. "It does not matter. I believe they will seek out the Homeland Gate. And that means they will come here, to Aktenzek."

"Even if those two failed experiments attack us here, we are not defenseless," Dendolet said. "We have the seraphs and Aktenzek's temporal shielding."

"We should still plan for the worst," Veketon said. "We cannot rely solely on Aktenzek's defenses to stop Vierj."

One of the Eleven cleared his throat and grinned. "Ahh, but what is life without its little challenges?" said Ziriken, Eleventh of the Eleven.

A wave of painful groans spread around the circle as they all glared at their most eccentric member.

"Must I continually remind you that we are dead?" Dendolet breathed.

"You are not helping matters, Ziriken," Veketon said. "Shut up or I *will* purge you this time."

"My apologies. It just occurred to me how exciting these next few days might be."

"Veketon, they are becoming quite agitated," Dendolet nodded towards the vast crowd of Aktenai sovereigns. "We should finalize what we are going to tell them."

"I will handle this." Veketon stepped out of the circle and walked towards Vorin. He stopped and spoke in a booming voice that filled the Great Hall. "We have finished our deliberations."

Vorin bowed deeply towards Veketon. "Venerable master, will you now reveal to us what you know?"

"First, let me state this." He traced his gaze across the stands. "We do not make this announcement easily, for we ourselves were in doubt until recently. However, upon careful consideration of the evidence at hand, we, the Original Eleven of the Aktenai, are prepared to reveal our discovery to you. And so it is with absolute certainty that I announce the following: this pilot Azeal is none other than our greatest enemy, the Bane of Ittenrashik!"

Cries of shock and disbelief erupted across the listening sovereigns. The entire Great Hall filled with thousands of agitated and frightened conversations. Vorin himself looked sick to his stomach.

"We regret the delay in revealing this information to you, our faithful servants," Veketon said. "But I am sure you understand we could not make such a monumental announcement casually. We, the Original Eleven, appreciate your understanding and your patience."

Veketon turned away from the stunned audience and returned to the circle of founders.

"A small drop of truth for a group of small minds," Dendolet said.

"This is a necessary risk," Veketon said. "Besides, letting them know who Vierj is may increase Aktenzek's chances of survival when she finally attacks."

"But, Veketon," Balezuur said, "it may lead them to discover that pilots—"

"No, I seriously doubt that, though I share your concern. Regardless of what is to come, we must be prepared. We should make arrangements for leaving Aktenzek."

"But where to?" Xixek asked.

"Zu'Rashik, the fortress planet under construction. That is our path of retreat if all turns against us."

The other founders nodded cautiously.

"In preparation," Veketon said, "we must move the thrones and our other research material to Zu'Rashik."

"The thrones are not ready for deployment," Dendolet said.

"No, they are incomplete. That does not make them useless in combat. And, I fear, we may need their power."

"But releasing them is dangerous. They are uncontrollable, even psychotic in some cases. We dare not use them."

"We may not have a choice," Veketon said. "But this is only a precaution. With fortune on our side, no one will ever know about the thrones until it is too late."

"Despite what we learned from Jack Donolon's seraph," Dendolet said. "We have not perfected how to transfer our personalities to the thrones."

"We have waited millennia for our divinity," Veketon said. "We can wait a little longer."

Quennin sat with all the *Resolute*'s pilots, medics, technicians, and even the Renseki in the recreation center. Vorin's hologram shimmered within a rough ring of tables, resplendent in his gold-trimmed coat-of-office as he explained the situation simultaneously to all Aktenai pilots across the fleet. They hung on his every word in breathless silence.

Azeal is the Bane! Quennin thought, grasping her trembling hands. She closed her eyes and took a calming breath.

A part of her didn't want to believe it, but the Original Eleven had spoken and had set all doubts aside. The seraph squadrons not only faced the traitor Jack Donolon and the hordes of archangels, but also the greatest foe the Aktenai had ever known.

Seth sat next to her, his fists clenched in rage. She rested a hand on his, understanding his anger all too well.

"It wasn't enough that he killed our son," Seth whispered, breathing in angry huffs.

"All seraph squadrons and fleet elements are being recalled to Aktenzek," Vorin said. "We have reason to believe an attack of enormous proportions is imminent, and we believe the Bane will participate. Those who can, return to us as quickly as possible."

The hologram flickered and vanished.

"Seth?" Quennin put a hand on his shoulder.

Seth stood quickly, face twisted in anger. His chair clattered to the ground behind him, and he walked out of the room.

Quennin watched him go and almost followed, but she knew Seth preferred to sort out his emotions alone, at least until some of the heat left his mind.

All six of the Renseki sat one table over from Quennin. Yonu had joined her parents there and now stood.

"Okay, not to put too fine a point on this, but how are we supposed to stop the Bane?" Yonu asked. "I don't know about the rest of you, but I don't have any idea how we're expected to beat this thing. This is the same creature that destroyed Imayirot, and it's coming after Aktenzek! Maybe some of you are made of sterner stuff than me, but I'm *terrified* by what that means!"

Quennin stood, her fingertips resting on the tabletop. "You are forgetting one very important thing. This is our purpose. This is what we have trained for all our lives. We as seraph pilots are the only people capable of stopping the Bane. Even though we've spent most of our lives fighting the Grendeni, *this* is what we were all born to do! To complete our Great Mission! To finally defeat the Bane!"

"And yet, a seraph pilot has allied himself with the Bane," Yonu said.

The memory of Tevyr's seraph being cut down stung Quennin's mind, and she looked away.

"I know. All I can say is we here are still true to the Great Mission, and it is our duty to carry it out."

Yonu sat down. Quennin saw a tentative hand go up from the EN table. The pilot seemed nervous, as if the very act of asking his question might be an insult.

"Yes, Pilot Daykin?" Quennin said.

Jared stood up. "Now, I hope I'm not making a fool of myself by doing this. Most of you Aktenai may find this question disturbing, but please bear with me."

"Of course, pilot. What do you need?"

"This is just for my own personal benefit, since I'm a simple guy from Earth," Jared said. "But could someone *please* tell me what this Bane actually is and how we're supposed to beat it?"

Several Aktenai stared at him in disbelief, but Quennin nodded, expecting this. Earthers did not share Aktenzek's long history, nor were they required to learn it as children. Concepts like the Great Mission, the horror of Imayirot's destruction, and the Bane's terrifying power were still foreign concepts to them, yet so important to what went into being Aktenai.

"The Bane is a creature that the Original Eleven and their followers, the Aktenai, created," Quennin said. "It is our great sin, and it became our Great Mission to right this wrong. This is what it means to be Aktenai, to be one of the Forsaken. The Bane is a creature that can manipulate time, speeding its passage or stopping it entirely, and can use this ability to lay waste to entire worlds.

"Our Great Mission, the reason we seraph pilots exist, is to kill this creature unchanged by eons, to kill that which cannot be killed ... for if we cannot, no one else will."

"So, how do we kill something that can't be killed?" Jared asked. "The Bane destroyed that gloomy planet we visited, right? What chance do we have?"

"Seraph pilots are immune to the Bane's manipulations," Quennin said. "Pilots and their seraphs, through the protection of their chaos barriers, cannot not be frozen in time or rapidly aged."

Jared nodded thoughtfully. "Well, that's better, I guess. The Bane may be able to slaughter everyone and everything we all care about, but at least we'll be safe in our cockpits. We still can't hurt that monster."

Quennin could think of nothing to say. Jared slumped in his seat and stared glumly ahead. After that the meeting began to break up.

Four of the Renseki left, but the twins Kevik and Kiro walked over to Jared and sat with him. Despite his gloomy disposition, he seemed slightly cheered by their arrival. Quennin wondered why.

Slowly, groups of people left the rec center. Some were quiet, while others loudly discussed these revelations. Quennin followed a large group of technicians out, determined to find Seth and check on him.

As she walked through the *Resolute*'s long corridors, her mind buzzed with activity. Something about Jared's question bothered her, though she couldn't quite pin it down. She had never given much thought to why a seraph pilot could fight the Bane, and up until now she never had reason to. It was always a given that this final battle should be a seraph pilot's true purpose in life.

So how can we resist the Bane's powers? Quennin thought. *What makes us so special? And how could anyone prove we have this ability? It's not like there were seraphs and seraph pilots around when the Bane destroyed Imayirot. The first seraph was created two thousand years ago, eighteen millennia too late for that battle.*

No, I'm missing something here. Something doesn't feel right.

The question lingered in the back of her mind, but she took a moment to link with the *Resolute*'s computer and call up Seth's position. He was near his seraph, as he often was when something got under his skin.

Quennin took a lift down to the seraph bays, working the questions through her mind. The more she thought, the more she found threads linking seraphs and the Bane. First there was Jack Donolon, hero and traitor in equal parts, allied with the Bane. Second was the Bane in battle: fighting them from within a seraph, defended by an impervious barrier, but still fighting very much like another pilot.

The Bane inside of a seraph ... the Bane can pilot a seraph ...

Oh no.

That train of thought was almost too horrible to comprehend. When the lift opened, Quennin burst into a run down the row of dormant seraphs. She rushed across the bay shelves, thankful that no one was around to see her, and spotted Seth donning his i-suit.

"Seth!" she called out, running towards him. "Seth!"

Her beloved looked up, surprise and confusion written on his face. She came to a stop next to him.

"What's the matter, Quennin?"

"Seth, I think I know why Jack—"

"*All pilots to your seraphs! All pilots to your seraphs! Aktenzek is under attack!*" The booming voice echoed in the cavernous bays.

Quennin and Seth exchanged looks.

"What is it, Quennin?" Seth asked. He must have seen her unease.

"I'll …" she paused, not wanting to burden Seth before the battle. "I'll tell you when we get back."

There was nothing more to do but prepare for battle.

Chapter 14

Return of the Bane

In full control of his seraph with vast fleets arrayed about him, Jack retreated to his inner thoughts, back to where he'd set all of this in motion seventeen years ago. In the three years after merging with his seraph, before abandoning Earth and his friends, a slow horror had begun to settle in. He'd suspected what he was, or rather what he was becoming, and had begun a search for something to prove himself wrong.

That search began with Aktenzek's mammoth but restricted archives. He used to spend hours sifting through those ancient digital tomes in a quest for answers, but they were few and far between. Even though the Choir undoubtedly knew a great deal about the Bane, the Gate, the destruction of Imayirot, the Exile, and other subjects, the archives held little of value.

The Choir hid the detailed technical data on those subjects. After all, how could the Choir know seraph pilots were immune to the Bane's attacks without such information? No, there was a great store of knowledge being denied to the seraph pilots, and perhaps even to the majority of the Choir.

But despite these attempts at censorship, small gems of information fell through the cracks, allowing Jack to choose a course of action. Most of this seemingly useless knowledge pertained to the Gate and its strange physical manifestation within this universe.

The Gate was a dimensional disruption, not unlike those a seraph pilot created when drawing chaotic energies into this universe. However, the Gate operated on a much higher power scale and far more precise organizational structure. It created a field effect around itself, nullifying other dimensional disruptions in close proximity.

And so, Jack surmised, as one approached the Gate, a seraph pilot would lose many of his or *her* abilities.

Jack turned his head to the right and let his wings flex outward slightly. Vierj's shadowed seraph hovered in space, ready and eager for battle. He wondered if he would succeed in the end.

But first I must find the Gate, wherever the Choir has hidden it, and to do that, we must assault Aktenzek and force its location from them.

"First wave has secured our entry," Dominic said, monitoring the battle from over a hundred light-years away. "We'll be sending the second wave through momentarily."

Thousands of warships floated serenely about him, waiting their turn to assault Aktenzek. In the cold calculations of war, every machine in this fleet was expendable if the Grendeni could wrest control of the Gate and hold it. To the Grendeni, the Gate was a means to an end, not the quasi-religious artifact the Aktenai held it to be.

If the Grendeni secured the Gate, they could force Aktenzek to stop the war. Even if the Grendeni could not physically destroy the dimensional rupture, they could theoretically move it to the heart of a star or throw it into a black hole.

The Aktenai would obey any demand to keep that from happening.

"How's the assault going?" Jack asked.

"It's a bloody massacre right now," Dominic said. "They had more ships in position than we anticipated. Plus their seraph squadrons were on high alert. First wave has taken heavy losses, but we have a breach in Aktenzek's fleet defenses. Losses are within acceptable parameters. We're sending the second wave through now."

Vierj opened a private channel. "I'm surprised by how anxious this waiting is making me."

"I know, but be patient. Let the Grendeni pay the price for entering Aktenzek, not us."

"Of course, Jack Donolon."

Hundreds of Grendeni warships, thousands of exodrones, and dozens of archangel carriers all powered up their fold engines simultaneously. Space rippled as each ship punched a momentary hole through space-time and vanished. Vast distortion rings expanded outward, turning space into a violently disturbed black pool.

Thirty archangel carriers were in the second wave alone. Each massively armored craft held four full squadrons of archangels. That was almost fifteen hundred archangels in a single wave.

"We've got an opening for you," Dominic said. "It's not much, but it's better than the hell the rest of the fleet is engaged in. Transmitting fold coordinates. Good hunting."

"Thanks, Dominic. We won't let you down."

The hypercast link shifted, and Dominic spoke privately to Jack. Or so he thought, at least. "Make sure you keep her under control. We want the Gate, not genocide."

"I understand, Dominic. And thank you."

"Just get us that location. I'm trusting you here. Don't prove me wrong."

"Oh, have a little faith, will you?"

The countdown reached zero. Jack and Vierj folded space to Aktenzek.

Fleets in the thousands dueled in the black skies above the fortress planet. Thick clouds of exodrones buzzed about them, disgorging salvos of torpedoes and stinging with internal lasers. Even the Earth Nation fleet participated, approaching cautiously from Earth and adding its own fire to the storm of beams, explosions, and death.

Aktenzek itself stood out, almost totally eclipsing the pale white smile of Zu'Rashik at this angle. Massive barrages of fusion cannons fired up from its surface, lacerating the Grendeni fleet. The seraph's scanners focused in, finding the closest entry portal and marking it with a digital nav beacon.

To Jack's side was Earth, visible as a sideways blue and white crescent lit brightly on its night side with human civilization. Lights from the sixteen Orbital Republics and the countless factories, ships, and edifices in space orbited around the planet. Even further away, beyond Earth and the twin fortress planets, was the Moon, its surface illuminated almost as brilliantly as Earth's.

Jack opened his chaos scanner to full gain, thankful once again that he could detect nothing through Vierj's barrier. All across Aktenzek, Earth, and the intervening space, little fireballs appeared, each a chaos-adept human. For a moment, Jack wondered why in a galaxy filled with human life, Earth alone had produced seraph pilots.

But that was a question for another time. Three Aktenai dreadnoughts came about and headed towards his position.

Jack flared his six blade-wings. Their edges ignited with blue fire, and he shot down towards Aktenzek.

Despite his speed, Vierj rushed to his side with ease. She extended an open palm and released a thin black cord of energy, almost imperceptible against the starry black of space. The cord whipped out, went taut near an Aktenai dreadnought, and the end expanded into a huge triangle. The Aktenai dreadnought fell through the triangle, but only shattered debris blew out the other end.

"Impressive." Jack focused his active scanners on the dreadnought's debris. Every piece had a temperature close to absolute zero, having cooled for millions of years in a heartbeat.

"That was just a warm-up." Vierj released two more black cords from her hands. They lashed across space and opened into triangles. Another two Aktenai dreadnoughts disintegrated from the ravages of time. "The Aktenai are such cowards to hide behind robots. And I sense something else from the planet below."

"What is it?"

"There is a field engulfing much of Aktenzek. It feels similar to a seraph's barrier, though much weaker and wider. Ah, Veketon. How clever of you."

"Vierj?"

"I almost died destroying Ittenrashik. I think I would die if I tried the same here."

Jack almost sighed in relief, but he caught himself.

"The Eleven planned for your return," he said instead.

"As we knew they would."

"Well then, it's a good thing we're not here to destroy Aktenzek."

"Hmm. Yes …" Vierj sighed with indifference.

Jack spotted the group of Aktenai seraphs flying up from the fortress planet's surface. "Six seraphs heading our way."

"Shall I deal with those malformed copies?"

"We'll take them together."

"As you wish. Lead the way."

Jack fed power into his wings and flew down to meet the seraphs. Fusion cannons fired up, but the tight beams splashed off his barrier without effect. He ignited his primary blade and dove straight at the leader.

As with all Aktenai seraphs, each stood out with unique personality and flair. The lead seraph ignited its dagger, bright green against the angular green-and-white of its body. The Aktenai seraph slashed up, and Jack cut down.

Their blades met, but this opponent was no Seth, nor was it among the elite pilots onboard the *Resolute*. This pilot had not been tempered by combating swarms of archangels. Nor had it engaged in desperate duels with other seraph pilots, and its blade and barrier were weak.

The Aktenai seraph's green dagger exploded apart from the force of their impact. Jack sliced through the torso in a single stroke, killing the pilot instantly. Two other seraphs were quickly at his sides.

Vierj crashed savagely into one, ripped its arms out of their sockets, then tore its chest open without even bothering to ignite a weapon. A shower of glowing red fluid sprayed over her.

Jack parried the third seraph's attack, then skewered it with his sword.

Whatever training these Aktenai pilots had received, they had never met nor imagined foes like this. From the right and the left, two more seraphs rushed in. Jack spun in a tight circle, his sword lashing out, shield at the ready. He blocked their attacks and cleaved both at the waist.

The last seraph turned and fled.

"I think not." Vierj lashed out with a black whip of energy and split the seraph in two.

Jack formed up with her. "We need to get down to the surface. Follow me."

They descended towards Aktenzek. A barrage of fusion beams shot up from the surface. They wove through, rare hits splattering off their barriers. Seraph squadrons diverted from other battles and began to converge on their position.

"Dominic, we're becoming awfully popular here."

"Yes, I see that. Sending reinforcements."

Eight Grendeni carriers folded in and released their archangels. Cannon fire from the Aktenai fleet and Aktenzek prioritized the new targets. They killed dozens, but the archangels were fast, nimble targets, and they swarmed over the Alliance seraphs as soon as the range dropped.

Ahead, four EN seraphs opened fire from the surface. Volley after volley from their rail-rifles slammed into the archangels, felling several of the skeletal machines. Jack flew past the archangels and dove at them.

The closest EN seraph didn't have time to ready its dagger. Jack slashed through it diagonally, cleaving through its wings, torso, and rifle with equal ease. The other three EN seraphs backed away and fired at him, but their rail-rifle bolts ricocheted off his barrier. One of the EN pilots shouldered its weapon, ignited a bright orange dagger, and sped in.

Jack slapped the dagger upward with his shield, then slipped inside the EN seraph's defenses and stabbed through its torso. The seraph's orange vent-like shunts turned black, chaos influx dying with its pilot.

Without a barrier providing resistance, the seraph slumped off Jack's blade. The broken remains clattered lifelessly against the pale armored surface of Aktenzek.

The two remaining EN seraphs backed away.

In a flash of dark motion, Vierj was behind them. She ignited her blade, gutted one from groin to head, pirouetted, then gutted the other from head to groin. Four seraph halves slumped to Aktenzek's surface, each sputtering streams of conductor fluid.

"Such weaklings are fools to stand against us," Vierj said.

Jack took off and gained some altitude from Aktenzek's surface. He found the navigational beacon for the entry portal.

"This way." Jack raced towards it.

Vierj fell in behind him. The Armor Shell of Aktenzek stretched out like a frozen sea of white metal. Vast pillars rose from it, forming a forest of towers kilometers high and tipped with dreadnought-caliber fusion cannons.

Jack and Vierj wove through the towers, dodging fusion beam volleys. The few lucky shots that hit only splashed against their barriers.

They sped out of the tower forest and through mountain ranges of white and silver domes, past mammoth drone control pyramids, until finally arriving at the entry portal. Even though the portal stood a full five kilometers square, it was dwarfed by the four drone control pyramids surrounding it and the fusion towers encircling those.

"Vierj, can you open it?"

"Yes. This field around Aktenzek should not interfere with a small display of my power."

Vierj flew up and stopped directly above the portal. A continuous barrage of fusion beams deflected off her invincible barrier. A black cord spilled out from her open hand, whipsawing back and forth until it came to rest just above the armored doorway.

The tip of the cord expanded, grew larger with frightening speed and became a square five kilometers to each side. The square sank down into Aktenzek and splintered a set of ten armored doors, each a kilometer thick.

They were in.

Seth folded into Aktenzek space and gasped at the scale of combat before him. He hadn't seen a fleet engagement this big in twenty years since the last battle at Earth. No one had.

The *Resolute*'s full complement of seraphs folded in around him. Quennin and the six silver Renseki seraphs appeared to his left. Jared's combined squadron folded in to the right, a total of twelve pilots out of an original twenty four.

"The fleets appear to be evenly matched," Quennin said. "Even with their archangels providing cover, our seraph squadrons and Aktenzek's defenses will eventually thwart this attack."

"They don't have to win." Seth sent the others coordinate data for a huge black square opening up near the surface of Aktenzek. "Look there. Near the surface."

"What is that?" Jared asked.

"The Bane has returned to the Forsaken who created it," Quennin said.

"We're going in. Follow me!" Seth descended towards Aktenzek's surface. The rest of the Alliance seraphs followed him in.

"Sir," Jared said, "even if we catch them, what can we hope to do? All our attacks against the Bane have failed to penetrate its barrier."

"We'll stop it," Seth said. "No barrier, however strong, is truly invincible. We keep hitting that monster until it falls."

The formation of seraphs flew in as space boiled over with cannon beams and torpedo explosions. The Aktenai and Grendeni fleets engaged each other in bitter duels. Aktenzek fired salvo after salvo from its surface cannons, tearing into the approaching Grendeni ships. Nearly three thousand archangels and hundreds of seraphs meshed in battle throughout the dying fleets.

Zo transmitted a set of coordinate data. "Seth, I am concerned about our fleet's positioning. Grendeni ships are moving into a gap in

Aktenzek's orbital defenses. If they succeed, they'll be able to screen approaching archangel squadrons."

"Yeah, I see it."

"I suggest you send Pilot Daykin's squadron to seal that breach while the rest of us continue after the Bane."

Seth knew that wasn't the real reason. He stole a glance at the blue seraph flying in formation near Jared's EN command seraph. But even knowing Zo's ulterior motive …

"Good idea," Seth said. "Pilot Daykin, take epsilon squadron and seal that gap. I don't want any more archangels reaching Aktenzek's surface."

"Confirmed, sir," Jared said, perhaps a little too quickly. Twelve seraphs broke formation and headed for the cluster of Grendeni ships.

Seth, Quennin, and the six Renseki continued onward.

"Thank you, Seth," Zo said privately. "You didn't have to do that."

"I understand why you asked all too well. Believe me."

"Archangels folding in directly ahead," Quennin said.

"Break through them!"

Seth rocketed out of formation at a speed none of them could match. Quennin and the Renseki opened fire. The twenty archangels were still reorienting themselves when seven fusion beams slammed home and obliterated five archangels.

Two archangels survived the hits, their barriers flickering weakly.

Seth ignited twin chaos daggers and closed with the stunned archangels. He cut through fragile wings and torsos with a pair of clean slices. Yellow fluid pulsed from deep gashes.

Seventeen more archangels closed in, but Seth did not stand against them alone. A second volley of fusion beams pounded into the archangel formation, vaporizing three more before the opposing forces collided. At full strength and in close quarters, the archangels would have struggled against eight fully functional seraphs, perhaps willing to accept a kill or two for their loss.

But this archangel formation had been utterly decimated, and the survivors found themselves dueling the elite honor guard of Aktenzek's Sovereign. The fight was over in seconds.

"Form up!" Seth said.

They pressed on towards Aktenzek, leaving the wreckage of twenty archangels in their wake.

"Grendeni dreadnought moving to block our path," Zo said.

"Take it down!"

The Grendeni dreadnought lumbered about. Torpedoes and seekers belched from its armored carapace, targeting the approaching seraphs. Seth and the others executed practiced evasive maneuvers, their conformal wing pods automatically ejecting clouds of countermeasures. Some of the seekers and torpedoes zeroed in on the countermeasures, exploding vainly in empty space, but others impacted against seraph barriers.

A short spasm of discomfort rang through Seth's leg as a torpedo found its mark, but he pushed relentlessly through the expanding nuclear fire. The dreadnought was directly ahead: as powerful and invincible a craft as Aktenai and Grendeni science could achieve.

It didn't stand a chance.

Seth fired six torpedoes from his leg weapon pods. The torpedoes activated their overloaded gravity drives and joined the others fired by Quennin and the Renseki. Forty-eight torpedoes wove their way through the thick layers of defensive fire. Railguns, lasers, and defensive seeker ports all contributed to the protective blanket of fire around the dreadnought. It shot down over half the torpedoes.

Twenty-two small suns erupted across the dreadnought's massive length, heating, cracking, and even vaporizing sections of the mnemonic hull. The dreadnought shuddered, its weapons and drives failing for a moment. Internal systems restarted. The armor cooled and began to close under carefully programmed forces.

Seth and the others fired eight fusion beams through gaps in its armor, precisely cutting into delicate vitals. The hull cracked at a diagonal, and the dreadnought broke apart. Each piece would continue to fight to the last, firing seekers and torpedoes and lasers until every last compartment was dead, but the threat of its centerline beam cannons had been destroyed.

Seth dove towards Aktenzek's surface, reached it, and skimmed across it. Vast fields of fusion towers passed underneath, all firing at the Grendeni fleets above.

"Archangels and exodrones are breaking through to the surface," Zo said. "Grendeni carriers are ramming their way through our defenses and actually crashing into the planet."

Tallies for the archangel forces on Aktenzek's surface came up. Nearly three hundred archangels had already made it through.

"That's a lot of archangels and a whole cursed swarm of exodrones," Quennin said. "Some are getting close to the breach in the armor shell. We can't let them get into Aktenzek."

Seth opened a channel. "Pilot Daykin."

There was a short pause before Jared replied, his voice strained and quick. "Go ahead, sir!"

"As soon as your squadron is free, I want them to blockade the breached entry portal." Seth sent coordinate data. "Keep the Grendeni out of Aktenzek."

"Confirmed, sir! We'll finish off the last few dreadnoughts breaking through and head down."

Epsilon squadron dove for the surface several hundred kilometers ahead.

Seth skimmed across the surface and came to an intact entry portal. The first of ten heavy mnemonic doors snapped open. He dove inside, followed by Quennin and the Renseki. The surface door sealed shut, and the nine doors below it opened. All eight seraphs rushed through.

Seth descended into Aktenzek, flying through rings of light and darkness. He cut around a sharp turn, flew straight for several kilometers, then dove into a massive abyss.

Unlike in the past, the interior of Aktenzek was far from defenseless, and the further down invaders traveled, the more kill zones they faced. Corridors often made sudden turns into armored doors edged with fusion cannons.

But for all these traps, Aktenzek's primary defense still remained its outer shell, and while formidable, the inner defenses were incomplete. Even after twenty years of buildup, Aktenzek's inner defenses had yet to be finished, since the full force of the planet's industries had focused on completing Zu'Rashik.

Seth linked with Aktenzek's security grid, bringing up the Bane's position.

"We're falling behind!" He flooded his wings with fresh power and surged forward.

"Seth, we can't keep up with you! Stick together!" Quennin said.

Seth forced himself to slow down, staying in a tight single-file formation with the other seraphs. A single barrier door opened just long enough for them to speed through. They passed the checkpoint and turned down a sharp descent. A row of armored shutters parted and then snapped closed as they flew down.

They turned at the bottom and entered a narrow horizontal passage, finally linking up with the Bane's path of descent through Aktenzek.

"They've already been through here," Quennin whispered, surveying the demolished kill zone. Armored doors and fusion cannons floated weightlessly in shattered, frozen pieces.

"We need to keep moving. Come on!" Seth shouted, descending further.

The other seraphs swept in behind him.

Chapter 15

Tyrant and Destroyer

Jack descended deeper into Aktenzek's interior. Once again, he took a sharp turn into a waiting kill zone. Four fusion cannons opened fire, searing his barrier. Tight strands of plasma ricocheted off and hit the walls with tremendous force. He grunted, raising his shield to protect his face. Hot needles prickled his armored skin.

Vierj rounded the corner and unleashed a thin black cord from her hand. The end bloomed outwards into a square, passed through the fortifications, and reduced them to frozen dust.

Jack sped through the demolished kill zone and turned down into a shaft blocked by a thin mnemonic door. He smashed a kick into its center.

The doorway split open down the middle. Its panels tore free of their moorings and tumbled into the great chamber beneath. Jack flew down into one of Aktenzek's habitat discs and then stifled a curse. Even though it had been twenty years, he hadn't expected new cities this close to the Core.

The habitat disc measured twenty-five kilometers across, its interior space shaped like a fat coin with a ring-shaped lake and wide central island. Along the edge of the disc rose the vast ringcity, extending sideways towers out of the wall. The lake stretched out from the edges of the ringcity and gently caressed the beaches of the central island. Towering spires of polished stone and glass rose from the island's center, forming this habitat disc's hubcity.

Jack glanced at the ceiling and saw a perfect simulacrum of a dark-blue sky and orange sun peeking over the horizon. Here in this habitat disc, it was early morning.

Vierj descended into the habitat disc and stopped.

For a moment, Jack thought she would destroy the city simply because it was there. She'd done far worse in the past, and he'd witnessed some of it.

Instead, Vierj summoned a point of black light over her open palm and dropped it. The point splashed into the lake, expanded into a seraph-sized triangle, and sank through the lakebed. Water drained out of the habitat disc, forming a whirlpool on the surface.

"You seem tense, Jack Donolon. I can feel it in your aura."

"The Core is close. We need to be careful."

"Are you, perhaps, concerned for the inhabitants of this city?"

How did she guess that? he thought.

"Sometimes I find it difficult to understand you," Vierj continued. "These creatures are so far beneath our notice as to be insignificant. What does it matter if they live or die? They present no obstacles to us, and so they live. If they impeded our progress, I would sweep them aside without a second thought."

"I used to be one of them, you know. It puts things in perspective."

Some brave soul ran out of a small wooden hut near the beach and fired a shoulder-mounted laser at her seraph.

Vierj sighed. With a snap of her fingers, the man turned to ash.

"Let's keep moving," Jack said.

"Of course."

They dove into the lake, water foaming around their seraphs. Jack flew out of the new kilometer-high waterfall.

Fortifications grew denser and more deadly as they pressed on, but Vierj made such obstacles trivial. In between the kill zones, they passed vast industrialized fields, long corridors choked with hovering cargo containers, and empty mined-out chasms.

Jack dropped into a dense field of giant mechanical silos that formed part of Aktenzek's vast artificial gravity network. The chamber stretched out in every direction, curving gently around an unseen spherical center.

Vierj reached out with her talent and cut open the floor. They dove through the breach and slowed.

The Core loomed before them: a smooth, white planetoid within the fortress planet, hovering in the center of a great spherical chasm. All along the ceiling, tightly packed mechanical cylinders buzzed with stored energies: the massive drives and fold engines of Aktenzek.

"Vierj, I'm not detecting any access to the Core's interior. Can you make an entrance?"

"A thin barrier shrouds the entire Core. It would be extremely taxing for me to use my talent here. I will focus on finding a more traditional entrance."

Jack felt a powerful spike of influx from the planetoid's surface and spun to face it. The Sovereign's Palace sat on the Core like an immense mirror-sloped pyramid. A lone seraph ascended from its peak.

This seraph resembled the Renseki, with elegant curls flowing up the limbs, torso, and wings. These stylized shunts glowed with brilliant red fire, but unlike the Renseki, its body shone with gleaming gold armor.

Vorin Daelus, Sovereign of Aktenzek, ignited his chaos dagger.

"You will go no further, traitor."

"Is that so?" Jack readied his sword and shield. "Stand aside, Vorin. You can't possibly defeat us."

"We shall see about that." Vorin spread his wings wide. Their edges flashed with crimson energy, and he raced in.

"Vierj, keep looking. I'll handle this guy!"

Jack accelerated towards the Core. His blade clashed with Vorin's in an explosion of crackling energy. Their weapons ground harshly against each other, showering the air with sparks.

Though Vorin didn't share Seth's agility, he'd piloted seraphs for two whole centuries, and his level of finesse was enough to catch Jack by surprise.

With the slightest turn of his dagger, Vorin let Jack's blade slide past him. He swung in with his fist and pounded into Jack's lower torso.

Jack groaned, a burning sensation radiating out across his stomach. He tried pulling his sword back, but Vorin grabbed hold of both his wrists, locking them together so that neither could strike.

"You are strong, traitor," Vorin said coldly. "But even you cannot defeat all the seraphs coming to my aid."

"Nice to see you too, Vorin!"

Jack headbutted Vorin. He headbutted Jack right back.

Their two seraphs spun above the Core, both men struggling for an advantage. No matter what Jack did, he could not twist his sword into the Sovereign's side, and the two finally crashed against the Palace's silvery slopes.

Sparks scintillated as they slid down the slope, tearing open a deep diagonal groove. Jack fired his wings, and they took off again, still locked and unable to break.

Jack let the energy sword on his left dissipate and transformed his right hand shield into a blade. It wasn't perfect. He had never been good with his right arm's weaponry shunts, but he forced the blade to extend through sheer strength of will.

Surprised and off balance, Vorin tried to pull away and block the attack, but his counter came too late. Jack cut into his shoulder and drove down diagonally towards the cockpit.

Vorin managed to deflect the attack at the last instant. His dagger clashed against Jack's in a flash of energy, and the attack went high, cleaving through the gold seraph without killing the pilot.

Jack pulled his dagger out of the chest cage, lopping off the seraph's arms, head, and all six wings. Red chaos-imbued fluid spewed from the long cut and splashed against Jack's barrier in an arterial shower. The legs and lower torso fell and crashed against the Palace slope, but that half's shunts still flickered red.

Jack's heart raced. He searched for any seraphs that had arrived during his duel with Vorin.

There were none. He and Vierj were still alone in Aktenzek's Core.

"Vierj, status!"

"I have just found the entrance." She transmitted coordinates.

Jack orbited the planetoid and stopped over a patch of white no different from any other. He reignited his sword and dove down. Two diagonal cuts and a strong kick allowed him to force his hands into the gap. Mnemonic forces in the armor fought to repair the damage, but he tore the armor open and dropped into the Core's interior.

Jack found himself between two tightly packed rows of clear cylindrical vats. A partially completed seraph floated within each container, suspended in a cloudy fluid. He folded his wings and walked deeper into the facility.

Some of the seraphs were bent over, their wingless backs exposed, spines open and ready for the artificial neural columns. Others were nothing more than copper endoskeletons awaiting their fibrous musculature, arterial pumps, and shunt fluidic transfers. All of the seraphs lacked their armored mnemonic skin.

Further into the Core, the containers held only parts of seraphs. To his right, dozens of nearly finished arms bobbed gently in their tanks. To the left, Jack saw neural columns being grown in thin vertical tubes. Some of the columns were fully grown and possessed an unmistakable brain-like texture. Others had yet to mature beyond thin gray strands suspended in clear organic slosh.

Jack shivered. No wonder the Choir didn't let pilots in here.

At the end of the seraph factory, he found a passage leading deeper into the Core's interior. He raised his chaos sword and paused for a brief moment.

His hypercast array received an incoming message.

"About time." Jack let the signal through.

"Hello, Pilot Donolon," Veketon said. "It's been a while."

"Hello yourself. I was wondering how deep I'd have to go before one of you would call, though I'm not surprised it's you."

"There is no need to proceed further, Pilot Donolon. I am sure we can discuss this rationally. You seek the Gate's location, do you not?"

"You know it, Vek."

"Yes, I do know that, among a great many other things. What I don't know is why you desire its location as well."

"Just helping out a friend."

"Really now? Vierj is many things, but I doubt she is your friend. You have poor taste in companionship, Pilot Donolon."

"To each their own."

“Indeed.”

Jack raised his sword again. “Enough stalling. Either give me what I want or I drop into the next chamber and start cutting at random.”

“Before I give you the Gate’s location, I want you to understand one thing.”

“What’s that?”

“You have less power over me than you might think,” Veketon said. “Yes, you could destroy the Choir and the seraph factories and even cause enough destruction to the Core that Aktenzek would cave in on itself, but you can’t harm me.”

“It’s always about you, isn’t it?”

“And why shouldn’t it be?”

“Like father, like daughter, huh? What did you people ever do to her?”

“Simple. We said no.”

“Ha! Nothing’s ever that simple with you, Vek. So why give me the Gate’s location?”

“Because the Choir wishes to beg for its collective unlives, and I speak as their representative. Besides, I loathe the chore of having to build all of this again.”

Jack smirked. “They can’t hear us, can they?”

“They hear something, but it is not this precise conversation.”

“Fine. Vierj and I will spare them.”

“Then we have an agreement.”

“Sure. Whatever. Now where is the Gate?”

“Why, the last place anyone would ever look for it. You see, we hid it within Imayirot.”

Jack blurted out a laugh.

Imayirot. The Dead World. A world slaughtered by the Bane.

Of course. The one place no one would ever look. A place both sacred and taboo to the Aktenai and the Grendeni. A place of such profound cultural grief that neither faction would ever desecrate it. Of *course* that's where the Original Eleven hid the Gate.

"I see you appreciate our choice," Veketon said.

"Oh, you have a twisted sense of humor," Jack said. "You'd better not be lying."

"I suppose you have every right to be suspicious, but you can verify it easily enough. Vierj should be able to feel its presence from low orbit."

"You're not afraid of her getting back to the Homeland?"

"Not really. Twenty thousand years ago, yes. But now, the situation has changed. Having her go through first and weaken the Keepers has a certain appeal. It's not ideal, but it can be of some use to us."

"You people really are a bunch of planet-sized buttholes, you know that?"

"We've been called worse."

"If you're lying, we'll be back," Jack said.

"Of course. I look forward to our next conversation, Bane."

Veketon's reply chilled the humor out of Jack. He walked back across the seraph factory and exited the Core.

"Quite a discovery," Vierj said.

"Yes." Jack wasn't at all surprised that Vierj had listened in. "Who could have guessed it would be Imayirot?"

"It seems somewhat obvious now. I hate that world. I almost died there, and the memory of that experience still haunts me. Even now, I am reluctant to return."

"Looks like we don't have a choice." Jack flew away from the Core. "Be prepared. They'll undoubtedly try to block our escape."

Jack and Vierj ascended through the Core's ruined security checkpoint and entered the gravity silo field.

Eight seraphs sped across the field straight towards them. Six had the unmistakable silver lines of the Renseki, though one stood out larger than the other: the honor guard's command seraph. Another possessed flame-red armor, with large kite-crystals burning with green fire.

And the final seraph, with its black angular armor and thin gray scars, flew ahead of the pack. Twin purple daggers snapped out of its forearms.

"Here we go," Jack whispered.

Seth charged straight at Jack and swung in. Their blades met in a fierce snap-flash of blue and purple light. A shockwave blew out, ripping through several gravity silos.

Quennin and the Renseki swarmed over the Bane's featureless seraph. On the way down, Seth had elected to engage Jack alone. He hoped his comrades could suppress the Bane until reinforcements arrived.

A force of over fifty Aktenai and EN seraphs now patrolled Aktenzek's shattered surface portal, along with four Aktenai dreadnoughts and three primitive Earth Nation dreadnoughts. Jared had coordinated the defense with shocking skill for someone his age and was even now organizing their descent.

All we have to do is hold them, Seth thought, struggling against Jack's raw power.

Seth found none of the earlier hesitation in his opponent. Both he and Jack fought with all their skill, cunning, and strength. They crashed their blades together, broke apart, then struck again. They wove through the endless fields of gravity silos, their blades colliding in massive displays of energy.

Seth's dagger grated against Jack's shield, showering the surroundings with short-lived sparks of blue and purple. Jack pushed in, his wings burning almost white with energy, and threw Seth into a gravity silo. Machinery crumpled as both seraphs crashed through.

Seth maintained his dagger integrity, even as they broke out the other side. They crashed into the ground and cut a long groove across it.

Jack lifted off and darted for the exit, but Seth fired his wings, skidded across the ground, righted himself, and shot after him. Jack spun around at the last second, bringing his shield up. Seth slashed down, and the blow rebounded off Jack's shield.

Jack countered with his sword, and Seth stabbed in with his second dagger. Their weapons locked, neither pilot giving ground. Seth felt the awesome strength of Jack's attack, the limitless power he infused into his weapons, and he forced his own dagger to maintain stability.

Jack threw Seth back, but had no intention of running this time. He swung his huge blade in from the left, and their weapons clashed again. Light exploded from the impact point and another two gravity silos went silent.

Seth glanced at the other battle. The Bane flung itself repeatedly at its foes but had yet to land a significant hit. Frighteningly fast, it forced Quennin and the other to approach cautiously.

Jack broke off suddenly and fell back towards the Bane. With Jack and the Bane so close, Quennin and the Renseki were forced to split their attention. Sensing their momentary distraction, the Bane lunged for Zo.

"Watch out!" Seth rushed in and interdicted its strike.

The Bane almost lopped Zo's head off, but Seth blocked the attack. The two blades released a violent display of black and purple lightning. Seth tried to hold, but the power at this creature's command was limitless. He pulled back before his own dagger disintegrated from the stress.

Seth regrouped with his comrades, the chamber's exit at their backs.

Jack and the Bane joined up.

"They'll try to break past," Seth said. "Be ready!"

Both enemy seraphs charged straight in. The Bane lunged at Seth with incredible speed, but he dodged left and thrust in from the side. His dagger slammed against the Bane's barrier just below the seraph's chest cage, and met an immovable wall of barrier energy. Seth pushed in, willing his dagger to burn brighter and cut deeper. He felt the Bane's barrier give just a little, even as a horrible freezing sensation crept up his arm.

His strength faltered for a moment, and the Bane's barrier snapped back into place. His dagger exploded, and he flew back, stunned. The Bane whirled around, weapon ready, and threw itself towards him.

But Seth was not alone in this fight, and suddenly Quennin was in front of him, blocking the Bane's approach. She met the monster's blade with her own dagger. But Quennin had overextended in a rush to aid him. The Bane saw this, pulled back, and struck again with a blur of quickness. Its dark blade chopped her arm off at the wrist.

"Ahhhh!" Quennin cried out.

Green fluid pulsed from the wound. Quennin recoiled, and the Bane pulled its dagger back for the killing blow.

Seth relit his own daggers and rushed to Quennin's aid, but he was too slow.

The Bane sliced into Quennin's seraph just below the chest cage. Quennin screamed in horrific, burning pain as the blade sliced effortlessly through her seraph's torso. The Bane pulled up and cleaved her seraph's head in two.

The screaming stopped.

"QUENNIN!" Seth screamed.

Her shunts died and the broken seraph fell. Two sections clattered to the canyon floor. Green fluid pulsed from the diagonal chest wound, turning black.

Seth swooped down and landed next to her crippled seraph, his daggers buzzing fiercely. She had to be alive! She *had* to be! He would cut down anyone who dared attack her now.

But no attack came.

Jack and the Bane fled across the gravity silo field, then darted up a narrow supply shaft. The six Renseki followed as fast as they could, but their quarry could both outfight and outrun them.

"Seth, hurry up!" Zo shouted. "We need to catch them before they reach the surface!"

Seth did not hear her.

"Quennin! Quennin, say something!"

Silence.

Seth knelt beside his beloved's broken machine. Zo and others continued to call out to him, but he ignored them. The entire universe could burn to cinders in his absence and he wouldn't care.

He brought his hand close, forming a bridge between his cockpit and Quennin's, locked his position, then forcibly severed his mind from the seraph. In the cockpit, he swooned from the unclean separation, then shook the fog from his head.

The cockpit expanded around him and opened. The seraph's zero field disengaged, and he walked carefully out of the cockpit, which slanted towards Quennin's seraph. He jumped down to his seraph's right palm.

Seth hurried across the hand's giant digits, then leaped down to the torso of Quennin's seraph. He wasn't even conscious of the tears streaming down his cheeks.

Under normal circumstances, a seraph would never open its cockpit hatch unless specifically ordered to by the pilot. But the seraph recognized the presence of a medical emergency and accepted Seth's command override. Mnemonic skin peeled back along three sides of a rectangle, forming the edges of the cockpit hatch. The hatch swung out, stopping when it pointed straight up.

He hurried over to the cockpit hatch and looked down.

Quennin's body lay still in the pilot alcove, arms spread, head lolling to the side. A diagonal slash along her i-suit was charred black, mimicking the damage to her seraph. That scorch pattern wasn't from external heat, but from the burning temperatures within her suit.

"Quennin!"

Seth climbed into the seraph, cold fear chilling him. He crouched down at her side and gently picked up her head and turned it to him. He wanted to see her face, to witness even the smallest sign of life.

But there was none. Her entire face was burned to a blackened crisp.

Chapter 16

Weapons of the Eleven

Seth leaned against the bulkhead just outside the *Resolute*'s medical ward, trying his best not to fidget, worry, or look nervous.

He was failing on all accounts.

It had taken the combined arguments of Zo, Mezen, and several sovereigns from the Choir to make Seth leave Quennin's cockpit, but despite his desire to stay, he understood their orders. He could do nothing for his beloved, whose life had hung by the merest threads, and Aktenzek needed every possible defender.

Seth had boarded his seraph once again and rejoined the battle. By then, Jack and the Bane had made their escape, but multitudes of Grendeni warships and archangels remained. Seth attacked their numbers with an unquenchable fury until the Grendeni forces began folding space towards Imayirot.

All the while, emergency response teams carefully transported Quennin's body to the medical facilities in the Sovereign's Palace. It took only minutes for the response teams to reach her, for they had already been dispatched to recover Vorin.

The Sovereign was expected to make a full recovery, but the same could not be said for Quennin. Her vitals had been secured and her body mended, but she'd suffered severe cranial damage. Once Quennin's health was stabilized, the Choir immediately transferred her to the *Resolute.*

With the Grendeni fleet on its way to Imayirot and the Gate, the Aktenai fleet had no choice but to follow. A sizable force of ships and seraphs still remained at Aktenzek, but the bulk of the Aktenai fleet now pursued the Grendeni at maximum speed. Even now, the *Resolute* made fold after fold in an effort to catch up.

Despite their haste, the Grendeni would reach Imayirot first.

Little of this passed through Seth's mind. Under different circumstances, he may have been surprised by the Gate's location in such a sacred place, but for now he gave the revelation no more than a passing thought. Instead, he thought of Quennin and wondered if the person behind the medical ward's door would be the woman he knew so well.

It doesn't matter, he thought, but his own reassurance felt hollow. Of course it mattered.

Fear kept him outside the medical ward, fear of what he might find within. Aktenai science could mend flesh and bone, but an injured mind could never truly be healed. Seth had looked down at Quennin's broken body once and only once before he had to turn away.

Her wounds matched those of her seraph: a fierce burn from just beneath the right rib cage, then up and through the head. Only her i-suit had prevented death from extreme organ trauma before medical teams had arrived.

Seth had thought he could handle the sight of her silent body. But dozens of surgical arms furiously wove her flesh back together, and the morbid view had been more than he could bear.

The doors parted, and Zo walked out, her face grim, eyes downcast.

Seth pushed up off the wall and stepped closer. "Well?"

Zo looked up with moist eyes. "It's pretty bad."

Seth's throat went dry, and he waited for Zo to continue.

"There was a lot of brain damage," she said sadly. "And while the physical damage has been repaired, her mind has …"

"Zo, just tell me."

"She's lost a lot of her memories. I don't know how many, but the prognosis says the losses may permanent. She didn't recognize me."

"I see …"

Zo gave him a cheerless grin. "But it's not all bad. She's asking for you."

Seth nodded and walked to the door. Zo stopped him with a gentle hand to his chest.

"Seth, something else happened to her. She'll never fly a seraph again. Her talent is gone."

"That doesn't matter." Seth brushed her hand aside and walked in.

Along the medical ward's ceiling were the robot operators: hemispherical machines with bunches of dangling insect-like arms. Seth walked further into the ward and stepped into the first partitioned room on his left.

Quennin lay on a futon with white covers over her body and underneath her arms. Few signs of surgery existed unless one knew where to look. An angry pink line traced up along her neck and through her face, passing through a line of scalp shaved of hair. Her skin was pale and her face weary.

Quennin looked up from her futon, her eyes meeting his, and he could see the recognition in them. Seth smiled warmly. He walked over and knelt at her side.

"Hey." Seth took her hand in his. "How do you feel?"

"Ehhh … not very good."

"You're doing a lot better than before."

Quennin chuckled weakly. "Yeah, I guess so."

"Do you need anything?"

Quennin shook her head. Her hand tightened on his. "Just stay here for a while."

"Don't worry," he said softly. "I'm not going anywhere."

"Seth, I'm having trouble remembering things." Quennin's eyes started misting up. "Important things."

"I know." Seth placed a hand on her forehead and gently brushed strands of hair out of her face.

"That woman said I may never regain my memories." Quennin tried to sit up in her futon. "She said the damage might be permanent."

Seth winced. *That woman is your closest childhood friend …*

"Yes, I know." He gingerly pushed her down. "But I don't care about that, and neither should you. You're alive. Nothing else matters."

Quennin rested on her back and stared at the ceiling. "But Seth, my mind is so clouded."

"You remember me."

"Yeah, I know who you are, but I can feel gaps where memories should be. I don't even know how we first met."

"Do you remember your first visit to the Sovereign's Palace?"

"No."

"Vorin brought you to the seraph bays. I saw you when I landed."

"And what went through your mind when you saw me?"

"I imagine the same thing most seven-year-old boys think when they see a young girl. Not a whole lot. I was more annoyed with Vorin than anything else. He'd interrupted a particularly fun duel between me and my father."

Quennin stared at the ceiling, but her eyes started to light up and a smile crept onto her lips. "I think … I think I might remember that. Yes, I do! Your seraph looked so *huge*. I saw it being lifted into the bay."

"That's wonderful, Quennin. See? Your memories aren't all lost. Do you remember what you thought when you saw me?"

"You were so … short."

Seth laughed a little. "Did you have to remember that?"

"And you had this mean scowl on your face."

"Anything positive?"

"Umm… Not really. I was so nervous when I saw you. I thought you were scary."

"That sounds about right."

"And then you made me cry!"

"Not on purpose."

"And why was that? Oh, now I remember! You didn't like my gift. I made a model of your seraph and you said it was stupid."

"I also said I was sorry."

"But only later." Quennin grinned. "I worked so hard on that model. I was sure you'd love it."

"In my defense, I do still have it."

"Really?"

"It's in my quarters if you need proof."

"Well, I suppose I'll take your word for it."

Seth gave her a reassuring smile. "What else can you remember? Let's start there."

“It’s strange. Some things I can recall perfectly. Others are so murky. That woman said I’ll never pilot a seraph again. I don’t really know how I feel about that yet.”

“Come on, Quennin. Let’s face the facts. You’re one lucky woman.”

“I don’t see how.”

“Quennin, you’re *alive*. You met the Bane in battle. You fought against that monster, and you’re still with us.”

“I suppose you have a point there.”

Quennin took a slow, calm breath. But then, her eyes went wide.

“The Bane!” she said. “I remember! I had something to tell you before we left! It was important!”

“Don’t worry about it.” Seth lightly brushed her forehead. “Just rest for now.”

“No!” Quennin sat upright in her futon. “No, it’s there. I can almost remember it. This was important, I know it! It had something to do with the Bane.”

Seth thought back to before the attack. Quennin had come running into the seraph bay with a look that had sent chills down his spine.

“*Seth, I think I know why Jack—*”

And then the Grendeni had launched their attack on Aktenzek.

“It had something to do with Jack,” he said at last.

Quennin nodded slowly. She put a hand to her forehead.

“Seth, I need you to do something for me.”

“Anything. Just name it.”

Quennin spoke in a soft, careful tone, enumerating a puzzling set of steps. The whole thing seemed nonsensical, but he agreed. How could he not do this for Quennin, even if the exercise appeared pointless at face value?

“Make sure you get another pilot to join in,” she said. “Like one of the Earth Nation pilots. I … don’t count anymore.”

“Of course. I’ll return when I’m done.” Seth stood up.

"And keep this quiet. Don't let the Choir know."

Seth nodded, hoping that this odd behavior wasn't a symptom of worse problems. He walked out of Quennin's room and linked with the medical ward. One of the operators moved silently across the ceiling and stopped above him. A single spindly arm reached into an internal compartment, produced a thin black case, and handed it over.

Seth opened the case and inspected the rows of ingestible capsules, each containing hundreds of microscopic sub-probes for monitoring bodily health. Normally, Aktenai robot operators performed surgeries with their own internal scanners, but sometimes a more precise on-site analysis was called for. Swallowing these capsules was one method for introducing the tiny probes.

Seth closed the black case, pocketed it, and exited the medical ward.

Yonu stood waiting outside the exit. "Is Pilot S'Kev …"

"She's doing better," Seth said.

"Is it true that she'll never pilot a seraph again?"

"I'm afraid so."

Yonu stared at the floor. She seemed to be summoning the courage for something.

"I can help," she said quietly.

"I'm not sure I understand."

Yonu looked up. "I can help. Without Pilot S'Kev, you'll need someone to watch your back. Let me do it."

"Thank you, but no. I am grateful for the gesture, but you must realize you are no match for the Bane or even Pilot Donolon."

"I am not useless! You and my mother sent us away because you both thought we couldn't help! But I can!"

Seth put his hands on Yonu's shoulders, looked into her eyes, and saw the terror in them. She feared what she was asking permission to face.

But in spite of that terror, she possessed the conviction to face it head on.

"I see why my son was so fond of you," Seth said. "But this is not your fight, and it is not your decision."

"You can't face them alone."

"I will face him no matter the circumstances, no matter the odds. Even if it means certain death."

"But—"

"Respect my wishes and do not ask again."

"I …" Yonu closed her mouth and looked at him sadly. Finally, she bowed her head. "As you wish, Pilot Elexen."

Seth palmed the thin case of biometric probes, wondering what Quennin hoped to find. Even though the probes could monitor anything in the human body, she was interested in only one function: their internal clocks. He couldn't fathom what she hoped to find, but he would carry out his beloved's wishes regardless.

The distant hum of the *Resolute*'s fold engines escalated sharply then ebbed away. The carrier had just completed another spatial fold on its way towards Imayirot.

The door to Jared Daykin's quarters opened and Seth walked in, surprised to find not only Jared, but the twin Renseki pilots, Kevik and Kiro. The three pilots sat around an Earth Nation board game his son had been fond of. Seth had never figured out its elaborate rules, despite Tevyr's numerous attempts to educate him.

Jared stood up. "Commander Elexen."

The twins rose as well and offered Seth polite nods.

Jared smiled and gestured to the twins. "Sir, I finally found some opponents I can beat at chess."

"You have hardly given us time to learn the rules, Jared," Kiro said in a strangely familiar tone. Or perhaps it was Kevik. Seth always had trouble telling the two brothers apart.

"Don't spoil the moment, Kiro," Jared said, all too informally, but the Renseki didn't seem to notice.

Ah, so that one is Kiro, Seth thought.

"Anyway, what can I do for you, sir?"

Seth produced the case of biometric probes and set it on the table next to the playing board. "I have a little experiment I want to run. I'd like you to help me, and if the Renseki don't mind, I'd like them to join in as well."

"Of course, sir. Anything to lend a hand."

The twins nodded curtly to Seth. "We'll join in. What do you require?"

Seth opened the case and selected a pill. "These are standard biometric probe capsules. I'd like each of us to swallow one."

"What are you looking for?" Kiro asked. "We are all in excellent health."

"I suppose I'll know it when I see it."

"I'll get some water." Jared headed over to the kitchen and poured four glasses.

Seth set the one capsule down in the center of the table. "This one will be the control. We'll use it as a reference for the probes we swallow."

"Shouldn't the control be inside a human being?" Kevik asked. "If this is something particular to pilots, I'm sure we can get one of the technicians to join us."

"That won't be necessary," Seth said. Just what did Quennin expect to find?

Jared brought over a tray of glasses and set it down on the table.

Seth placed a capsule in his mouth and washed it down with water. The other three pilots did the same. Once all of them had swallowed the probes, Seth linked to the wall screen. The vista of a mountain range from Earth disappeared, replaced with five biometric displays including the control probe on the table.

Kiro glanced over the data. "Everything appears normal. Our stress indicators are all high, which is to be expected. Jared's blood pressure is elevated, but still within the acceptable range for being at rest."

"Well, I always get a little nervous during medical checkups," Jared said sheepishly.

"I do not see anything noteworthy here," Kiro said.

"There is one particular metric I wish to check." Seth linked with the displays. Data disappeared, replaced with each probe's internal clock. Seth then zeroed out the data and brought it up as a ratio to the control. In theory, all the probes should have displayed values of 1.000, as their internal clocks matched perfectly with the control's.

That did not happen. Seth read the numbers, wondering why they didn't match and how Quennin could have known. Now arranged in a column, the numbers read:

SETH ELEXEN	0.958
KIRO TORVULUS	0.994
KEVIK TORVULUS	0.994
JARED DAYKIN	0.985
CONTROL	1.000

"What do you suppose this means?" Kiro asked.

"I have no idea," Seth said quietly.

"Could the probes be malfunctioning?" Jared said. "You know, maybe a bad batch?"

Seth shook his head. "Four out of five probes faulty? I think not."

"Why don't we swallow another batch," Jared said. "Just to be sure."

"I agree," Kiro said. "Let us take no chances with this discovery."

The four pilots swallowed another set of probe capsules, then looked up at the wall screen. Seth linked to the new probes, bringing up their data in the same ratio format. The numbers did not change.

"Have you considered why the numbers are different for each of us?" Kevik asked. "And why my brother and I are identical?"

"Yes, that is strange," Seth said. "This seems to indicate a pattern of sorts."

"Well, we're all pilots," Jared said. "Why not bring up our coefficients and compare? Maybe we'll see a pattern."

Seth nodded, linking to the wall screen again and displayed their coefficients in a new column.

CONTROL	1.000	0
KIRO TORVULUS	0.994	1120
KEVIK TORVULUS	0.994	1120
JARED DAYKIN	0.985	1300
SETH ELEXEN	0.958	1840

"Look, as the coefficient rises, the ratio drops," Jared said.

"Yes, but that does not explain why," Kiro said. "There seems to be a pattern, though it is not completely linear."

"Perhaps you have to reach a certain threshold before the effect takes hold," Jared said.

"Perhaps," Kiro said.

Seth stared at the numbers. What did they *mean*?

The other pilots turned expectantly towards him.

"Well, Seth," Kevik said. "This was your experiment. Surely you must have some idea what it means."

"Not really," Seth said. "I'll let you know when I figure it out."

Seth departed without another word, leaving three confused expressions in his wake. He quickly made his way back to the medical ward and returned to Quennin's side. She looked up at him and frowned when she saw his expression.

"Well?" she asked, her tone slightly worried.

Seth knelt beside her. "I ran the test, and none of us matched the control. We were all lower."

"Your number was the lowest, wasn't it?"

"That's right. Do you know what this means?"

Quennin turned her head away from Seth and rested against the pillow. She nodded slowly.

"Then what is it?"

"My fears have been confirmed," Quennin said.

"Fears? What fears?"

"Don't you think it's odd that the Bane can pilot a seraph?"

"Well … I suppose it is. I never gave it much thought. We were all too concerned about facing the Bane and not some other pilot."

"And what about our resistance to the Bane's attacks? How would anyone know this?"

"I …" Seth stopped and pondered the question carefully. "I guess I always took it as a matter of faith that the Choir and Original Eleven knew it to be true."

"So did everyone else. But it's an important question, and the answer is now clear."

"What answer, Quennin? You can tell me."

Quennin turned around and looked straight into his eyes. "Pilots can slow time in their bodies, Seth. We can affect the passage of time subconsciously. And this ability increases as a pilot becomes stronger.

Don't you see? The reason pilots can defend against the Bane, the reason the Bane can pilot a seraph, and the reason pilots can affect time is all the same. All these abilities are related. Chaos energy can combat chaos energy."

"You don't mean …" Seth began.

"We are all the thing we have been taught to hate. We are all banes."

Seth turned away, the realization finally dawning on him. He clenched his fists and let out a jagged breath. Blood and rage boiled within him.

"That's why Jack betrayed us," Quennin said. "He figured out what he was becoming."

Seth wanted to scream out at the cruel universe, to vent his anger at anything and anyone around him, but he held it in and let Quennin continue.

"Our leaders have betrayed us," she said. "They haven't been trying to make weapons to defeat the Bane."

Tears now ran down Quennin's pale cheeks.

"They've been trying to make more."

Chapter 17

Birth of the Dead Fleet

Veketon turned from his fellow founders and surveyed the angry mob in the Great Hall. The enraged chatter from thousands of sovereigns assaulted his ears. Veketon had never seen them so unruly, though he understood why.

Sovereign Vorin Daelus stood shakily across from the Original Eleven at the base of the Great Hall's circular auditorium. He had suffered grievous injuries in his battle against the still-maturing Bane Donolon. Yet despite his pain and weakness, he stood proudly with only a metal rod for support.

"Is this true?" Vorin shouted. "Answer the charges against you!"

"Has the Great Mission been about nothing more than creating banes?" one of the dead sovereigns shouted.

"Do not hide behind silence!" shouted another. "Answer for your sins!"

Veketon turned away from the mob.

"This is rather unfortunate," he said to his colleagues. "We must do what we can to salvage the situation."

"Can we not conjure up a suitable story?" Xixek asked.

"No," Dendolet said. "The evidence against us is too great."

"We should not have revealed the Bane's existence," Balezuur said.

"And what *should* we have done?" Veketon asked. "Wait for them to discover it when the Bane attacked Aktenzek? We only provided information they would have learned on their own. Nothing would have changed this outcome, only its timing."

"Perhaps we should throw ourselves at their mercy?" Ziriken asked.

Veketon gave him a dry chuckle. "Their mercy? We would be fortunate to survive. Look around you. They will purge us if we submit."

Ziriken shrugged his arms. "But surely we can come to some agreement."

"No. The Aktenai have been faithful pawns for many long years, but their usefulness is at an end. And all is not lost. Far from it, for we have the thrones and our research safely on Zu'Rashik. It is time to make our escape and join our prizes there. We have planned for this, and I say we carry out those plans."

Slowly and with some reluctance, each of the Original Eleven accepted this new direction.

"Excellent," Veketon said. "The decision is unanimous. We have survived much, my colleagues, and we will continue to survive without the Aktenai."

"Shall we leave now?" Dendolet asked.

"Not quite yet. I want a final word with these peasants."

Veketon turned from the circle. He took several steps towards the center of the Great Hall and Vorin. The Sovereign held his ground and met Veketon's harsh stare.

"You wish for us to answer your charges?" Veketon's voice boomed over the noise. He passed his gaze over the surrounding stands. "You wish for us to answer for our crimes? What right do you have to judge us?"

"You have defiled the Great Mission," Vorin said.

"And why not? We created the Great Mission and your entire society. Both were ours to use and defile from the very beginning."

"Long have we walked the path you laid before us, only at the end to find you misled us every step of the way."

"You think you understand what is happening? Look at you, nothing more than children scrounging around in the dark, cherishing whatever scraps we feed you."

"We have grown beyond you," Vorin said, his voice reserved but no less forceful in the Great Hall. "And we will survive without you."

"Those are truly brave words, child, but they ring hollow," Veketon said. "However, for the sake of clarity, I will answer your charges. First, you are only partially correct. The Great Mission does exist, and we intended to destroy the Bane. However, the only way to defeat such a creature is with another bane or even an army of banes. You yourself, Sovereign Daelus, like so many of your kin, are nothing more than a stepping stone in our weapons research."

Shock spread through the Great Hall, and Veketon did not let it die out before continuing.

"You have always known that we, the Original Eleven, created the Bane, and that we were expelled from the Homeland for this sin. All of this is true. But did you know that we planned to return to the Homeland in order to conquer it? Imagine, returning to the Homeland with endless legions of banes at our command. Not even the Keepers could stop us!"

The anger built in the surrounding stands. Veketon watched with a sense of pleasure as Vorin's face twisted in rage.

"You will be purged from the Choir for your sins!" Vorin said.

"I think not, child."

With a thought, the transfer began. All around Veketon, light and sound dissolved to nothing, then snapped back into place with sudden clarity.

The Original Eleven were alone within the new Choir in Zu'Rashik's Core.

"We must work quickly," Veketon said, signaling his colleagues to begin.

Space exploded around them into large maps of tactical data. The solar system appeared with Earth, Aktenzek, Zu'Rashik, and the Aktenai fleets all shown in vivid, hostile red.

"We are initiating the takeover," Dendolet said.

Veketon nodded, watching the surrounding screens.

Zu'Rashik was the first to fall, its systems subverted by the Original Eleven. The entire planet changed in hue from red to green.

"We have complete control over the fortress planet," Dendolet said. "Walls are in place to prevent the Choir from reentering. They will find them impossible to breach."

"Excellent," Veketon said. The plan was working. It had to work.

Slowly, the red icons of the Aktenai fleet changed to green as the Original Eleven gained complete control of the robotic ships. The subversive software spread across the entire fleet until nearly one-third of the ships were under his command.

"We are receiving interference from the Choir," Dendolet said. "They are attempting to halt our fleet takeover."

"They appear to be succeeding," Veketon said.

More ships fell to the Original Eleven, but the rate dropped significantly. Great duels waged in space while ships once in formation now turned guns on one another. A few ships were lost when the Aktenai focused their fire on isolated craft, but not enough to disrupt the plan.

Wherever possible, ships folded away, rushing towards a rendezvous point that Zu'Rashik itself would soon join.

"We have a little over half the Aktenai fleet at our command," Dendolet said. "Not as good as we hoped, but sufficient for our needs. The Choir's response came faster than we anticipated."

"Indeed," Veketon focused on Zu'Rashik. "Why have we not folded space?"

"The Aktenai have deployed a negator on Aktenzek's far side," Dendolet said.

Fusion cannons all across Aktenzek opened fire.

"And they are now targeting us."

"Return fire. Destroy the negator."

Space between Aktenzek and Zu'Rashik erupted with tens of thousands of plasma lances.

"We will need to bring some of our fleet in to finish off the negator," Dendolet said.

"Do it." Veketon watched Aktenai and Earth Nation ships closing on Zu'Rashik. A group of six craft, small and hard to spot amidst the immense chaos, sped towards the Original Eleven's final refuge.

"Six Earth Nation seraphs are approaching," Dendolet said. "They are heading straight for a gap in the Armor Shell. Veketon, they're going to get inside."

"Let them. Open a path for them to the Core and see that they follow it. We'll send the thrones out to meet them."

"But Veketon, we cannot control the thrones!" Dendolet said.

"It's too dangerous!" Xixek said.

"We don't know what those creatures will do!" Balezuur said.

Veketon turned from the screens and appraised his fellow founders carefully. “We have nothing else that can match seraphs in battle. There is no option. Release six of the thrones. Hold the rest in reserve.”

The screen zoomed in on Zu’Rashik’s interior. Six red icons sped through the long stretch of shafts and corridors, guided by the Eleven’s lack of resistance.

From near the Core, six green icons came to life.

Dendolet leaned over to Veketon and spoke in a whisper. “If this goes badly, we will have to abandon the planet.”

Veketon ignored her. The two sets of icons approached one another, and he permitted himself a confident grin when they meshed. A screen appeared to his right, showing a live visual feed of the battle.

The thrones were roughly the size of seraphs, but where a seraph could be considered passably humanoid, the thrones were slender and almost human in shape. A single halo-wing spun rapidly behind each of their torsos, wider than their shoulders and not physically connected to the main body. The inner and outer edges of the halo-wings and vents across their bodies burned with blue fire. Their perfectly white mnemonic skin gleamed from nearby cavern lights.

The EN seraphs fired their rail-rifles and fusion cannons, but every shot rebounded off the thrones. Without daggers, the thrones tackled the EN seraphs. They pierced through the seraphs’ barriers with clawed fingers and ripped open their armor.

One of the thrones pulled a pilot free of the cockpit and crushed her in a spray of gore.

Veketon let out a satisfied sigh. “Ah, what savage beasts we have created.”

All of the Eleven turned from their tasks. Fluids sprayed from amputated limbs and disemboweled chests. The thrones tore through the seraphs. Only two managed to light their daggers, but the thrones caught their arms and ripped them free of their sockets.

"What have we made ...?" Balezuur whispered.

"And to think that this is only a fraction of their power," Veketon said.

The thrones finished the EN seraphs, leaving nothing but dismembered corpses and scraps of twisted armor.

Dendolet turned from the scene and reviewed the solar system's fleet status. She cleared her throat loudly. "The fleet has concluded its destruction of the Aktenai negator."

"Then let us fold."

A moment passed, and fortress planet Zu'Rashik vanished from Earth orbit.

Assistant Administrator Dominic walked to the front of the *Virtuous Executioner*'s control room. A transparent dome on its side peered into the interior of the archangel carrier, where a full four squadrons stood ready in their bays. Dominic thought the design similar to the interior of a schism, with its open center and four neat rows of archangels lined up in different quadrants of the cylindrical hull.

Officially, Dominic didn't have to risk his life with the fleet. Except for the archangel pilots and their support crews, the carrier was entirely automated. But he had a good reason for believing the carrier was safer than the schism *Righteous Anger*.

"Dominic, pay attention for a change," Gurgella said. He eyeballed one of the carrier technicians who passed through his hologram.

"Certainly, administrator." Dominic walked back to a wall of glowing screens showing Grendeni and Aktenai fleet positions. "I am, of course, as surprised as anyone."

"Naturally," Gurgella said. "The Aktenai are fighting each other!"

"Yes, it has all the appearances of a civil war. Though, unfortunately, we have no idea what the root cause may be or if one of the factions may be inclined to assist us."

"That, Dominic, is wishful thinking. It's bad enough we unknowingly sided with the Bane, of all creatures. No, I think the Executives will be extremely cautious with any future outside help."

"Administrator, as I said before, we had no way of knowing Jack Donolon's ally was indeed the Bane until we were able to analyze her attacks at Aktenzek. In fact—"

"It doesn't matter." Gurgella gave him a brusque arm wave. "That man provided what he promised. We now know the Gate's location and can move to secure it, though the Executives' impetuous decision to attack bothers me."

"But administrator, surely there will never be a better time to strike Imayirot," Dominic said. "With the Aktenai fleets concentrated around the fortress planet, we will reach Imayirot first and in greater numbers. This latest development only strengthens our position."

"You forget the defenders around Imayirot. Our Forsaken brothers and sisters have activated the planet's defenses."

"I have not forgotten that detail," Dominic said. Indeed, how could anyone forget the swarm of orbital weapons surrounding Imayirot? Year after year, Aktenai and Grendeni had met at Imayirot, adding and modernizing the weapons that protected this world. The history of Imayirot was etched deeply into both cultures, and it alone could bring together the Forsaken and the Fallen.

And now, even that has been betrayed by the Aktenai. To think that the Gate would be there. To think that we were duped into defending what we sought to possess.

And now those silent leviathans had come alive and would open fire on anything near Imayirot, destroying Grendeni and Aktenai with equal prejudice. Dominic supposed it had been a necessary design compromise when constructing the defenders. Both factions could activate the swarm, which would stay functional for years before returning to standby.

"It is really academic for us to argue the point," Gurgella said. "The Executives have already made their decision to proceed with the attack."

"Of course, administrator."

Dominic studied the long range exodrone images from Imayirot. The planet itself stood out against space as a small black sphere, completely devoid of light or life. A vast shade eclipsed the sun, preventing light and heat from despoiling the dead world now preserved at the moment of death.

The shade, a disc thirty thousand kilometers in diameter, held its position between the sun and Imayirot, anchored deeply into both gravity wells. Along the circumference of the disc were thousands of heavy beam cannons: the merest fraction of Imayirot's military power. Around the shade and Imayirot floated thick clouds of orbital weapon platforms, many surpassing dreadnoughts in size, power, and resilience.

Those robotic defenses now stood at high alert, firing on any vessel that approached the dead world. Already, the first wave of observational drones had been mercilessly gunned down in an attempt to reach Imayirot's surface and begin searching for the Gate.

Dominic zoomed in on a single dreadnought attempting to run the swarm's orbital blockade.

Black spherical defenders spun in space, bringing their weapons to bear on this new target. Lances of white light shot out and savaged the dreadnought's hull from every angle. Somehow, the dreadnought survived this first volley, its outer hull an ugly patchwork of white glowing lines.

The second volley came from the shade itself, more than one hundred fusion cannons firing in unison, focusing on the lone target as if through a lens. Not even a dreadnought could withstand that sort of punishment, and it blew apart into a cloud of glowing gas and debris.

"We did perhaps too good a job building the shade, I think," Gurgella said.

"What of Jack and his companion?" Dominic asked.

"We've requested they land on the *Righteous Anger* so that we can coordinate the assault on Imayirot. So far, they seem to be cooperating."

"Administrator, I strongly suggest you do not allow them to land."

"What? And pass up an opportunity to capture their seraphs? Come on, Dominic. They're dangerous in their seraphs, but once we get them outside, they're just regular people. We'll kill the Bane and capture two more seraphs as a tidy bonus."

Dominic grimaced. "Perhaps, just to be safe, you should evacuate the schism."

"Are you joking?" Gurgella scoffed. "There's no call for that."

"Administrator, I feel very strongly you should not allow those two to approach the schism."

"What are you getting at?" Gurgella asked. "This will be one of the greatest victories in all of Grendeni history, and I get to be at the forefront. Don't tell me you're jealous."

"That's ridiculous, administrator, I … Gurgella, would you please listen to me for once. Do *not* let them land."

"We need to double check our preparations. Thank you for your opinion, Dominic. I'll be in contact soon."

The hologram vanished.

No, Dominic thought. *You're already dead.*

Chapter 18

Their Unbreakable Will

It seemed like a good idea at the time.

With Imayirot's defenders activated and the Aktenai fleet on its way, why not coordinate one last time with the Grendeni?

Jack and Vierj took a tram from the archangel bays and entered an isolated corridor within the *Righteous Anger*'s factory zone. It was then that the floor split open.

"Oh crap!"

Jack slipped towards the widening gap and the star-speckled darkness below. A powerful air current roared out and made his ears pop. The chamber was decompressing!

"Vierj!"

The howl of the air drowned out his scream. He lost his grip on the floor and plummeted away.

"VIERJ!"

The roar stopped. He dangled over a black chasm that no longer had stars. Vierj had sealed it with her talent.

Jack looked up and saw Vierj floating over him, his hand in hers. Six great wings of black energy flexed out from her back. She drew him up so that he could wrap his arms around her waist.

"Thanks, Vierj."

"It seems these peasants no longer consider us allies."

"Yeah, I think we've overstayed our welcome. Let's get back to our seraphs."

"No," she said firmly.

"Vierj?"

"Remember what I said about people being beneath our notice."

"Yeah? As long as they don't try to stop you."

"That line has been crossed."

Vierj flew to the far end of the floorless corridor and caressed the airlock with her fingertips. It shattered and blew open.

Jack placed one foot on the ledge and staggered in.

"Look, I can have my seraph here in less than a minute."

Vierj landed next to him. Her wings vanished into a mist of black specks.

"This way, Jack Donolon. I can see a great many eyes watching us, and their sources all converge in a nearby tower. We will go there."

"Why bother? We should just leave and head for Imayirot."

"Not until I have a word with whoever tried to kill us."

Jack followed Vierj deeper into the schism, dread filling his stomach. He couldn't see any way this would end well.

The corridor led them straight ahead. A dozen heavy mnemonic doors slammed in their way, but Vierj turned each of them to frozen ash.

"I doubt the decompression was the only trick they have," Jack said. "We should really turn back."

"This will not take long."

"Look, they can still kill me."

"I will ensure no harm comes to you."

Vierj cast the last door aside and caught sight of an empty elevator shaft. She stuck her head in and looked up.

"Maybe you should hit the call button," Jack said.

A rhythmic hum echoed down the shaft.

"Uhh, is something coming down?" he asked.

"Yes."

"That can't be good."

Vierj backed away from the shaft. The elevator car arrived and opened, revealing a fat cylindrical device that filled the car from end to end.

"That's a nuke!" Jack shouted.

Vierj put her hands on her hips and let out a slow, frustrated sigh.

The Grendeni fusion warhead exploded. For the briefest of moments, it flooded the entire corridor with blinding light. Then, as quickly as it started, the light was gone. Where the elevator car had been, a black cube stood in its place. Vierj let the cube fizzle into a rain of soot.

"Damn, they set off a nuke inside the schism," Jack said.

"That weapon was controlled by the people above us."

"Crazy bastards. Maybe the top of this tower is fortified."

"Whatever defenses they have will not stop me. Come, Jack Donolon. Let us ascend."

Jack wrapped his arm around her waist. Vierj unfurled her black wings and flew up the elevator shaft at breakneck speed. Near the halfway point, the shaft's exterior became clear, providing a view of the schism's northern factory.

A Grendeni dreadnought entered the factory zone from the space dock and turned its main guns towards them.

"You have got to be kidding me!" Jack shouted.

"Close your eyes," Vierj said calmly.

Jack scrunched his eyelids shut and buried his face in Vierj's shoulder.

The dreadnought fired. A lance of plasma obliterated the elevator shaft and a wide stretch of factories behind it. Except for a brief moment of seeing the red of his own eyelids, Jack felt nothing. When he opened his eyes, he found a black circular shield between them and the dreadnought.

Vierj sent the disc flying outwards. It engulfed the dreadnought and reduced it to cold, floating scrap.

"Jack Donolon?"

"Yeah?"

"I have decided how I will punish these peasants."

"What are you going to do?"

Vierj grinned at him. It was not a cheerful expression.

"You will see."

The top of the tower looked like it could serve as some sort of oval-shaped transport craft. It disengaged from the upper remains of the elevator shaft, letting the clear, half-melted frame fall away. The transport lit a pair of drive blades at its base and began moving away.

Vierj snapped her fingers. The oval transport halted, its drive blades gone.

"Let us greet our would-be executioners." Vierj lifted them to the transport and cut a triangular hole in the side. Its mnemonic hull was over five meters thick.

Jack stepped in. "No wonder they weren't afraid of setting off that nuke so close."

"They should be more afraid of me." Vierj landed next to him and took the lead.

Jack followed her into a round chamber, its walls taken up by screens showing their seraphs, the decompression corridor, the elevator shaft remains, and the dreadnought's debris.

Eight technicians formed a rough line with railguns leveled at Vierj. The stubby weapons shook in their hands. A short, bald man cowered behind them, his green jacket emblazoned with golden administrator sigils.

"Gurgella, you idiot," Jack spat.

One of the technicians fired. The bolt ricocheted off Jack's hand when it should have blown it off.

"Ouch! Damn it, that stung!" Jack sucked on the back of his hand.

"You have made a grave mistake today," Vierj said.

Another technician aimed his weapon at Jack and fired, but this time he was ready. He dashed aside with inhuman speed, let the bolt fly past, then rushed his attacker. With a brief grunt of effort, he formed a dagger of blue energy in his left hand and cleaved the man's head off. Blood spurted out of the stump, and the corpse flopped limply to the ground.

Gurgella put his back against the wall. "W-w-what are you people?"

"Didn't anyone tell you?" Jack gave him a frigid grin. "We're monsters."

"Drop your weapons," Vierj said. "Or fight and die. Either way, you cannot harm us."

"Help is coming," Gurgella said.

"It will not be enough." Vierj walked towards him. "Make your choice."

"You'd better do as she says," Jack said.

"D-drop them," Gurgella stuttered.

The technicians threw their weapons to the group and hurried out of her way.

"There. We've done as you asked. We're completely at your mercy."

"You were defenseless before you dropped those toys." Vierj stopped in front of him. "Nothing has changed."

"What are you going to do to me?" Gurgella asked.

"This."

Vierj stabbed Gurgella with her bare hand. His ribcage provided all of the resistance of wet tissue.

"Gah!" Gurgella gasped and looked down, unbelieving. He grabbed her arm with shaking hands.

Vierj twisted her wrist and pushed in further.

"Nngh!"

Tendrils of black energy spread from Vierj's hand, running across his chest and up his arms.

Gurgella's eyes bugged out and he screamed. It was a sound of absolute, indescribable pain. And when he finished screaming, he filled his lungs and screamed again, lips foaming with spittle and blood.

One of the technicians dove for his gun. Jack grabbed him by the shoulder and threw him into the wall. The technician hit with a wet thunk and crumpled to the ground unconscious.

Gurgella sucked in a gurgling breath and cried out again. The tendrils of energy spread further, enveloping his chest, running down his legs, and sliding up his neck. They reached his mouth and poured down his throat.

His eyes were the last part of him still visible, frantically turning every which way before the black liquid encased him.

Vierj slid her hand out of his chest.

The darkness dispersed, and Gurgella reappeared, locked in his last pose. Vierj tapped a finger against his forehead, and he crumpled into a pile of glittering, frozen dust.

Vierj closed her eyes, spread her arms, and manifested her wings.

"Now hold on," Jack said, reaching for her.

Her black seraph arrived at the transport, clutched it with both hands, and broke it in half. The technicians cried out and fell to the factories below.

"Whoa!" Jack shouted, only to be buffered softly to the seraph's open palm. A thin barrier formed around him, sealing in a portion of breathable air.

Vierj floated backwards into the seraph's cockpit.

"You don't have to do this!" Jack shouted.

From within the seraph, Vierj held Jack aloft, then stretched out the seraph's free hand. A ball of black energy appeared. She cast it into the factories below, linking herself to it with a thin strand of darkness. The ball hit the surface and rushed across the factories in two directions until it met above, forming a continuous ring around the schism's interior.

The black ring parted down the middle, then began moving in opposite directions. It engulfed the entire factory zone, the space dock, and pushed into the northern city. Chilled debris spat out the other side.

"Vierj, stop!"

"You are too soft, Jack Donolon." The voice reverberated from the barrier around him. "You must harden yourself if you are to survive, for you are still vulnerable to attack. Even this vacuum I shield you from is deadly to you. Do not show these lesser creatures pity, for they deserve none."

The twin rings expanded out faster, consuming the forests, mountains, lakes, and quaint villas within the schism's cylinder. It ate through the southern city in seconds, then enveloped the southern factories and space dock.

When it was over, a ragged field of dark, cold debris was all that remained of the *Righteous Anger*, its two cities, and millions of inhabitants. His seraph floated amongst the wreckage, completely unaffected by the attack.

"There, it is done." Vierj spoke those words with an air of boredom.

Jack knew he alone was to blame for awakening this sleeping beast. If he had not set out on his fool's errand, the Bane would still be in hiding. But Jack had suspected when he set out what he was becoming, and the terror of that revelation drove him to act.

He had found the Bane. He had earned this murderer's trust. And now he stood on the cusp of helping this creature return to the place she was banished from.

But Jack could not let that happen, *would* not let that happen. The Gate, his goal and the Bane's goal, remained the key. Even now, as powerful as he was, Jack could not harm her. No one could. But near the Gate's dimensional rupture, this creature's powers would weaken.

She would be vulnerable to attack.

So many had died to provide Jack this one opportunity, and no one, not even Seth, would stop him. He would kill anyone who stood between him and his goal. In the end, at the very edge of this universe where the Bane was at her weakest, Jack would finally kill her.

Seth slipped his arms through the i-suit coat. A wall screen in his quarters displayed the black silhouette of Imayirot, transmitted to the *Resolute* by surveillance exodrones. Lines of white light lashed back and forth around the dead world, signs of the growing battle between Grendeni ships and Imayirot defenders.

Quennin stared down at her clasped hands. "Seth, I want you to reconsider."

"I don't have a choice," he said, sealing the front of his i-suit.

"Of course you do. There's always a choice."

Seth stopped. After a long pause, he nodded slowly.

Yes, you're right, he thought. *I do have a choice, especially after all that's happened.*

The reality he knew was disintegrating before his eyes. Jack, a trusted ally and friend, had killed their son. The Choir, their eternal and indivisible leadership, had splintered. The Original Eleven, founders and masters of the Aktenai, had betrayed them.

The Bane, a being of incomprehensible power and malevolence, had returned.

And we're all attempts to recreate that abomination, Seth thought, then pushed the fact away, burying it beneath layers of resolve.

Quennin came beside him. "And?"

"I'm still going."

She smiled sadly. "Somehow I knew you'd say that."

"My duty remains clear, even after all that has happened."

Quennin picked up his gloves and handed them over. When he finished putting them on, she placed her hands around his.

"I know what you're thinking," she said. "But everything we've fought for is a lie. You don't have to go."

"But I do," Seth said. "We cannot let the Bane pass through the Gate. I will not throw away what little purpose we still have."

Quennin sighed. "I suppose there's no way I can change your mind."

"You know I have to do this. My blade lies at Aktenzek's side, now and always."

"You cannot stop them."

"Maybe." Seth let go of her. He picked up his sidearm and set it firmly into his holster.

A thin smile slipped onto Quennin's face. "You have always been the stubborn one. There's no reasoning with you sometimes."

"You would know best."

"I won't be able to watch your back. I think that's why I'm so scared for you this time. Even with the holes in my mind, I don't think I've ever been afraid like this. I want to be out there with you, protecting you even as you protect me. Instead, all I can do is sit here and wait."

"Quennin, I understand why you don't want me to go." Seth picked up his sidearm and set it firmly into his holster. "But I cannot deny who I am, nor deny my path when it is so clear. The Bane must be stopped."

Quennin placed a hand on his cheek. "Then I will not ask again. Fight well today, beloved, and come back to me."

"I will."

Seth stepped up to Quennin and looked long into those beautiful green eyes, recognizing all the tumultuous emotions behind them. Perhaps his beloved's injuries had not changed her at all. Now that she could no longer be at his side, actively confronting her fears, those long denied emotions had surfaced.

Perhaps she merely hid her fears for my sake, just as I hide mine from her. We are not so different, my beloved.

Seth brought her close and kissed her gently on the lips. Quennin wrapped her arms around him and squeezed him tight. They stayed like that for what they both wished could be an eternity, both afraid that this might be their last moment together.

After more than a minute, Seth broke away, and they looked into each other's eyes.

"I will come back."

Quennin only nodded with moistening eyes.

"You will see." Without another word, Seth left for the seraph bays.

He took the lift down to the bay shelf and looked up at his seraph. Two Grendeni swords were docked against the wing clusters. All the seraphs onboard the *Resolute* now possessed refitted arms for using the Grendeni weapons. Seth was the only pilot who would carry two into battle.

Will these weapons be enough? Or do I go to my death?

Seth knew he had to stop Jack and the Bane, but he was no fool. Only the crucible of battle could judge now.

I must try to engage Jack alone if I am to have a chance. Either these swords will grant me the edge I need, or I will die trying.

Seth accepted his helmet from the waiting technician, donned it, and boarded his seraph. He leaned into the pilot alcove and let the cockpit close in around him. The ethereal connection with the seraph surfaced in the back of his mind.

Seth closed his eyes, letting the sensations of his physical body fade until they constricted into a small pearl of consciousness. The seraph's senses supplanted them, growing in strength and clarity. The white lights of the bay, the restraints of the catapult system, the heft of the swords and conformal pods, all this filled Seth's mind.

Seth didn't pilot the seraph. He *was* the seraph.

He let a trickle of power flow into his chest cavity's arterial pump. Pressurized fluid pulsed through his body, carrying raw chaos energy to his arms, legs, and wings. Shunts on his armored skin blazed to life, burning hotly with purple fire.

Clamps descended on rails and latched onto his wings. A catapult shutter snapped open beneath his feet, and the clamps thrust him downward. He cleared three shutters and flew out into the emptiness of space.

Seth unleashed the full yield of his talent. His barrier shimmered with tiny sparks of purple electricity. He spread his wings and filled them with power. Their edges burned with light and he shot forward, clearing the cylindrical bulk of the *Resolute*.

Eighteen other seraphs launched and joined him. All six Renseki and all twelve of the pilots in Jared's squadron stood ready for his orders.

"Epsilon squadron at full readiness, sir," Jared said. "Fold engines fully charged and calibrated."

"Renseki standing by," Zo said.

Seth called up the probe data from exodrones near Imayirot.

Nearly four hundred Grendeni warships fought against the automated defenders with more ships folding every minute. The Grendeni would pour every available ship into this fight. They had to know the Aktenai fleets were out of position and weakened by civil war. Already, they had succeeded in driving a wedge through the orbital defense grid, though they had paid for it with over sixty smashed warships.

The Aktenai fleets would attack regardless of the skewed odds, and Seth led only a fraction of the two hundred seraphs committed to the attack.

A hypercast message carried the Choir's orders to all seraph squadrons.

Seth started a squadron-wide countdown. "Fold on my signal. We'll come in directly behind the Grendeni formations with our fleet in tow. Do not engage the defenders unless absolutely necessary. Focus on the Grendeni ships and watch for archangels. They'll show up shortly after we do."

"Confirmed, sir."

"Understood."

The countdown reached zero. Nineteen seraphs folded to Imayirot.

Space exploded around them.

Hundreds of beams crisscrossed between dense formations of ships and the orbital defenders. Thousands of fusion torpedoes and tactical seekers blossomed into white-hot suns wherever they hit.

Seth oriented himself with the Grendeni fleet ahead. The enemy ships flew towards Imayirot and away from him, beams converging on their formations from all sides. Grendeni frigates and dreadnoughts died by the dozens, smashing themselves against the weakening orbital defenses.

The great black shade, a disc thirty thousand kilometers across, no longer rested between Imayirot and its sun. It now orbited the planet, slowly approaching the weakest part of Imayirot's defenses. Cannons all across its circumferences fired on the Grendeni ships.

Light caressed Imayirot for the first time in millennia, illuminating its lifeless landscapes. No atmosphere hung above its barren surface. No ocean washed up along its cold shores. Cities that once stood tall and opulent now existed as rubble and debris. Domes lay scattered about its surface, some cracked open, revealing dilapidated cities and long tunnels leading deep into the planet.

Far below the orbiting weapons, yet hundreds of kilometers above the planet, was an incomplete patchwork of reflective mirrors and metal canopies. Like the domed cities, these had been Imayirot's attempt to stave off the brutal forces of entropy while its inhabitants tried to live without a sun.

Somewhere within the long, endless tunnels of Imayirot, the Choir hid the Gate, Seth thought. *And the only people who know the exact location are the Original Eleven.*

Behind Seth, the Aktenai fleet began folding in, its colossal ranks of frigates and dreadnoughts pursuing the Grendeni. Orbital batteries, not caring who intruded into Imayirot's sacred space, wheeled about and opened fire.

The battle was joined.

Seth marked the closest Grendeni dreadnought as a priority target. Jared moved epsilon squadron up and opened fire. Fusion beams and rail-rifle bolts shot across space, impacting against its glowing, deformed hull. White beams vaporized armor and breached the hull.

Torpedoes struck the wounded warship, and not all of them from Jared's squadron. Shoals of weaving, dodging projectiles spewed forth from the defenders. The torpedoes took heavy losses penetrating the dreadnought's defenses, but over half slammed into its hull.

Warheads exploded across the dreadnought's full length, sundering it.

But even as the ship died, two more dreadnoughts folded in behind it, along with over a hundred archangels. Like vast clouds of copper skeletons, the archangels wheeled about, and bore down on epsilon squadron.

"Archangels!" Seth reached for his chaos swords. He gripped the extended handles and pulled them free from his wing clusters. "Take them down!"

Seth brought the twin swords in front of him and let chaos energy flow down his arms and into the blades. With almost no effort, the edges ignited with brilliant fire. Seth readied the blades and flew up to meet the closest archangels. Six Renseki seraphs followed him, their own chaos swords ready and burning with vengeful light.

Behind Seth, Jared's EN seraph gun-line opened fire with their rail-rifles, protected by a screen of six Aktenai seraphs. Kinetic bolts tore through the archangels, but the huge mob pressed on.

Seth closed with the first archangel and cut in. He met the archangel's sword with his own, and the two flashed brightly as they met. But even though this foe had the same technological edge, it had none of his strength, and its blade faltered almost instantly.

Seth cut through sword and torso, hewing the archangel cleanly in two.

More archangels dove in, and Seth rocketed through them, slashing apart any in his path. Behind him, the Renseki cut a vicious path through the archangels.

Epsilon squadron volleyed their fusion cannons and rail-rifles again into the archangel swarm, pulverizing scores of the copper machines. Seth pulled up and away, a trail of hewn corpses behind him, his twin swords blazing with purple fire.

The archangels began to thin under the onslaught of Renseki swords and epsilon squadron guns. Seth flew back into the swarm, and archangels fell in around him with suicidal focus. Two archangels approached from his right, and he spun around, bringing a massive sword through both foes in a single cut. Another came at him from behind.

It never had a chance.

Seth flipped, shearing the archangel's sword arm off with the first blade and cleaving the archangel down the middle with the second. Space thickened with dismembered bodies and blackening fluid.

Far ahead, almost unnoticed in the grand battle of Aktenai versus Grendeni and seraph versus archangel, two seraphs folded in, one white and one black. They flew across the head of the Grendeni fleet and dove through the weakest section of Imayirot's defenders.

All nearby Grendeni craft opened fire on the traitor seraphs. Seth supposed it only made sense. Not even the Grendeni would knowingly ally with the Bane. They must have figured out the truth at some point.

More archangels folded in, but not all of them near Alliance seraphs. Whole squadrons arrived at the head of the Grendeni fleet formation, oriented themselves towards the planet, and dove after the two traitor seraphs.

Perfect.

Seth opened a private channel with Zo.

"Go ahead, Seth."

"Zo, take command here. I'll head across the Grendeni formations and do what I can to delay the traitors. Join up with me when you can."

“Now hold on, Seth! That’s crazy! We break through their lines together.”

“No offense, but you’ll just slow me down.”

He spread his wings and shot into the heart of the Grendeni fleet.

“Seth, you don’t stand a chance alone!”

But he ignored her words. Seth had spotted the only foe that mattered, and nothing short of death would stop him.

Chapter 19
Where It All Began

Jack looked over his shoulder at a horde of over sixty archangels. They weren't all clustered together, but still, that was a lot. He descended towards Imayirot, flanked by massive spherical defenders. They spun around to face him.

Vierj lashed out with twin cords of black light. They whipped through space, expanded into flat triangles, and swallowed the defenders whole. Cold, broken husks drifted out the other side, and the triangles vanished into fields of winking black motes.

The swarm of archangels closed in from above.

Jack descended with his back to Imayirot. "Can you feel where the Gate is?"

"Not yet," Vierj said. "There is something here interfering with my talent, but I am unsure where it is coming from. I will try to locate it."

The first archangels dove in. Jack ignited his shield and blade, opened his wings, and flew up to meet them. The lead archangel came at him, raising its sword above its head.

Jack shot past it. Two halves of the archangel separated slowly, fluid pulsing from the wound.

A dozen archangels fell in around him. Jack wove through their ranks, cutting and slashing at targets of opportunity. As clumsy as they were, each archangel posed a very real threat. A solid hit from their swords could cripple his seraph or even kill him.

An archangel came in from the right. Jack spun around, deflected its sword strike with his shield, then cut up and through its torso. A dozen chopped-up archangels floated near him within a cloud of spilling conductor fluids. Twenty more archangels moved in for the next attack.

"Damn, there are a lot of you!" Jack shouted.

The seraph did not speak.

"Yeah, I know!"

Jack sped down and away from the horde, regrouping near Vierj. More archangels kept folding in, bloating the size of the swarm. They waited this time, gathering their numbers into one decisive clump. He didn't know if he could handle so many at once. One mistake on his part, and that was it.

"Vierj? The Gate?" Jack asked urgently.

"I believe it is here. There *is* something here interfering with my ability, though it is quite weak and distant. I need more time."

Fifty archangels charged towards him. Jack darted out of the way, let the leaders sail by, then flew into the side of the formation. He dismembered two archangels in the first seconds, clipped a third with a sharp kick that sent it spinning out of control, and stabbed his sword through the head of a fourth.

Archangels turned slowly and came in from all sides. The swarm was almost a solid suffocating mass around him. Jack fought against them alone, killing them over and over again with brutal repetition. The swarm constricted around him without the slightest hint of fear.

Below, Vierj hovered over Imayirot, perfectly still.

Jack cut down two, sometimes three, archangels with every attack. Severed limbs, broken torsos, and dark fluid choked the space around him. Archangels pushed through the floating detritus, swinging their swords in slow motion compared to his blinding speed.

Jack butchered his way through the swarm. He killed and killed and killed until only a few remained.

The last four archangels charged him together.

Jack stabbed the point of his shield through the rightmost archangel cockpit. From the left, three brought their swords crashing down. Jack met their combined attack with his own blade. The blow released a flash of energy and rang through his body like a hot, burning spasm.

Jack cried out. His blade flashed brighter, and he threw the three archangels back. His foes tumbled wildly and he closed in, cut two down in a single stroke, and thrust forward for the final kill.

Jack kicked the archangel off his blade and checked his surroundings. "Vierj?"

"I am not getting anywhere. The Gate is here, but I cannot pinpoint its location."

"Do we need to get closer?"

"That may help, but I want to try something first." Vierj spun around and lined up with Imayirot's orbiting shade. "We shall move to a different position over the planet. Follow me."

Vierj took off towards the shade and Jack followed her lead. Orbital defenders opened fire on them, but they darted through the crisscrossing lines of white light.

The shade loomed close now, a tall black oval against space, ringed with turreted weapons. Beam cannons all across its circumference poured continuous fire into the Grendeni fleet, and a few plasma lances impacted against Aktenai ships folding in behind the main Grendeni force.

Jack focused his active scanners on the Aktenai ships, searching and cataloguing the massing ranks of dreadnoughts, frigates, drones squadrons, and yes, seraphs.

Where are they? he wondered.

Jack sifted through the raging battle, looking for six silver glimmers in a tight formation or a distinct black and red seraph pair. He couldn't find either, but that wasn't surprising, given the scale of the battle. Even his chaos scanner was useless. Between the seraphs and archangels, all the influx signs blurred into a single bright slurry.

Vierj passed underneath the planetary shade and slowed.

"I'll try to sense it from this angle," she said.

A formation of three Grendeni dreadnoughts broke away from their main lines and headed for the Imayirot shade at maximum power. At first, Jack thought the gesture useless, but then he noticed the relative velocities between the three dreadnoughts and the shade.

Shade fusion cannons fired, tearing into the three Grendeni dreadnoughts. Two of them broke apart under the torrent of plasma. The final dreadnought was nothing more than a glowing shard of ruined armor when it struck the shade and vaporized.

The shade trembled from the impact like the head of a drum. A circle of armor six kilometers across blew open. Shockwaves rippled outwards, tearing its web-like support lattice free and silencing cannons along the perimeter.

Great rips formed like star-filled oceans, but the shade's automated systems continued fighting. The outer ring had been damaged, but functional guns across its circumference resumed firing.

"I think I am starting to narrow down my search," Vierj said. "We must descend. Follow me."

"Right behind you."

The swarms of defenders began to thin the lower they flew. They entered part of Imayirot's jagged and broken mirror shell, each fragment permanently anchored to the planet's gravity well in a short-ranged mimicry of geosynchronous orbit.

Vierj stopped above a continent-sized shell fragment, pitted and breached in hundreds of locations across its massive girth. The outer surface of the mirror shell was deathly black, even as the system's yellow sun lit it for the first time in millennia, but the inner surface held a vast warped mirror.

"Any luck, Vierj?"

"I'll have to descend down to the surface. And once there I should remain motionless. Moving about in orbit is making this difficult."

"But you can find it, right?"

"Yes. It must be very deep in the planet or perhaps on the far side, but I will locate it."

A rapidly approaching object caught his attention. Jack turned to see a lone black seraph fly clear of the Grendeni fleet.

So, Quennin did fall, Jack thought. Vierj's attack hadn't passed through the cockpit, but enough feedback could kill anyone.

"Vierj, head on down to the surface. I'll stay up here and join you later."

"Why?"

"There's a seraph on approach. I'll deal with him. You focus on finding the Gate."

"One of your former comrades?"

"Yeah."

"Perhaps I should stay."

"No. This is my fight. If anyone is going to kill him, it should be me."

"If that is your request, then I shall honor it. Fight well."

Vierj descended towards Imayirot.

A squadron of archangels folded in and intercepted Seth. They wouldn't delay him long.

First your son, then your lover, and now you, Jack thought. *Come at me, Seth. Do your worst. God knows, I deserve it, but I won't let you stop me. I've paid too high a price for this to fail now.*

Jack wanted to call out to Seth and explain everything, but he buried those feelings. He could send no message Vierj might intercept. Absolutely nothing he did could reveal what he planned, for Vierj needed to be unguarded at the last moment, or all the death he'd wrought would be for nothing.

Jack lit his blade once more, and waited above the shell fragment for the inevitable.

"Get out of my way!" Seth shouted.

He spread his swords to either side and charged into the archangel squadron. The closest two raced in, and he flew past, swinging his swords horizontally like a giant pair of scissors and cleaving them at the waist.

More flew in and more died. Seth tore through their ranks without mercy.

The Archangels tried to overwhelm him. They tried striking from multiple directions at once or crowding in from of his path to delay him or even colliding with him so that others could move in for the kill. They tried all they could to stop this force of nature, but nothing worked. Seth cut and slashed and fought his way through their ranks like a madman.

Finally, Seth broke free of the archangels, flashed his wings full of energy, and surged towards his true objective, leaving the sluggish remnants of the Grendeni imitations in his wake.

Behind him, the battle continued. No matter how many Grendeni or Aktenai ships died, more flooded in. Neither side was willing to give up the Gate, regardless of the cost. Seraph squadrons and archangel swarms dueled amongst the fleets, and Imayirot defenders continued to pour fire into the increasingly cluttered combat zone.

None of it mattered to Seth. His mind was made, his will set, and he flung himself towards Jack, who waited above a fragment of the mirror shell.

Seth sped through the last of Imayirot's defenders and dropped altitude until his orbit came level with the shell fragment. He checked the Bane's position, now dropping towards Imayirot. Whatever misdeeds the Bane might commit down there, it was still *down there.*

Jack was alone.

Seth received a hypercast signal and acknowledged it.

"I regret it must end this way between us," Jack said.

"What's your friend doing?"

"Going on ahead. This fight is between you and me."

"At least you have that much right. Too bad about everything else."

"I cannot let you stop me, Seth, and I will kill you if you approach."

"You can try!"

Seth lunged, his twin swords burning with purple light. Jack spread out his wings and flew up to meet Seth. Their blades met with terrible force. A sharp flash of energy exploded from the contact point.

They fought against each other, splinters of light cascading off their blades. Seth pushed in, driving Jack's sword back. He sensed the edge the Grendeni swords gave him, and readied his other sword for a killing strike.

But as much as the Grendeni swords leveled the field of battle, that was all they did. Jack bashed in with his shield. Seth spun around the attack and arced a sword towards Jack's side. Jack angled his wings and flew back, leaving nothing but dead space for Seth to slice through.

The two seraphs flew across the mirror shell, drive wakes pulling the shell's skin loose. Seth stabbed in, and Jack met him. A shockwave blasted out from their blades and rippled across the shell fragment. Shards of silver blew off the support lattice.

Jack brought his sword crashing down with such force that he threw Seth off balance. Seth broke through the mirror shell in a rain of splinters. Jack rushed in, but Seth crossed his swords into a rising block.

Jack smashed into the block, raised his sword, and struck again. The fiery edges of Seth's swords wavered like turbulent water.

"You're still no match for me," Jack said, pressing in.

"Then finish me, if you can!"

Seth willed his swords to hold. He pulled one back and brought it around in a glowing arc. Jack raised his shield, and the two met with a blast of energy.

"Damn, that hurt!" Jack exclaimed.

Jack kicked Seth in the stomach and flung them apart.

Seth fell back and spread his wings to regain control. Jack rushed in and the two clashed again. They broke apart and flew like two comets locked in a tight orbit, spinning about each other as they attacked and retreated.

No longer was this a match of unequal opponents. Once, Jack Donolon held the upper hand, but Seth's weapons and determination granted him the edge he needed. The two opponents darted in and out, testing defenses and resolve, neither possessing a significant advantage. Seth held the advantage in speed and agility, but Jack remained the undisputed powerhouse.

Seth pulled away from his opponent and regained his bearings.

Their battle had led them across the tattered mirror shell to a large structure in orbit: a fat disc with a bowled center. Machines the size of cities rose along the edge of the bowl, and a long spike protruded from the center, aimed away from Imayirot.

Seth recognized the silhouette. Once encased in accelerated time, Imayirot's people had united in an attempt to drill outside the temporal axis. The spatial drill had failed and now orbited in silent testament to the Bane's power.

Jack hovered in front of him, blade ready at his side, the huge drill behind him.

"Come at me, Seth. I know you haven't had enough."

"Not nearly."

Seth threw himself forward, and their blades collided in a momentary flash of light. But Jack didn't offer his usual resistance and instead let Seth's momentum carry him forward.

Jack slashed in with the edge of his shield. Seth pulled away, but the edge of the shield cut up across his arm.

The shunts in Seth's arm flickered, and the edge of his sword wavered like turbulent water. Bright purple fluid gushed from the wound. Pain burned up his arm and through his mind. Within a small pearl of understanding, he saw red medical indicators blossom across his real forearm. The i-suit went to work, extruding nano-cilia into his scorched flesh.

Likewise, the seraph's repair systems engaged. Programming for the mnemonic skin altered and sealed the breach. Valves along the arterial lines closed and bypasses opened. The wavering shunt flared back to life, and the edge of his sword reformed.

"That was nothing!" Seth brought a sword down onto Jack's shield. The impact sent pain ringing up his arm.

The edges of the shield wavered and dissolved into a bluish fog. Seth fired his drive shunts and tried to force his way through, but Jack's moment of weakness passed. The edges of the shield regained sharpened and straightened.

Jack threw him back. Seth crashed into the spatial drill's bowl, his wings carving long grooves in the surface. He pulled up and righted himself, ready for Jack's follow up.

But it didn't come. Jack broke away and descended towards Imayirot.

"Don't you dare run from me!" Seth flew after him. The surface rushed towards them. Directly below, a city-sized dome rose like a diseased blister from the planet surface.

Jack spun around just before reaching the dome. Their swords clashed, and destruction blasted out from them. A wave of chaos energy peeled away the top of the dome, leaving nothing but frail girders to protect the desiccated city within.

The two seraphs fell past the opening and crashed into the city's highest tower. They plummeted through, shattering the tower floor by floor. Ashen debris blasted out, punching through nearby buildings.

Jack accelerated out of the dust cloud and headed towards the Bane's seraph. Seth exited the dome and pursued him across the ravaged landscape. They flew across empty riverbeds, dried oceans, and ancient battlefields choked with the blasted husks of ground vehicles and crashed aircraft.

"You see this, Jack? Is this legacy of death what you want to be a part of?"

Jack turned around and held his ground. Seth shot in and swung. Their blades met, scraping against each other in sharp crackles of energy. Jack shoved him away, and they hovered above the blasted landscape.

"I know this legacy all too well," Jack said. "But I will not turn away now."

"Being like the Bane does not justify siding with that monster."

"Is that why you think I do this? You couldn't possibly understand."

"And I don't want to!"

Seth charged in. Their blades slammed together and locked. The two seraphs faced off, weapons grinding against each other with snaps of blue and purple light.

"You're too late, Seth. We've found the Gate."

"And you will die before you reach it!"

"You won't stop me!"

Jack fired his drive shunts and threw both of them into the ground. Their impact sundered the frozen earth and released a shockwave of dust and ash. Jack pushed off, spun around, and headed for the Bane. Seth burst free of the debris and followed him past domed cities and great chasms that plunged deep into the planet.

Ahead, a great circular tunnel opened, and above the entrance hovered the Bane's black seraph.

But instead of standing and fighting, the Bane and Jack descended quickly into the tunnel.

Seth hesitated at the entrance. Above him, the battle in space continued to rage on. The Renseki and epsilon squadron were nowhere near his position. The same was true for all other Alliance forces.

"Zo, report," Seth said.

"We're trying to reach you, Seth, but these archangels just don't stop coming!"

"Keep at it."

He was alone.

With or without support, his path was clear. He dropped down the tunnel and fell into darkness. Only the glow of his shunts lit the walls.

Seth descended for several kilometers, keeping an eye on Jack's position with his chaos scanner. The tunnel thinned until Seth's seraph could barely fit through, then it turned at a sharp angle and ran horizontally.

Seth entered a rectangular cavern several kilometers long, partially natural, but mostly cut out by human technology. The ruins of its city lay heaped amongst the rubble of a forgotten war. Part of the ceiling had collapsed, apparently not by natural means. The broken remains of strange fighting vehicles dotted the ruins.

He gave the sight little thought and dropped down a small hole at the far end.

The passage tightened and soon began zigzagging back and forth at random. Every turn was littered with broken turrets and wrecked vehicles. He hurried on through the twisting passages, came to another wide vertical tunnel, and followed it down to a huge spherical chamber.

Seth was hundreds of kilometers underneath Imayirot's surface now, yet the civilizations of this era were almost as advanced as those on the surface. He detected layers of sophisticated insulators packed around the sphere's outer shell. A spiked globe floated in the center, still hovering after all this time.

The entire inner surface of the sphere was densely packed with buildings, all reaching towards the sphere's center. Over half the stalactite towers had fallen on the buildings below, filling the bottom of the sphere with rubble.

Two seraphs stood on a peak of rubble, apparently confused about their next direction. No less than seventeen passages intersected the sphere-city from various angles.

Seth dove at them.

Jack spun around, but the speed of Seth's attack caught him off guard. Their swords met, and the force sent Jack crashing backwards through the rubble at the sphere-city's bottom.

The Bane lunged at him from the side. Seth dodged back and swung in with one of his blades. He sank the chaos sword into the Bane's side, and its black barrier vibrated like the surface of a beaten drum, then broke apart.

Seth could see the machine underneath, still mostly black, but with long ovals of silver across the limbs and wings, each with a cross-hatch of black shunts.

Its barrier snapped violently back into place, throwing Seth across the sphere-city. But Seth knew he had a chance. The Bane's defenses had weakened, if only for a moment. It could be killed!

Seth charged in again.

The Bane raised an open hand. Black light blossomed in front of Seth, growing and billowing outwards until it wrapped completely around him.

Seth stopped and floated within a bubble of absolute darkness. The Bane had trapped him within a pocket of different time.

He flew up to the barrier and pressed in with a fist. The bubble's surface gave easily to the pressure. He kicked the barrier. It bulged outwards and rippled around him like disturbed water.

Seth raised his swords. "Enough of this."

He slashed down, crossing his blades in the form of a large X-cut. Strangely, in his mind he thought he heard a young woman scream. He shook the thought away, docked his swords, and jammed his hands into the breach. With a grunt of effort, he ripped the bubble open.

Tattered strands of darkness disintegrated around him. He flew out and swept his view across the sphere-city.

Jack and the Bane darted down a narrow passage near the sphere's equator.

Seth accelerated towards the passage but stopped as black light filled it. The dark film expanded outwards and halted at the entrance. When it faded, the tunnel was a solid mass of cold rock ten kilometers thick. The sight of it made him wonder just how precisely the Bane could control its talent.

"Commander! Hold up!" Jared said.

Seth checked the sphere-city's upper portal. Seraphs exited one at a time until eight floated down to meet him. All six Renseki along with Jared and Yonu had made it to the sphere-city.

"Glad to see you broke through the Grendeni lines," Seth said.

"No thanks to you," Zo said sharply. "But at least we didn't slow you down."

"You know what we're facing as well as I," Seth said. "If I'd died delaying that creature, it would have been worth the price. As such—"

"As such, it's a shame Quennin isn't here," Zo said. "You at least listen to her."

"This is no time for half-measures, Zo."

"Look, as fascinating as this conversation is," Yonu said, "don't we have a job to do?"

"Yeah, what are we waiting for?" Jared said. "Let's go kill the Bane!"

Chapter 20

One Will Fall

Jack and Vierj descended through the twisting passages and gaping city-caverns underneath Imayirot.

"How much further?" he asked.

"I am … not sure. We are getting closer, though."

"Do you feel that? It's like my seraph is becoming sluggish."

"Yes, I feel it, too. The Gate is interfering with my talent."

"Are you at risk?"

"No. The barrier around this machine is failing, but those weaklings will not be able to harm my body."

"That's good to hear."

Jack wondered if Vierj was downplaying her vulnerability. *She might even be killable this close to the Gate.*

The seraph did not respond.

Yeah, you're probably right, Jack thought. *Best to be absolutely certain. I only get one chance at this.*

They dropped down a sloped connecting tunnel between two large rectangular caverns. Each settlement was more primitive than the last.

Jack's runic shunts flickered. "The interference is getting *much* stronger."

"I know. We are getting close." Vierj's opaque barrier fizzled into snaps of black energy.

"If those seraphs find us, they might use conventional weapons. Our barriers won't take much punishment in this condition."

"I'll protect us. This machine is failing, but my talent remains strong."

"You sure?"

"Yes. This fake seraph appears to be more vulnerable to the Gate's disruptions than I am."

"Could be the influx amplifier," Jack said. "It might be boosting the interference, too."

"Perhaps."

The tunnel widened below them, revealing a vast artificial cavern shaped like an upright cylinder. The chamber was two kilometers across and more than twenty kilometers deep.

Tiers ringed the chasm every few hundred meters, and along each tier sat the remains of a vast city. Some of the tier-cities jutted out, with wide bridges spanning the middle. Others huddled against the walls or retreated back into them. Some of the cities appeared almost as advanced as those on the surface, while others were appallingly primitive, as if built from the rubble of a greater society.

Jack gazed down the cylinder, and his seraph's computers quickly counted fifty-five cities stacked one on top of the other. Many of the cities were in ruins, but some of the more advanced structures remained standing, frozen in false serenity.

Over a hundred passages led out of the tiered chamber, some ending in cul-de-sacs, others proceeding deeper into the planet.

Jack hovered near the top. His drive shunts sputtered, and he fell like a rock.

"Whoa!" He angled his wings and flooded them with power. The shunts glowed briefly, cushioning a landing on a third tier spanning bridge. Vierj touched down next to him.

"I am having trouble flying," she said.

"Same here. The Gate must be close."

"Yes, but behind which passage? There are too many to choose from."

"No time. Above us!"

Two Renseki seraphs entered at the top of the chamber. Their wings gave out, and they landed with graceless stutter-steps on the highest tier-city. One aimed its fusion cannon and fired, but instead of focusing the warhead into a coherent beam, the seraph's arm exploded.

A nuclear detonation leveled the highest tier-city. The Renseki fell back, its arm and part of its chest missing. Debris rained down from the top tier, fell past Jack, and tumbled into the dark chasm below.

Seven more seraphs emerged from the top: another four Renseki, a sleek blue Aktenai seraph, an EN seraph with command bars on its shoulder, and Seth. They all landed clumsily on the blasted remains of the uppermost tier-city.

The EN seraph ran to the ledge and launched a spread of six tactical seekers. The projectiles darted out and passed through tiny black triangles. Frigid debris rained out the other side.

"I will disable their weapons." Vierj raised both hands, palms up. She released a cluster of hair-thin cords that whipped out like angry snakes. They latched onto the enemy seraphs, cutting through swords, disabling launchers, and ruining cannons—but wherever they touched a seraph's skin, they stopped.

Seth stepped forward. He grasped one of the cords and pulled it taut. The cord snapped.

"Ah!" Vierj gasped painfully. The other cords vanished.

"This is going to be messy." Jack tried to light his sword. Small particles of blue light gathered ahead of his left forearm but refused to coalesce. "This is going to be very messy. Do you know where the Gate is yet?"

"No. I need more time."

"Then we stand and fight." Jack clenched his fists.

"Agreed."

Two Renseki leaped down and stuck hard landings onto the third tier bridge. This deep within the planet, gravity had lessened to half Earth's, but seraphs remained massively heavy machines. Their impacts left a pair of craters in a thick bridge.

Without weapons or daggers, the Renseki charged in for the only remaining course of action: direct physical contact.

They paired off, one rushing Jack, the other going for Vierj. Jack threw a kick into the Renseki's stomach and catapulted it back across the bridge. The Renseki crashed through a row of buildings near the edge of the tier.

The second Renseki grappled with Vierj. She slammed her fist into the Renseki's side. Barriers flashed. Armor crumpled, and the Renseki fell back, clutching its bleeding chest.

Someone kicked Jack in the small of his back. He skidded across the bridge and crashed into support pillars at the far end. The blue Aktenai seraph raced towards him, followed by the EN seraph.

Jack shook out his wings and rose from the rubble. He clenched his fist and struck the blue seraph with a swift uppercut. It flew up from the force of his blow.

The blue seraph lit its drive shunts, but only a faint mist of energy exhausted out. It hit the edge of the second tier and fell away, crashing into bridges and tiers as it rattled down the dark abyss.

Jack had no time to dwell on the pilot's fate. The EN seraph rushed in and punched. Jack swept his arm up to block, but the enemy's fist slid past and hammered his face. His barrier flickered. The armor underneath bowed, and the side of his face sizzled with heat.

"Damn!"

Jack clubbed the EN seraph's arm away and snapped a kick straight into its crotch. The strike sent it flying upward. The EN seraph hit the bottom of the second tier and fell in a heap in front of Jack's seraph.

Jack grabbed the downed seraph's wings and threw it off the edge. The EN seraph spun out of control through the dark chasm, crashing into bridges, tiers, and buildings before it careened into the abyss.

"And stay down there!"

The seraph did not speak.

"Damn it!"

Jack checked the third tier bridge and found it littered with Renseki limbs but nothing else. The fighting had moved elsewhere. He checked down the abyss and spotted Vierj fighting Seth and three Renseki about six tiers down.

Jack took a running leap off the bridge and fired his drive shunts to aid the descent. He landed chest-first against a tier's protruding edge.

The tier buckled under his sudden weight, but held together. Jack pulled himself over the edge and ran into the tier-city. Three Renseki turned and faced him. Beyond those seraphs, Vierj and Seth fought a brutal duel.

Jack dodged the first punch and grappled against the Renseki. With a quick sidestep, he pushed the Renseki past him and elbowed its back. The force of his strike sent it skidding across the ground. The Renseki groped for purchase, flew off the edge, and disappeared into the abyss.

"Honor guard? Ha!"

The last two Renseki tackled him to the ground. One of them kneed his side. Burning pain branched out from his ribs.

Jack headbutted one, causing it to stagger back. He threw his leg out and tripped the second Renseki. It flew off its feet, hanging motionless to his accelerated, chaos-infused senses.

Jack rose and smashed his fist into the Renseki's back. Its armor imploded in. The seraph's endoskeletal spine snapped, and the Renseki folded back onto itself unnaturally. It collapsed into a ruined heap. Rents in the armor spewed pressurized fluid.

Jack grabbed the downed Renseki and whirled it around like a club. He hit its comrade and sent them both flying. They crashed to the ground twenty cities down and did not get up.

Jack limped into the tier city.

"Ah, crap."

Dozens of yellow and red indicators appeared on a mental image of his seraph, each with lengthy repair estimates. His endoskeleton was warped at several points and the artificial musculature was torn in his leg and chest.

Jack ignored them and rounded two blocky structures, emerging into some sort of city square.

Vierj was down with Seth standing over her, raising his fist. A severed arm from her seraph hung over a building, and two of her broken wings lay on the ground. Black oil pooled underneath her.

Seth was also injured. Conductor fluid bled from his torso, and his armor looked like someone had beaten it with a mallet. But he was standing, and Vierj wasn't.

Jack staggered in from the side and threw a punch. Seth backpedaled and caught his fist, but Jack swung a second punch and connected with Seth's battered chest. Purple barrier energy crackled, and the armor tore open, but Seth held his ground and lashed out with two quick punches to Jack's abdomen.

Two of Jack's arterial lines ruptured, and blue fluid spluttered out.

"Just give up already!" Jack shouted.

He raised an arm straight up, then brought his elbow crashing down onto Seth's head. Seth dropped to his knees, the seraph's head warped out of position. Before he could recover, Jack slammed a knee into his chin.

Seth fell back and landed on his side. He rose slowly, armor mending itself, fluidic lines closing off and rerouting. Then, with a sudden burst of speed, he gathered his fists into a ball and pounded Jack's knee.

Jack staggered to the side and fought to regain his footing. He grabbed Seth's arm, lowered his stance, and threw the black seraph over his shoulder. Seth crashed through four buildings before finally coming to rest.

He didn't get up.

"Vierj, you okay?" Jack limped back to Vierj's downed seraph.

"Yes … a little … disoriented. I am not accustomed to such sensations."

"The Gate. Do you know where it is yet?"

"Yes. I will guide you to it. Come closer. This machine is ruined."

Mnemonic skin peeled away near the seraph's cockpit hatch, and Vierj climbed out. Even though the tier-city existed in a vacuum, Vierj needed no pressure suit and wore none, unlike Jack. Black wings unfolded from her back, and she rose above the wreckage.

Jack held out a hand and let Vierj land on it. He wanted to crush her, but even at peak performance he doubted it would be any easier than squeezing a diamond with his bare hand. As Vierj stepped onto his seraph's palm, he could feel the temporal barrier around her body, almost as powerful as ever.

Almost, he thought. *It has weakened. This can work, but I need to get her closer.*

Vierj held up nine fingers, then pointed down.

"Nine levels down. Got it."

Jack walked to the main chasm of the tiered cities and spotted a ledge on the opposite side nine tiers below.

He jumped and fired what little energy he could from his wings. The seraph landed and stumbled forward on the ledge protruding from the target level. All around him, the ancient structures on this tier seemed to blend together, not so much a collection of tightly packed buildings as one super-building. From his palm, Vierj pointed straight ahead.

Jack lurched forward, walking more easily with time. Repair systems had bent some of his endoskeleton back into shape, and the skin ruptures had finally been sealed.

Vierj motioned for him to stop. She spread her wings and floated down to the tier's surface.

A narrow passage existed directly ahead. But as far as he could tell, it ended in a small cavern-habitat.

Jack knelt and segregated himself from the seraph. The cockpit widened around him, and he took a careful moment to check the seals on his pressure suit. He pulled his sidearm out of its holster, clicked the safety off, and set it firmly back in place. Satisfied that everything was ready, Jack linked the outer hatch open. The seraph's zero field disengaged, and Jack found himself under a moderate gravitational pull.

The darkness was absolute. Jack summoned a point of chaos light above his hand and let it float upward.

He climbed down the seraph, dropping first to the seraph's left hand, then the right, and finally to the tier surface.

Jack walked over to Vierj, who motioned to the narrow passage ahead of them. But before Vierj took her first step towards the passage, she whirled around and looked up.

His body would not move.

In Seth's mind, he saw the red indicators all across the seraph's frame: endoskeleton cracked, muscles torn, and two arterial chambers punctured. He didn't have time for repairs.

Seth commanded his body to stand, but it remained still. His connection to the seraph felt distant, slippery. He pushed, prodded, and willed it to stand. Chaotic influx surged weakly through his body. He began to move.

Rubble sleeted off his back. He pushed free, grabbed a nearby building, and pulled himself upright. Indicators across his legs blinked red. They needed more time to repair before they could safely support his weight.

Seth stood, not smoothly, not steadily, but he wasn't on the ground anymore. He limped towards the edge of the tier-city and spotted Jack's powered down seraph. He zoomed in and for the first time saw the Bane. She was looking straight at him.

A woman?

Seth had never given the Bane's appearance much thought. Everyone knew it had once been human, but he hadn't expected a young woman that didn't look any older than Yonu.

A body protected from the ravages of time, he realized.

The Bane and Jack had left the safety of their seraphs, but Seth had no functional ranged weaponry. He hobbled over to a building, tore a heavy column loose, and flung the chunk of debris.

The column arced towards Jack and the Bane, its aim true, but the projectile never reached the intended target. A black rectangle materialized in front of the Bane, expanding like a shield of darkness. The column smashed into it and shattered like glass.

Jack and the Bane turned away and headed for a narrow passage.

I need to get down there.

"Pilots, status," Seth said.

"Uhhh, that hurt," Yonu said. "I'm fine, but my seraph is trashed. I can't even connect to it anymore. Pilot Daykin is down at the bottom with me."

"Yeah, I'm okay," Jared said. "I've lost most of my conductor fluid, though."

"Same goes for the Renseki," Zo said. "We're all in poor shape. Looks like you're the only one still standing."

"Barely standing."

Seth eyed the drop. He test-fired his drive shunts, but the wings generated insufficient lift.

He walked back to the chamber wall, took off at a sprint, and leaped off the edge. The joint in his right knee blew apart, and his leg flopped loosely below the joint. He sailed over the chasm and dropped away, falling towards the ninth tier below.

He almost jumped the full distance.

Seth reached up with both arms and grabbed the tier's edge as he passed underneath.

"Ah!"

Musculature snapped loose in his left arm, but he held on with the right. With one arm, Seth pulled himself up, managed to get one leg onto the ledge, then the other, and finally rolled onto its back.

Seth took another look at his repair status. In his mind, the seraph was solid blob of red indicators.

He disconnected from the seraph effortlessly. His real body had suffered a few nasty burns, but his i-suit had the injuries under control. Damage was minor compared to the thrashing his seraph had received.

My weakened connection to the seraph must have acted as a buffer.

Seth checked the seals on his i-suit and made sure he had his sidearm. He didn't know why all the seraphs had lost power, but chaos energy was chaos energy. The Bane's own abilities *had* to be suffering. Perhaps, just maybe, Seth would be able to kill the creature.

And even if I can't, Jack is only human.

Seth signaled the hatch to open and climbed out. Total darkness stretched forth in every direction. He switched on a light in his helmet and slowly made his way down.

His seraph lay on its back, broken limbs splayed about. Seth had some trouble getting used to the half-strength gravity but found it made climbing down the seraph's side easier.

Seth linked with the seraph's scanners and regained his bearings. The last thing he wanted to do was run blindly into darkness and fall off the tier. He ran around one of the seraph's mangled arms and sprinted towards the narrow passage Jack and that woman had headed down.

Seth ran through a seemingly endless field of inky blackness. He finally reached a towering structure, its sheer face rising up into infinite black. At its base was a plain archway barely large enough for two people side by side. Seth hurried through the archway and entered a long, dark passage.

The passage went on, turned slightly down, then straightened. Seth could see nothing at its end. On and on it went until at last Seth came to an open space.

Some primitive culture, perhaps the remnants of the tier-city societies, had carved out this chamber. To either side, small nooks had been cut into the rock walls. A long, open space stretched down the middle, marred by bits of debris. Everything now lay in ruins.

Where did Jack and the Bane go?

Seth looked around. His pressure suit's light caught the edges of the decrepit structures. He decided to head down the middle and took off at a run for several minutes, until he came to the stone wall at the far end.

A door had been built into the stone wall, and as Seth approached, the door split open.

It has power! I must be close.

Seth proceeded through the door and into an airlock. Light flooded the chamber, and Seth squinted, his eyes watering. The data link from his i-suit indicated a breathable atmosphere. The airlock finished cycling, and Seth walked into a long tunnel with a metal grate floor.

Seth drew his sidearm and proceeded deeper into the powered complex. He came to another door, but unlike the airlock, these had been forced open. Pushed and bludgeoned into opening—*not* aged.

Perhaps the Bane was weak here. Perhaps she could no longer precisely control her powers.

Hope dared to rise in his heart. It mingled there with intense, almost numbing fear.

Seth pressed on. A distant thrumming began to fill his ears.

The tunnel opened until it became a suspended walkway, passing above and beneath vast machines. Small roach-like robots skittered about the machines, repairing and maintaining the devices. However, the machines closest to the walkway were twisted and idle, perhaps damaged by the Bane. Robots clambered over them in the hundreds.

Seth ran on, past rooms of machinery and more security doors, each just as mangled as the first. The walls ahead of him seemed to bow away at the visible edges, as if he were heading deeper into a series of concentric spheres.

If so, then he had to be close to the center.

Seth passed through another set of security doors and found himself in a wider tunnel that bent to the right, the walls and ceiling thick with metal pipelines. Seth crept along the path, sidearm ready.

A sound from ahead clapped out like a thunder. Then two more just like it, closer and more distinct.

The tunnel turned down, then gently arched towards the sphere's center. Seth could hear a voice ahead: an angry female yelling in the Aktenai tongue, her thick accent similar to those of the Original Eleven.

Seth slowed, coming at last to the end of the tunnel. He edged closer to the entrance and peaked into the heart of the massive layered sphere.

The central room was a hollow sphere with a metal walkway looped around the equator. Near him, the walkway extended out towards the center. And at the center—

Seth didn't really know what he was looking at. Some shape existed in the center, but light slid off it, around it, and back at him, so he not only saw the other side of the room, but also every part of the room and himself when he looked directly at it.

It was a halo of light surrounding a mercurial reflection of everything near it.

The Gate to the Homeland.

Seth only had a moment to take it in. To his left, the Bane stood calmly with her back to him, a deadly sword of dark light in her hand. Opposite and facing her, Jack had also manifested a short blue dagger.

Jack no longer had his pressure suit helmet on. Blood oozed from a vicious cut along his temple, dripping over one closed eye. He glanced to the side, and when he saw Seth, an unmistakable look of relief filled his face.

Suddenly, Seth *understood.*

The Bane turned and faced Seth, but kept her sword pointed at Jack. She studied him with cold, stern eyes.

Seth raised his sidearm, stabilized it with both hands, and fired a single shot. The bolt ricocheted off the Bane's barrier in a flash of black light. Seth fired again, but that shot rebounded, too.

The woman smiled coldly. A black cord of energy snaked from her fingertips. It snapped out and struck Seth across the chest, throwing him against the wall. He collapsed onto his side. Gasping for breath, he struggled to his hands and knees, still holding the sidearm.

Jack charged the Bane. He feinted once, then lunged, the edge of his dagger slashing through the Bane's barrier. Black energy swirled around her for a moment, and vanished. Her barrier collapsed, and his blade cut into her arm.

She cried out in pain and thrust her sword into Jack's side. Blood splattered across the walkway.

Seth raised his sidearm. The Bane's barrier was down, and he fired.

The bolt punched straight through the Bane's heart. Darkness exploded outward, throwing Jack across the room and knocking Seth onto his back. Jack hit the wall with the horrible crunch of bones shattering on impact.

Dizzy, stars in his vision, Seth struggled to his feet again.

The Bane turned to face him slowly. She looked at Seth, her face twisted into a horrified expression, then gazed down at her chest. Gingerly, she touched the bleeding wound.

"I … I can't stop it. It won't stop. Why won't it stop?"

She fell to her knees. Blood continued to pour out of her heart, and she collapsed.

The Bane was dead.

Seth held the sidearm firmly in both hands. He edged up to the Bane and turned her over with a boot. She stared at the ceiling with lifeless eyes, blood soaking her shirt.

The Gate shuddered. Its reflective surface roiled like stormy waters, but Seth had no way of knowing if this was something to worry about. And even if it was, what could he do about it?

A painful wheeze drew Seth's attention. He walked over to Jack's prone body. A thousand evil thoughts poured through his mind. He looked down at the sidearm in his hands, then back at Jack. The Bane's weapon had cut through Jack's abdomen and spilled out his intestines.

Seth thought about his son, about Quennin, and all his fellow pilots now dead by this pair.

But now, in this place, Seth felt his pain eclipsed by what had been accomplished. He now understood what Jack had done, at least partially. The urgent need for retribution left him. Jack had succeeded where twenty thousand years of human civilization had failed.

The central purpose behind all Aktenai society, their Great Mission, had been achieved.

But my son is dead, Seth thought. *And I don't have to kill Jack. I can just walk away and let him die.*

He winced at this idea. *What would that accomplish? What would that prove?*

That I am nothing more than a slave to revenge?

Just like the Bane?

Seth shook his head. *No. No, I am nothing like that monster!*

At last, he flung the sidearm away. It clattered across the metal walkway and fell into the spherical pit.

He removed his helmet and broke the i-suit seals around his waist. Jack was dying, and Seth wore the only thing that could save him.

Chapter 21
Two Wrongs Made It Right

"Ohhh ..." Jack moaned. Consciousness and coherent thought slowly returned. He blinked and looked around.

How did I get here?

Jack thought he recognized the airlock at the entrance to the Gate complex.

His eyes watered. Needles of pain shot through his abdomen and danced across his whole nervous system. He clutched his side and found something thicker and more rubbery than a pressure suit.

My intestines seem to be on the inside. That's an improvement.

Jack became aware of new data in his neural link. This suit, something called an interface-suit, provided details on his current medical condition. He tabbed through the data and frowned. Bones had been set, blood loss stopped, organs returned to their proper locations, but he remained in poor shape.

Oddly, all the damage came with repair time estimates.

Jack focused on breathing. Each lungful burned him inside and out. He sat up and leaned against the wall.

Seth Elexen crouched against the opposite wall and stared back at him with a neutral expression.

Oh crap …

Jack shifted his posture, back to the wall, and rested there.

"Hey, Seth."

"Hey."

Jack tapped the i-suit. "Is this yours?"

"Yeah." Seth wore a white form-fitting pressure suit with a black fishbowl helmet at his side.

"Thanks. I guess I—damn!" Jack grunted and clutched his side.

"Jack, why didn't you tell me?"

"Oh, I don't know." His words were heavy with labored breathing. "What would I have said? 'Hey, Seth! I just figured out today that I'm turning into another Bane!' How would you have reacted? How would anyone have?"

"You should have told me what you planned, especially after you found that thing."

"I wish I could have, Seth. Really. But the Bane can … heh, she *could* listen to hypercast."

"That's impossible."

"Yeah, well, so is stopping time. I suppose the two might be related. Plus she was very observant. It sometimes caught me off guard how sharp she was. Gnnnngh! Is it supposed to feel like a thousand needles digging through my side?"

"Yeah. Pain means it's working."

"Some painkillers would be real nice."

Seth linked with the i-suit and released the painkiller inhibiters. Wonderful, blissful happiness spread out from his abdomen.

"Oohh … that's more like it." Jack breathed easier.

"It's normally held back. Painkillers dull our connections to the seraphs."

Jack took a deep breath and sighed. "So, what now?"

Seth glanced down the passage leading to the Gate. "Something's wrong. I talked to the Choir, and they think the Gate is going to bust loose. Our fight with the Bane damaged some sort of anchor that holds the Gate in place."

"Are we in danger?"

"Not right now. We've got some time before it rips free. The Choir said it will most likely shoot straight up, exiting the planet's gravity well. We should be in our seraphs ready to move when it does."

"Well, that solves the problem of getting out of this pit," Jack said. "As soon as the Gate leaves, our seraphs should be back at full power. Can your crew get out when that happens?"

"The seraphs are prioritizing their repairs accordingly. We'll be ready to leave."

"That's good."

"And since we have some time before the Gate leaves," Seth said, "why don't you explain to me how you concocted this crazy plan of yours?"

Jack sighed. "Well, you remember when I left, right?"

"How could any of us forget? It was so sudden."

"I was actually running away."

"Running from what?"

"Everyone. I figured out what I was becoming, Seth. I knew that I was going to become a bane, though I still have no idea how long the process will take. Do you have any idea what it's like suddenly realizing you're going to turn into some monster everyone hates?"

"Can't say that I do."

"Well, I did. Hell, your entire *society* is centered around killing the Bane. And I'll admit it. I was scared. Hell, I was terrified. And so I ran away."

"You went looking for the Bane."

"Well, my goals evolved over the years as I searched. By the time I did find her, I figured if I could defeat the Bane, it wouldn't matter if I was turning into the same creature. I'd done a lot of research on the Bane, the Gate, and the Exile before leaving, and that bastard Veketon let slip more than he thought. So I was able to come up with a plan to lure the Bane here. I thought if I could kill the Bane, it'd be proof to everyone that I wasn't like that creature."

"But it didn't turn out like that," Seth said.

"Seth, I know I screwed up. The plan seemed simple enough from the start. Find the Bane. Get it to the Gate. Spring the trap. But it all got mucked up when I actually found her. The Bane was smart and suspicious. And there was no way I could send a transmission of any kind to anyone about my intentions, because she would know. I was alone and in over my head."

"So you used the Grendeni?"

"Well, I knew I needed to get the Gate's location. Seth, the Choir would never have just *given* me the location. Me turning into a bane is bad enough, but I had the original in tow. You think asking nicely can make up for that magnitude of crap?"

Seth shook his head. "No, I suppose not."

"I thought about going in alone or with the Bane. Alone was suicide, plain and simple. I'm good, but I'm not that good. Going in with the Bane might have worked, but too many seraphs would have swarmed us, and the Bane would have fought back hard. She could have done to Aktenzek what she did to Imayirot. Seth, you might not believe me, but I used the Grendeni because I wanted to minimize casualties."

"No, I believe your intentions," Seth said.

"And even that blew up in my face. The Bane killed one of their schisms. Just wiped it out without a second thought, like the millions of people living there were nothing but vermin."

"You helped us kill it. That counts for something."

"Seth, I'm sorry about your son and Quennin. I know words can't right what I did, but please believe me, they're sincere."

Seth's face twisted up at the mention of his dead son. He closed his eyes and took a deep breath.

"I won't ever forget what you did." He steeled himself with another slow breath. "But I will forgive you for the death of my son."

"And Quennin? Is she …" The words caught in Jack's throat.

"The Bane almost killed her, but she survived."

"That's good to hear." Jack sighed heavily. "I'm glad. You know, it's a small miracle we didn't kill each other. Despite all my planning, I still needed your help in the end."

"What are friends for?"

Jack gave him a tired smile. "Yeah."

The ground trembled.

"Should we be getting out of here?" Jack asked.

"Yeah. Seems like the Gate is getting ready to break free."

Jack tried to stand up, but his legs wobbled even in the low gravity. Seth stepped over and helped him up. They walked out side by side with Seth supporting him.

At the airlock, both pilots checked their seals. Seth put on the black fishbowl helmet.

"It's amazing these things still work," Seth linked over. "The Eleven built to last when they hid the Gate."

"Why not use my pressure suit?" Jack asked.

"It has a big hole in the side, remember?"

"Oh, right."

The airlock opened and the two pilots walked out into the darkness. Seth guided Jack every step of the way

"Where are we going?" Jack asked.

"Straight ahead. The exit isn't too far."

"Can you see anything?"

"Yeah. This helmet has quite a few imaging options."

"I'm glad one of us can see."

"Your i-suit has a light."

"Okay." Jack linked to the suit and switched on the light. It illuminated a small patch of the gloom. "Well, that's a little better."

They walked down the narrow tunnel to the tiered cities. Seth guided Jack through the dark until they reached a pale structure. It took him a moment to realize he was staring at his seraph's leg. He was so used to feeling the seraph's presence that its absence caused him to shudder.

He closed his eyes and tried to command the seraph to move.

Nothing.

"I can't get to the cockpit like this," Jack said.

"Right. Stay here. I'll be back."

Seth propped Jack against the seraph and disappeared into darkness. A minute went by, then two. Five minutes later, the ground shook violently and Jack slipped onto the ground. He again tried to will the seraph into motion, but nothing happened.

Ten minutes ticked by.

"Seth?"

"Hold on. My seraph doesn't want to move."

Three more minutes passed. Jack was alone and in darkness except for the i-suit's meager helmet light.

Finally, a black shape approached so suddenly Jack flinched away. He looked up and saw the arm of Seth's seraph reach down through a curtain of black, its hand settling directly in front of him.

"Hurry up and step on," Seth said.

Jack stood up and limped onto the giant hand.

"Hold on."

Jack wrapped his arms around the thumb. The hand moved up and across, stopping by his seraph's cockpit. He let go, crawled on his hands and knees, and dropped inside.

Jack collapsed into the pilot alcove, his thoughts once again melting and merging with the seraph's.

"Ahh. There you are, buddy."

The seraph did not respond.

Images and sensations opened in his mind. Thoughts of his own body shrank away. He became the seraph once more. Around the edges of awareness, an uncomfortable fuzziness existed, perhaps a side effect of the painkillers. He found that tasks required more concentration than normal.

Power trickled through his body. Repairs were incomplete, but all critical damage had been patched up or bypassed.

A tremor shook the ground, the most violent yet.

"That didn't feel good." Jack rose from the ground and flexed his wings.

"That Gate is becoming more unstable," Seth said. "Hey, Jack?"

"Yeah?"

"I've discussed what has happened with the Choir. We know pilots are just attempts to recreate the Bane. The Choir … they want you to return to Aktenzek, and … and I agree with them."

"Thanks, but no thanks. Those corpses have already messed with me enough."

"Jack, the Original Eleven are gone. They've fled the Choir."

"*What?*"

"They fooled all of us. You, me, all the pilots. Even the Choir. Jack, we were all used. You don't have to face this alone. Despite what has happened, you belong with us, and you know it."

Jack sensed the sincerity in Seth's words. The offer truly was tempting. He missed Seth and Quennin, and he wanted to repay them for all the wrongs he had committed. However, seventeen years on his own, free of the Choir's machinations? *That* was something he did not regret.

"Sorry, Seth. I'm tempted, but I'm not going back."

The tier cities shook with tremendous force. Power surged through his body. Shunts ignited with brilliant light.

"Jack, you don't—"

He closed the channel.

The edges of his wings blurred with radiant energy. He lifted off the ground and floated into the middle of the tiered cities.

Nearby, other seraphs powered up.

Jack flew out of the cylinder and headed towards the surface. He wove through the planet's interior chasms.

Massive seismic motion spread throughout the planet. The Gate had broken free and now ascended in a wild spiral. It also grew in size and intensity, tearing Imayirot apart from the inside.

Jack reached the surface and accelerated into low orbit. He turned around and watched for the Gate to emerge.

Already, vast cracks gaped all across Imayirot's surface. Cities and domes crumbled as the ground convulsed underneath them. The entire planet, long dead and cold, now quaked on every continent. The planet's crust opened and heaved. Nine badly injured seraphs flew out of the planet, moments before the passage collapsed behind them.

Jack zoomed in on the point where the Gate should exit. The crust collapsed inward in an expanding ring, like a funnel of rock and ash.

The funnel deepened and widened, rock flowing inward like water. It appeared as if the entire planet was being sucked into itself. Then the bottom of the funnel rose upward, first as a bulge, then as a tight spiral of debris. A point of light burst out the end.

Imayirot disintegrated. A full half of the planet exploded outward with violent force. Jack dodged a boulder the size of Europe. He pulled into a much higher orbit, watching Imayirot's planetary remains expand. Some of the debris followed the fast-moving Gate in a strange, ragged comet tail.

The Gate accelerated, faster and faster until finally it vanished from sight.

Jack checked his scanners. Somehow, the Gate now traveled faster the speed of light.

"So much for everyone's prize."

Jack set his fold coordinates and vanished from the system.

Only two weeks had passed since the battle at Imayirot, and yet everything had completely changed.

"I still can't believe you killed the Bane." Quennin rode in Seth's seraph-hand, a bubble of chaos energy shielding her from the wind.

"You do know that I had significant help from Jack."

"So? It was your shot that killed the monster." Quennin winked and blew a kiss towards the cockpit.

"Are you trying to distract me? It's going to look really bad if I crash into the Sovereign's Palace."

"For you, Seth, I think they'd build a new Palace every day for the rest of your life, just so you can crash into it."

"Not *funny.*"

Seth descended through Aktenzek, passed the final security checkpoint, and headed to the Core and the Sovereign's Palace. The massive mirror-plated pyramid rose up from the white planetoid, and a thin landing platform extended out from the side. He zoomed in on the crowd of thousands on the landing platform.

"Uhh ... *people,*" Seth muttered.

"It'll be over quickly."

"That doesn't mean I have to like it."

A bulbous circle tipped the landing platform. All manner of craft docked along its circumference. Seth counted thirty-one seraphs: one full squadron from both the Earth Nation and Aktenzek, along with all six Renseki and the Sovereign.

Seth touched down on the outer lip of the landing platform. He folded his wings and let clamps secure him in place.

With a moment of concentration, he separated his mind from the seraph. Quennin joined him outside the cockpit.

"Ready?" she asked.

"Yeah. Let's get this over with."

Seth and Quennin walked across a plateau that separated them from the dignitaries below. Only a select few joined them up top.

The Renseki stood to his right, resplendent in perfectly tailored storm-gray coats splashed with silver. Next to them waited Sovereign Vorin Daelus, his own gold-adorned coat looking even more immaculate than usual.

Behind the Renseki and their Sovereign were two rows of seraph pilots, the elites of both the Earth Nation and Aktenzek. Jared stood rigidly at the far left of the EN row, appearing even more uncomfortable than Seth with this formality. Behind Jared, Seth thought he could just make out Yonu over the first row's shoulders.

But Seth found his attention drawn to the three men on his left. The trio wore dark green jackets and black trousers, gold sigils on their right breast announcing their rank. They were Executives of the Grendeni, and they had arrived one week ago, offering a temporary cease fire with hopes of negotiating a more permanent peace.

As one, the Aktenai on the plateau all dropped to a single knee, bowing their heads towards Seth. The Grendeni Executives also bowed their heads, but with less enthusiasm than their hosts. The Earth Nation pilots clapped and cheered, as their bizarre culture dictated for such events.

"At least smile," Quennin whispered into his ear.

Seth tried.

"And try not to look like you're in pain when you do it."

He also tried this.

Finally, the Aktenai on the plateau rose, and Vorin stepped forward.

"Venerable master." Vorin bowed his head, addressing Seth with the deepest respect any Aktenai could address another. "If you would, please follow me."

"Sovereign, you don't have to call me that."

"How else shall I address the Slayer of the Bane? Please, come this way."

Seth followed him to the front edge of the plateau and looked down at the sea of people. The crowd noise evaporated into nothing.

Vorin's amplified voice boomed across the landing platform. "Citizens of Aktenzek! Citizens of Earth! I present to you the Slayer of the Bane: Pilot Seth Elexen!"

Thousands of people bowed in his presence, and many of them fell to one knee in a show of even deeper respect. Seth bit into the inside of his lip, the magnitude of their silent praise almost overwhelming him to the point of tears. The few hundred Earth dignitaries clapping boisterously failed to ruin the effect.

Seth inclined his neck to the crowd.

With a hand on his shoulder, Vorin guided him to his seat. Seth, the other pilots, and the Grendeni Executives sat down. Vorin cleared his throat and began his speech.

For such a momentous occasion, his speech remained short and to the point. He touched on the Great Mission, the Bane's defeat, and what this meant for Aktenzek. He also mentioned the treachery of the Original Eleven, their exposed lies, and the danger Zu'Rashik now posed to everyone.

But most importantly, Vorin spoke of the peace accords between the Aktenai and the Grendeni. The reasons behind the endless feud had evaporated: the Bane was dead, the Original Eleven were now hated equally by both sides, and the Gate they both coveted had slipped through their grasps.

Vorin acknowledged that peace would not be easy to establish or maintain, but he stressed that it was a worthy goal to strive towards. Seth saw two of the Grendeni Executives nodding thoughtfully. The third seemed more reserved.

Vorin ended his speech on this note, but his was not the last. Aktenai pilots and Earth representatives came forward and spoke. Personalities from the Choir and even one of the Executives took their turns as the day dragged on.

Eventually, the dignitaries atop the plateau broke for dinner, and Seth found himself in the Sovereign's private residence.

Fluted half-columns supported the dining room's high ceiling. Three long wooden tables formed a U, their sides carved and painted with seraphs by the Palace's artisans. Immaculate artwork of seraphs in combat against the Bane dominated each table's center. Seth thought a certain angular black seraph, scarred with gray lines and imbued with purple runic shunts, had been featured a bit too heavily in the paintings.

Seth sat at the head of the middle table, Vorin to his left and Quennin to his right. Servants rushed about, bringing out the trays of hot food and cold beverages. Seth took a sip from his spiced juice and set it down.

He turned to Vorin. "Sovereign, do you believe we'll actually have peace?"

"Eventually," Vorin said. "Though it will be a long and difficult road. However, there are many reasons to be optimistic. One, the Original Eleven were the very reason Aktenzek never listened to past Grendeni peace offers. Those manipulators constantly fanned the fires of war for their own gains. Two, the war has been carried out mostly by robotic ships. Though both sides have committed atrocities, they have, thankfully, not been the norm. I believe our peoples will adjust to the peace."

"We also now have a common enemy," Quennin said.

"Absolutely," Vorin said. "With the Eleven in possession of Zu'Rashik, its industrial base, and half the fleet, they pose a very real military threat. The appearance of those thrones, which the Choir knew nothing about, only deepens my concern. The Grendeni fear the Eleven's intentions, and that fear may open up some interesting discussions in the days to come."

"Can we trust them?" Seth asked.

"Perhaps. We shall have to see, but I remain hopeful that we can forge a lasting peace. In fact, securing the Gate may prove to be our best opportunity to unite our two peoples in a common task, and I plan to raise this point with the Executives."

Seth nodded at this. "That might actually work."

"And on that topic." Vorin turned from his untouched meal and spoke softly. "We have been in touch with Pilot Donolon."

"He actually contacted you?" Seth asked.

"Yes, I was surprised myself. However, now that the Eleven are gone, he is free to return to Aktenzek. The Choir and I have discussed the matter thoroughly and have pardoned his crimes, given his role in killing the Bane."

Quennin tensed up and bit harshly into her lip. Seth put a hand on hers and squeezed.

"It will be a long time before I trust that man again," she said.

"We will be guarded in our dealings with him as well," Vorin said. "After all, he nearly killed me. But common enemies lead to strange partnerships, and Pilot Donolon has no love of the Eleven."

"Is that why he contacted you?" Seth asked.

"That, and he has volunteered to track the Gate's location for us."

"Why?" Quennin asked.

Vorin leaned close. "Because if we or the Grendeni control it, then the Eleven do not."

Jack folded into a nameless star system, near a baby blue gas giant and a glittering set of icy satellites. He checked his scanners, observing the after-effects of the Gate's passage through the system. Gravity clearly had an effect on the Gate, both decelerating and attracting it, but Jack couldn't figure out the particulars.

The blue gas giant hung in space with a tight hole punched through its center, large enough for the Earth to pass through. Three of its satellites now orbited as expanding fields of crushed ice, each damaged by the Gate's passing.

Jack flew in for a closer look, but stopped abruptly and turned.

Fourteen ships folded into the system: two dreadnoughts and a squadron of frigates. At first they registered as Aktenai, but critical seconds ticked by, and he failed to receive valid IFF codes.

"The Eleven's fleet, huh?" Jack angled his wings and accelerated to engage the enemy forces. "So even the dead covet this Gate. I wonder why."

The seraph said nothing.

To be continued in

THRONE OF THE DEAD

Book 2 of the Seraphim Revival

Thank you for buying *Bane of the Dead*. I hope you enjoyed reading it as much as I enjoyed writing it.

As an independent author, I don't have the exposure of being on bookshelves or the support of a marketing department from a major publishing house. Instead, I rely on fans like you to help spread the word. If you would like to help, please consider doing one of the following.

A) Post a review on Amazon.
B) Rate on Goodreads.
C) Like the book at **http://www.facebook.com/seraphimrevival**
D) Tell a friend or family member about the book.
E) Follow my blog at **http://holowriting.com** to hear about my next book.

Again, thank you for buying my book. And don't be shy. I'd love to hear from you. You can reach me through my blog or say hello directly at **holojacob@gmail.com**.

Jacob Holo

Photo by Keith DeLesline

About the Author

Jacob Holo is a former-Ohioan, former-Michigander living in sunny South Carolina. He describes himself as a writer, gamer, hobbyist, and engineer. Jacob started writing when his parents bought that "new" IBM 286 desktop back in the '80s. Remember those? He's been writing ever since.

Fueled by the soul.
Exiled by the dead.

Quennin S'Kev was a seraph pilot before injuries scorched her mind and stripped her abilities. Exiled by her people for reasons she does not understand, she lives on without honor or purpose. It is an existence so repulsive to her that she openly considers ending her own life.

All that changes when enemy commandos kidnap Quennin and bring her before the renegade Veketon. He claims he can restore her talents, even make them stronger, and offers her a place in his army worthy of her skills. It is everything her heart secretly desires.

His price?

She must swear allegiance to the worst traitor her people have ever known.

THRONE OF THE DEAD

Book 2 of the Seraphim Revival

Thrilling giant robot action from Jacob Holo

Coming Soon in Print and eBook
holowritingstore.com

J A C O B H O L O

THRONE OF THE DEAD

Book 2 of the Seraphim Revival

Fueled by the Soul. Exiled by the Dead.

"The strong action scenes are fast-paced throughout ... the dialogue flows well, and the fictional world is detailed, plausible and well-designed ... Well-written, sincere and undemanding military sci-fi adventure."

– KIRKUS REVIEWS

"After the fast opening, chapters rarely pass without a big, life-or-death battle, which leaves the novel in a nearly continuous intense state."

– KIRKUS REVIEWS

61086379R00178

Made in the USA
Charleston, SC
15 September 2016